ANGEL'S TEMPER

A PARANORMAL ANGEL ROMANCE

ELEMENTAL ANGELS

AIMEE ROBINSON

AMR PUBLISHING LLC

Angel's Temper

To Big Magic

ELEMENTAL ANGELS

Angel's Target

Angel's Duty

Angel's Devotion

Angel's Light

Angel's Temper

Angel's Conquest

CHAPTER 1

It only took one stolen glance at her boss's laptop screen for Molly Resnick to realize her career was over. The unplanned intrusion into her restaurant's back office had been exactly that and would have remained so had it not been for the tri-folded paper on the floor taunting her OCD with its sharp corner poking beneath the door. If it had been anyone else's office, she'd have assumed the poor thing had been the victim of a breeze through the small open window. Because it was her boss's office, however, odds were good that the messy precursor was due to his gorilla-like organizational skills instead.

Jeffrey Buchanan may have been the owner of the most popular restaurant in Northern New Hampshire, but he had the coordination and care of a male silverback foraging through the African forests. Instead of snapped shoots and torn leaves, papers, coffee cups, and empty wrappers from a week's worth of breakfast sandwiches littered his habitat.

Marie Kondo he was not.

Molly used to think it was a big fat blessing that Aurora's health department stuck to inspecting only the restaurant's food service spaces. Now, however, with the weight of the municipality's raised seal pressing against her palm as she clutched the court document and analyzed the screen in front of her, she wasn't so sure.

A writ of seizure and sale. They were words she'd never heard in that combination before. More to the point, they were words she absolutely couldn't reconcile with the restaurant's banking information that had been left up on the screen.

Zero after zero after zero, all preceded by a glaring negative sign. All painted with the angry shame of New England's favorite sinful color: scarlet.

Molly tore through the court notice again and desperately sought out what she was missing, because surely, she had to be missing something.

To: Police Chief Ethan Montgomery of Aurora, municipality of Drake County, or court-appointed bailiff.

Under an order of this court, you are directed to seize and sell the real and personal property of JEFFREY BUCHANAN, OWNER/OPERATOR OF SERENDIPITY RESTAURANT, LLC, and to realize from the seizure and sale, the following sums with compounded interest . . .

Numbers and names blurred into a kaleidoscope of confusion after that. Molly obviously identified the restaurant's address, but the other properties and figures made no sense. Establishments she'd never heard of in zip codes she couldn't afford to breathe the air in, let alone live in. Vehicles whose makes and models had more numbers than names attached to them. Even two other restaurants elsewhere in New England.

What *did* make sense on some horrific level was what a bank statement looked like when debt, overdraft fees, and nonpayment notices piled up.

And these were all for the restaurant's business and payroll accounts. The restaurant she was the current sous-chef at and had been working her hind quarters off for, hoping to be tapped as the new chef de cuisine once the current one retired within the next year.

Outside the office door, the usual sounds of the midmorning prep stations did little to dislodge her stomach from her throat and punch it back down to her abdomen. Soft taps of blades on boards and cleaned ceramic being stacked rankled, rather than reprieved. Two hours ago, she'd thrown her feet into her black Danskos, cinched her apron, and readied herself to be elbows-deep in her morning produce inspection. Those early hours had always been reserved for her precious sanity and the rote aspects of inventorying ingredients.

Now? With her holding a modern-day wanted poster sporting her boss's name, and a bank account statement ensuring that next week's paycheck, not to mention the food orders she'd just approved, wouldn't be funded? Well, she hadn't realized just how precious her taken-for-granted sanity truly was.

And like all other precious things, it had turned out to be just as finite and far too costly.

Molly froze, bent over the cluttered desk, even as adrenaline fueled her limbs to flee. Mr. Buchanan had rushed out of his office about twenty minutes ago with a phone clutched to his ear. Would he be back? Were the police on their way? Did she simply shut the door, join the staff, and do her paranoid best to pretend like she could muddle through the Wednesday lunch and dinner services without having a panic attack?

As soon as the questions fluttered through her mind, a deeper, louder question bullied its way to the forefront, causing her to strangle the court-ordered career death warrant in her grip.

Why is it always a freaking man?

And just who the hell insisted on lining up a blockade of Y chromosomes in front of her whenever her culinary profession's advancement was on the line? She'd knocked every one of them down, of course, but that didn't mean she wasn't tired of the routine.

Molly leaned into the familiar indignation with the long-held practice of equal parts disbelief and disillusionment. Then she dropped the writ, shoved herself away from the laptop, and forced her flyaway waves back behind her ears.

This was not happening. This was absolutely not happening.

On the third deep breath, she composed herself enough to show her face to the staff. She was just about to leave the office when her phone went off. Benny, her butcher chef and kitchen ride-or-die, flashed across the screen, and some of that earlier dread pushed its way to the surface.

"Benny? Everything okay? You're off today."

"Are you alone, Mol?"

She shifted the phone against her ear. "Um, I can be."

"Good. Get it done and let me know when you're settled." The deep timbre of his warning belied any false bravado she'd been working herself up to, effectively giving her permission to freak the heck out.

She sank back into the office and shut the door. "I'm alone."

Benny didn't speak. Instead, rhythmic tapping filled their air space until it was punctuated with a melodic *swoosh*. "I just sent it to you."

Molly pulled the phone away from her ear and opened up the article he'd just texted. She'd only managed to comprehend a few of the words in the headline before her palms turned clammy, threatening her grip on the phone.

"Real estate investment scheme . . ."

"Scammed foreign investors . . ."

"Tax evasion . . ."

"Benny." Her throat cracked on her friend's name, and she struggled to clear it. "What am I looking at?"

"I'll spare you the details and just give you the trumped-up headline." Concern coated his normally confident delivery. "Mr.

Buchanan, along with our own fucking head chef, was embroiled in a real estate investment scheme that turned south. They've been working with the CEO of a regional developer who scammed foreign investors out of millions of dollars while promising to build a new resort in the White Mountains. Instead of funding that project, however, they used investors' money to buy vacation homes, cars, pay off loans, open *more* restaurants, and generally live like Scrooge McDuck diving into piles of money."

Molly's apron strings tightened around her waist, compressing her stomach with each breath she took. Investment scheme? Tax evasion? From the same men who threw the restaurant's holiday parties and organized a freaking meal train for their hostess when she was involved in a car accident and laid up at home for a month?

Benny might as well have revealed that Mother Teresa hadn't been a nun but a notorious madam of a brothel, counting her cash as well as her clients.

And then she recalled the document that drew her into this office in the first place. "Do you, um, know what a writ of seizure and sale is?"

"Fuck." An exhausted breath cushioned the groan that swept through the phone. "I take it you're looking at one for Serendipity?" She nodded, and as if he knew she'd gone nonverbal, he chimed in to answer her. "It's a court order that allows a creditor, usually a bank, to take ownership of a property. It's pretty drastic, though. A bank won't go to those lengths unless there have been repeated nonpayments for extended periods of time. I'm talking about a year at the very least, usually longer. Shit, that means Buchanan defaulted on the building's mortgage."

"How?" Molly croaked, pushing past the emotion clogging her throat. "How did this happen? We haven't had an empty table at a service in at least six months! And the reservations—" She quickly tallied the tables from when she'd last peeked at the reservation program. "We've got to be booked out for just as long. I've been here for two years, and I can't remember closing out a service where we didn't meet, or exceed, our profit margins. For God's sake, we were written up by a national food critic! How the hell can there be no money? There isn't even enough to cover the next payroll!"

"They funneled it all into their private accounts. Any assets left are going to be confiscated and frozen real soon, if they haven't been already."

Too many things had decided to bleed out of Molly, in no particular order. Fear for her colleagues and concern over her own finances crept toward the top of the list, sure. What sat at the zenith of her encroaching despair, however, was the culmination of countless fourteen-hour days on her feet cooking someone else's food. It had been the promise of a dream paid in years she couldn't get back. The excitement of being offered a sous-chef job at a barely known restaurant in a sleepy New Hampshire town, then watching in awe as all of New England beat down the door for what she could give them.

For what *they* were supposed to give *her* in another year. The role of chef de cuisine. Her own menu. A partnership in the business.

All gone.

She didn't even have time to mourn a loss that was so new, the reality of it hadn't reached her frontal cortex yet. Even as she clutched the phone to her ear, her legs were still itching to begin her morning rounds and check in at the prep stations. Desperately searching for a loophole, Molly grasped for another possibility, *anything* that could explain this all away as a bad dream or a Jupiter-sized misunderstanding. "But what about—"

An audible thud echoed from outside the office, rattling the framed newspaper reviews that adorned the paneled walls.

"Staff meeting. Now!" The barked orders of her head chef

straightened her spine instantly, though whether her response was out of fear or familiarity, she couldn't be certain.

"Chef's here. Got to go."

"He's not your chef anymore, Mol." A note of bleak resignation colored his whispered words. "Call me when it's over."

When it's *over*? When *what* was over?

Her numb fingers darkened the screen, and Molly scurried to the kitchen to join the rest of the staff. Half a dozen line cooks paused the methodical setup of their stations, seemingly sensing that whatever was to come was far more than a last-minute menu change or announcement of a guest critic at dinner service.

Chef Mark Tourneau stood beside Mr. Buchanan in front of the swinging door that separated the kitchen from the front of the house. The executive chef, who had always carried himself with an approachable yet firm demeanor, now did his best to affix that discerning gaze on anyone who *wasn't* holding a knife in their hand. He wasn't wearing his black chef's coat or even his glasses. Instead, his thinning hair had been hidden beneath a ball cap so old that the apparel sported a team's logo that had since been redesigned, twice. Worn flannel hung limply from sunken shoulders, and the sight struck Molly dumb. How had such a frame ever managed to carry the weight and respectability of the region's most popular restaurant?

Turned out, it hadn't, which meant . . . it was all true.

Her head chef's eyes increased the torque on the vice already twisting Molly's insides. She'd *trusted* this man. Trusted her career and the livelihoods of all the staff to his storied tenure and vision. For what? *Cars?* The proverbial extensions of what all women knew men like these two lacked between their legs? She'd have laughed at the cliché's absurdity if the imagery didn't starkly remind her of her newly dire circumstances. Betrayal crowded out the curious murmurs around her, until Mr. Buchanan quelled the chatter with a bracing clap of his hands.

Hands adorned with not one but two walnut-sized gold rings she'd never noticed before.

Because she never thought jewelry would be a precursor to jail time.

"Look, uh, there's no easy way to say this, so chef and I are just going to come right out and rip the bandage off. Effective immediately, Serendipity is closing its doors. Final checks will be in the mail next week."

The raucous uproar around her was the only thing that had adequately matched her expectations since she'd walked into the restaurant that morning. Shouts rivaled the insistent pounding of pans. Kitchen towels met the floor with resounding slaps of equal disgust. Outrage volleyed among the line cooks until it hit her square in the chest, then settled around her in a curtain of her fractured reality.

"No, they won't," she whispered toward the floor through quivering lips. "There won't be any checks."

No one heard her, and no one knew. Colleagues who'd hacked off literal pieces of their fingers cooking for this restaurant huddled around the counters, eyes pleading for any explanation from their supposed leaders, and still, they were lied to. *She* was being lied to.

"Hey, come check this out." Juliette, the salad chef, had her nose buried in her phone, while her free hand waved the rest of the former staff over. Judging by the gasps and curses, they were reading the same article Benny had sent her. The same one outlining, in lurid detail, what all their hours of exhaustion had paid for.

"*Two* McLarens?"

"This lists a ten-bedroom beach house in Puerto Vallarta under chef's name!"

"Mr. Buchanan had off-shore accounts?"

Molly's eyes slid toward the men in question who, as each new accusation was uncovered, slunk farther away from the kitchen, until the front door to the restaurant slammed behind them with an audible jolt.

They were gone faster than it took Buchanan to spew his empty promise of a final paycheck.

Juliette turned off her phone but not before extending a choice finger in the direction their former bosses had escaped. "That's it. I'm out of here. No freaking way am I being associated with any of this. I do catering on the side anyway. I don't need this type of risky exposure." She shrugged out of her apron, grabbed her roll-up knife bag, and stormed past Molly.

"Right behind you." Martin, the appetizer chef, added his apron to the pile and followed in Juliette's wake.

One by one, the entire staff filed out of Serendipity, which, up until five minutes ago, had been the single greatest stepping stone for all of their careers. They walked through the dining room, furiously hip-checking tables and kicking chair legs, as if the very furniture, which had hosted some of the region's most famous celebrities and esteemed food critics, had betrayed them as well.

A handful of minutes later, the final pair of footsteps left behind their echo to bang around the abandoned cavern of Molly's former dreams.

Should she follow everyone out? How long before the police raided the property? *Was* that something they even did, or had she been watching too many crime shows?

Alone, and with far more questions than answers, she did the only thing her frozen limbs could manage and walked back to the office. She needed to call Benny, tell him more about what he undoubtedly already knew. What he'd rightfully predicted.

Call me when it's over.

At fifty-two, the man had spent more years in the restaurant business than most restaurants *stayed* in business. Would he leave her, too? Did any of them have a choice?

Stiff fingers pulled the phone from her pocket. Benny picked up before the first ring even hit her ear.

"It's over," she croaked.

"Did you see chef and Buchanan? Did everyone leave?"

"Yes. Effective immediately, everything's shut down. Buchanan mentioned something about final checks going out in the mail next week, but we both know that's crap." A bitter laugh escaped her lips. "We fill orders for freaking thirty-five-dollar entrées night after night on the *cheap* end, and there's nothing to show for it, not even a final paycheck."

Nothing to show for it . . .

Years of her life invested into a career, climbing her way to promotions the head chefs had no choice but to award her, always giving them ten reasons to choose her for every one reason to choose her male counterparts. Always fighting, always taking on more where others did the bare minimum. And then the sous-chef opportunity at Serendipity came along, and it was, quite literally, serendipitous.

It hadn't just been a promise of a step up the ladder but an investment in her future. Validation for the hard choices made for the sake of her dream she refused to let die. It was one more tool in her arsenal to combat the terribly unlucky star she'd been born under. It was . . .

An investment.

Molly eyed the crumpled court document at her feet, then lunged at the thing as if it were a treasure map she'd only just figured out how to decipher. She smoothed the stiff paper against her thigh and took in the ominous words again, this time through a different lens. "Hey, Benny? If one were to pay the bank the full sum it's owed, plus compounded interest, do you think that would satisfy the writ and keep the property from going into foreclosure?"

"I guess, in theory, that makes sense," he mused. "But the worth of the restaurant isn't just in its property value. In order for the business to be purchased, it would need to be assessed, appraised, insured, reinspected—"

"I'm not talking about buying the business. I'm talking about keeping the property from going into foreclosure." Molly's mind whirled with an unsteady rhythm born of a loose axle as she mentally tallied every spare cent in every bank account to her name, even marking the recent IOU money her best friend, Drea, had just paid her back. Nothing was left out of her frantic analysis, not even the dozen or so savings bonds she'd received for her bat mitzvah eighteen freaking years ago that *still* hadn't fully matured. She ticked off all available lines of credit and cash advances like they were items on a grocery list, along with any family members who might be convinced to pony up the money if she spun the investment angle the right way.

Then there was The Account. The private account she'd been squirreling money into ever since she'd first thrown on an apron in a professional kitchen and decided she wanted to feed people. Her vision-board seed money that would one day fund her restaurant. Money she'd been meticulously hoarding and nurturing with quiet low-risk investments. It wasn't nearly enough on its own, but perhaps altogether . . .

The result of her mathematical mesmerism slowly staggered out of its dizzying rotation until it landed approximately on the final payment the bank was seeking, interest and all, to prevent the property from going to auction.

"Molly . . . Earth to Molly . . . You still there, girl?"

"Yes," she breathed out, gathering her thoughts to deliver the first clear and sure sentence she'd spoken all day. "And I'm going to buy the building."

CHAPTER 2

It hadn't been enough. Even with the cash advances, both from her emergency credit card and her *For Real, Do Not Use Unless You Want to Eat Cat Food for The Rest of Your Life* backup emergency credit card, it hadn't been enough. As soon as the last pair of her former colleagues' work clogs shuffled out the door, Molly grabbed a stool, squatted her ass down, and threw every morsel of tunnel-vision motivation into making the numbers work. She'd called all her banks, including, begrudgingly, the bank of mom and dad, and then she'd called *the* bank—the bank of record on the court document.

Turned out, money talked a heck of a lot louder than she'd thought. And corporations, especially financially minded ones, well, they sure as heck listened. It had been surprisingly easy to broker the terms of the sale, provided she could pony up the cash before the close of business the next day.

Cash she was still several grand short of. Slight snag, there.

Until Benny, saint that he was, found her still slouching on the same stool hours later and offered her the biggest lifeline in the forms of a promise, payment, and, perhaps the most needed of all, pizza.

"This is a pity pie, isn't it?" Molly mumbled around a mouthful of pepperoni and cheese. "A consolation prize for the fastest attempt to rack up the most debt in the shortest amount of time." She pumped her fist in the air unenthusiastically and drolled, "Yay, winning."

The creases at the corners of his eyes deepened, mirroring the weathered lines on his forehead that spoke of not only years of grueling labor but the mental anguish of a world not doing right by you and the tenacity to power through regardless. His arthritic hand, gnarled at the knuckles from years of butchering everything from prime rib to pancetta, grabbed a plain slice and —*gasp*—folded it in half before shuttling the tip into his mouth. "Only thing pitiful is what went down here," he said between bites. Then he shook his head. "None of us came this far only to get kneecapped at the finish line, which is why Marisol wanted me to give you this, with her blessing."

Benny shifted to the side, pulled out a folded piece of paper from his back pocket, and handed it to Molly between two fingers as casually as one offered a messy-faced child a napkin. She tried not to wince at the mental comparison.

"What's this?" She quickly wiped her greasy fingers on an *actual* napkin before accepting the note.

What she unfolded was anything but.

Molly leaned forward to confirm what she held and nearly teetered off her stool before she managed to catch herself. The check in her hands was for the difference she needed to complete the property transaction, plus a hefty amount extra.

"I promised Mari I'd give her a proper retirement when it came time, take the two of us back to the Dominican Republic. She'd get to be with her sisters and the rest of her family, and I'd finally spend my days in a sailboat under the sky catching and filleting my own fish instead of all this farm-raised crap."

Under normal circumstances, Molly would have whole-heartedly echoed the man's sentiments regarding his pesca preferences, except for the small fact that farm-raised canned fish was pretty much the only protein she saw herself being able to afford over the next few months.

A situation potentially remedied by the check weighing down her palm and the warmth spreading throughout her chest caused by what Benny was offering her.

Molly summoned a voice thick with heavy emotion. "You're not retiring. You're only fifty-two. Oh, P.S. and by the way, I can't accept this." She thrust the paper toward him like it was on fire but only watched, mildly aghast, as Benny ignored her in favor of another slice.

"You know as well as I do that this career puts the *long* in longevity, and not in a good way. Longer hours, longer work weeks, longer time before a promotion comes your way, if you're lucky and manage to use the right set of skills to impress the right people." His rejected crust nubbin landed next to its sibling on the paper plate. The sound was as insistent and final as the sincerity Benny pressed into his words. "Very few cooks get to have any form of real retirement. Most of us can't afford to stop working and only do so when we no longer have a choice, either because our bodies finally give out or our adult children finally give us an ultimatum."

Her friend paused for a moment. His lip twitched on a memory, and Molly's stomach tightened. "Neither of those options work for me or my Marisol. We never had any children, and while I'm no young buck anymore, I've still got some appreciable strength left in me to serve her right by." He slapped his stomach in affirmation, which was only beginning to show signs of aged softness. His eyes misted over, and a secret smile deepened the grooves at the corners of his mouth. "She deserves more than the leftovers she'll get when this career is through with me. And helping you buy this place—in exchange for part ownership," he said pointedly, knowing full well the offer was already on her tongue, "well, that's about as good a ticket to paradise as we could get."

"I don't . . . I can't . . ." God, where were her *words*? Never in her entire life had she been short on things to say, and there she was, sputtering like a bad engine starter. Molly's mother had often joked how, at birth, she was only given a certain allotment of words to use for the rest of her life, and at the rate she went, she'd use them all up by the time she turned eighteen.

If fate had chosen this moment to prove her mother right, Molly would eat her apron.

"Sure you can," Benny replied, smugly *not* trying to keep his amusement at her distress out of his words. "Whatever you want to do with this place, it's yours. We just want to help you get there. Menu, style, interior design, all that crap is beyond my pay grade. You do what you like, and I'll cook it. All I ask is to remain here and see you through this next venture until Marisol calls me home and books those one-way plane tickets to paradise." The table legs groaned against the wood floor as he stretched his bulky frame and worked a knot out of his shoulder. "As I figure it, I've got at least another ten years of professional cooking in me, but it ain't my call. Those years are Mari's." Then he winked at her. "But she's happy to consign me out to you for the time being. Told me so herself last night in bed after we—"

"I adore your wife, but please, under no circumstances, will you finish that sentence."

The vibration of his teasing chuckle only added to Molly's internal tremors. Was this really happening? Had her friend just handed her—she glanced down at the check again—the monetary equivalent of her dream?

Benny slapped his hands on his thighs and stood. "Call the bank in the morning and get it done. You and I both know they'll take your money faster than it takes to overcook a steak, but closing on this property and getting those keys in your hot little hands ain't no twenty-four-hour turnaround." He walked over to a table, one that had been ceremoniously hazed by the other staff on their way out, and righted one of the chairs. Once he gently pushed it in like it was occupied by royalty, he smiled at her. "What do you say? You want your restaurant or what?"

Molly swallowed around the emotion that was quickly being overtaken by a familiar determination. She shot to her feet, threw the check into her back pocket, and heaved herself at the man. He caught her weight like a guy used to lifting burdens and giving bear hugs. "I'm going to make you and Marisol so stinking proud of me."

He laughed into her hair before rubbing her back encouragingly and settling her down. "Then go get it, girl."

NEVER, in all her years of working in the hospitality industry, had Molly said no to more customers and been so freaking happy doing so. And there she was, hanging up on the third caller within the hour clamoring to make a reservation at Aurora's newest breakfast-and-lunch eatery, Suerte and Honeysuckles.

A reservation, she itched to reiterate into the phone, that would never be procured, because when Molly had finally spawned her beloved brainchild of a restaurant into existence, she had included one hard-and-fast rule: no reservations. Like, ever.

"Was that another paying customer you just hung up on?" Benny's rumbling chuckle was a punctuated chord amid the symphony of a kitchen in full swing. An egg cracked sharply against the flattop before falling to the sizzling surface below. Its weighted plop was barely perceptible amid the instant sputter of bacon grease crisping the egg's edges and kissing the air with the unmistakable smell of all things breakfast. Another egg joined its mate and firmly hunkered its golden yokey butt down next to two extra-thick-cut slabs of applewood smoked artisan dry-cured bacon.

Now, *this* was luck. The hard-won kind, with the mouthwatering texture of all her dreams finally realized. Well, *mostly* realized. In all Molly's unspoken imaginings of her dream breakfast-and-lunch joint, there hadn't ever been quite so much debt. Or so much *merengue* music, for that matter.

Not that she minded that last one a single bit.

"I didn't hang up on them," Molly remarked over her shoulder while she punched in an order with the back of her pencil. "I just kindly informed them that we don't accept reservations."

Benny flipped his griddle spatula in the air in time with the tamboura solo pumping from the small speaker next to the stove and executed a perfect hip swivel that was far too much excitement for such an early hour, but who was she to deny the man his indulgence? Had she had hips half as limber, she'd most likely salsa down the aisles of the grocery store just because she could.

Molly turned away from her view of the dining room's bustling patrons and leaned back against the counter so she could admire not the fancy front-of-house glitz but the solitary kitchen and exuberant chef she'd helped rescue.

Or who had helped rescue *her*.

Once the bank turned over ownership of the property to her, it had taken a good three months to tear down the stains of Serendipity and plant the seeds of her future.

Suerte and Honeysuckles. *Suerte* meant luck in Spanish and was a nod to Benny and Marisol's heritage, though luck, by conventional standards, had about as much to do with her success as kissing babies at a pep rally had to do with a politician winning an election. On the surface, her restaurant was pretty as punch, but beneath the glossy veneer lived years upon years of being told no, of being turned down and passed over for colleagues and applicants with nothing more to offer over her except for what hung between their legs.

Benny had been the sole exception in her culinary life, even though she'd only known him for two years, but damn did it feel good to see that man happy. When they first put their heads together to strategize about the restaurant, he'd remained true to his promise: whatever she wanted, he was on board with, provided he and Marisol were cared for and he got the freedom so often denied those who gave their lives to restaurant kitchens. The idea for it all slammed into her on a wave of gratitude and exuberance she hadn't had time to question—nor did she want to. Suerte and Honeysuckles would be a banner to all those who made their own luck. Simple yet elevated fare available to everyone, regardless of wallet size or reservation-making assistants. Together, she and Benny would produce delicious food that would pour out of a place that Molly hoped would become as invasive to the touristy town as the regional flowers she'd named her restaurant for. It would be both unapologetically New England and unapologetically her.

Also, not allowing reservations meant not answering to others' promises or expectations. An open-promptly-at-six and close-promptly-at-three establishment. No late nights. Plenty of family and friend time. With just enough left over to nurture a woman's lifelong dream, piled high with the best damned vintage cheddar and sourdough grilled cheese sandwiches, if she did say so herself.

"Hey, I'm with you. We don't need reservations." Benny gestured toward the full tables out at the front, reminding Molly she had about another twenty seconds before she needed to get back out there and start refilling coffees. "What we need is a hand to take care of the dishes and clear tables. You can't keep doing that all on your own, girl."

The urgency to grab as many coffee pots as she could and

turn tail in the opposite direction of the impending conversation caused Molly's face to heat.

"I'm managing," she huffed out with all the petulance of a kid being called on the carpet for offering to do the group assignment by herself so she'd be sure everyone would get a good grade.

"Yeah, managing to shave a few years off your life. And I promise you, if my arthritis is anything to go by, those years won't be the junky ones at the end like you're expecting." He regripped his fingers around the spatula before brandishing the thing at her in accusation. "You had a brilliant idea paring down the place to just short-order breakfast-and-lunch service. Expenses are a quarter of what Serendipity had."

She *had* been quite proud of that brilliant idea, now that he mentioned it. And if that coffee pot would stop dripping in the next quarter of a second, she'd grab the thing and it'd be a monumentally splendid way to end the conversation. She gripped the handle, staring down the final drips while expressing no small amount of need for it to wrap the heck up—

"But you still need staff. Not in my kitchen, mind you." Benny punctuated the fact with a knobby finger that expressed stubborn ownership she knew better than to question and, any other day, would be more than a little bit fond of. "For you. You can't run this place, handle the menu, inventory, marketing, maintenance, cleaning, and everything else by yourself."

Aaand there it was. The same point he'd been hammering her with ever since the new drywall went up and the signage was hung a month ago.

"I know." She cringed at the supplication in her voice. In the entirety of her career, when had she ever resorted to whining? The third Tuesday of never, that's when, and yet . . .

Benny flipped a row of sausage links and put down his spatula to lower the music. Crap. Not good.

The utensil was back in his hand a heartbeat later, and his words were everywhere she couldn't escape.

"It's early December. The tourists have hit Aurora hard. The holiday season is in full swing. We're already starting to have a hard time filling takeout orders. I can cook the menu with my eyes closed, but that won't wash these dishes any faster or clear those tables or, hell, even bag up some orders and answer the damn phone." Benny said all this while never removing his eyes from the stove. His arms and hands moved despite the thorough dressing-down he'd delivered, once again reminding her how she wasn't the only one who'd manufactured her own fortune to get where she was.

She wasn't the only one who needed this place to thrive, needed it to deliver on borrowed promises her heart had made before her head had caught up with it.

Molly folded her arms over her chest and slid her gaze toward the dining room again. Two tables had been vacated, one by a family of four who had asked for extra plates for every entree and one by a party of six who, judging by the unpushed-in chairs and food under the table, were more than used to being picked up after. A trail of crumpled napkins littered the floor. She watched as a crowd of eager patrons milling around the door stepped aside, making room for those exiting.

Patrons she didn't have enough tables for. More people she'd have to either say no to or ask to wait until she'd have time to bag up their takeout orders.

The traitorous coffee pot finally beeped, heralding the end of its brew cycle, and Molly sagged against the counter. Coffee had suddenly become the least of her concerns.

"I hadn't been prepared to hire staff yet," she said, knowing full well it was a weak-ass excuse. "I was hoping the restaurant would shore up its earnings a bit more first." She'd wanted to hire people. Oh, how she wanted to, but there had always been that niggling thought of *what if*. What if the restaurant had a bad month, or three? Could she really hire someone at this stage of the game, with that type of uncertainty hanging over her head?

She caught Benny's glare between ladles of cinnamon and cardamom-spiced pancake batter hitting the griddle. As she was fluent in all things Benny, there was no need for translation: *Bull. Shit.*

"Hope has nothing to do with it. If it did, you think you'd have done what you had to in order to purchase this place?"

He had her there.

Decidedly not, you infuriating man.

Benny scooped up a generous portion of corned beef hash, which had a *very* healthy week-long-cured corned-beef-to-potato ratio, and nestled it onto a plate next to the most perfect over-easy eggs dusted with smoked sweet Hungarian paprika. Another order to complete the five sitting on the counter, ready for her to take to the dining room. "The money will be there when it's supposed to be. It always is. Until then, take this sucker by the horns and do what you need to do." Molly loaded up the tray and hefted the thing to her shoulder, but not before Benny tossed a knowing wink in her direction. "Because Marisol would have my ass if she saw how much I'm letting you do around here."

Molly hip-checked the door. "You're not *letting* me do anything."

"Make sure you tell *her* that!" His bark of protest was cut off by the swinging door and drowned out further by the bustling dining room. To Molly's left, a crying three-year-old just spilled his apple cider under the table. To her right, three eager hands clutching empty coffee mugs all shot up into the air in a communal summons.

And the line at the door now spilled onto the sidewalk, threatening to swallow the bicycle racks and parking meters.

Molly lowered the tray onto a rack and began dispensing

orders. Once she'd been relieved of the weight, however, her shoulders still tensed under an unseen burden.

Did she really have a choice?

Dammit, Benny.

She grabbed a rag, dropped to her knees, and silently cursed her friend's name while cleaning up fallen food and musing over how one worded a job ad for a position they couldn't afford to post.

Wanted: Dishwasher and other TBD kitchen duties, with opportunity for advancement. Maybe.

CHAPTER 3

Of all the small towns in the world, Aurora seemed as good a place as any to descend into complete and utter madness. After nearly two thousand years of torture, Brass, a fallen sentinel, could hardly keep his head above the tar threatening to pull him under.

Especially when the threat's poisoned tentacles were mere weeks away from ensnaring his mind altogether.

Three weeks, to be exact. Then he'd see just how accurate his own hell would be compared to the one mortals threatened their so-called sinners with.

Brass tightened his grip on the motorcycle's throttle and jerked it toward him. Even after millions of years living in the mortal realm, he'd never developed the fondness for motorized vehicles his brother sentinels had. What he wouldn't give to trade his BMW's handlebars for horse reins and kick the beast into a frenzied gallop. To feel the panting horseflesh heaving against his strong thighs as he gave the animal leave to churn up the earth with wild unrelenting abandon. Uncaged, unencumbered, with only the will of the animal and the freedom of its primal urges to answer to.

The power of answering to no one save for the rider and his reins. The pulsing, pounding ardor finally released—

An electric vehicle blew the yield sign and whipped onto the lane in front of him. Brass clenched his teeth and braked his bike hard to the right. Tires squealed against the newly slick asphalt, still damp from the morning mist that hadn't fully burned off yet. The engine sputtered and growled beneath him, voicing its annoyance at being stalled.

"Mages dammit!" Brass whipped his head forward and caught the faint glow of the small car's brake lights pulsing through the thin fog. "Oh, *now* you brake?" The red rectangles briefly blinked their acknowledgment, or perhaps mockery, of his situation as the vehicle proceeded to speed up while approaching the amber traffic light instead of slowing down.

It all happened before Brass even had time to call the rage back. The snap in his mind resounded through him like a bone crushed beneath stone. He mentally leaped for the flapping tether of restraint, which now danced taunting circles in the hollow of a mind he barely recognized.

His power answered before his conscience could. A twist of his fingers into a fist saw the vehicle not only braking before it hit the light but slamming to a halt by an unseen anchor. Lights sputtered and metal groaned. Even from this distance, he could hear the vehicle's various alarms casting out their cries for help.

Help is not coming. It will never come.

The whispered warning in his mind locked his joints, imprisoning him further against his cursed nature as he cast out his power. His metal sought out every molecule of copper and zinc that held the vehicle's vital bits together and gave it all a new master: him. Wires sparked. Batteries bled. Wheel axles whined beneath an unknown weight. Through the haze of rampage, he could make out limbs. Bystanders tugging at door handles, the driver beating against the closed window to get out and flee, to run and escape.

There is no escape.

The voice rumbled through his mind like an avalanche, crooning and coaxing him with its unrelenting power. Just before it crashed into his soul for good, however, it burst into a spray of cascading ice shards that rained down its cackling torment.

Ice he could melt.

"Nooo!" In a blink, he tossed himself from his bike, ducked into an empty bus stop shelter, and welcomed the burn of his angel fire roaring to life. The last celestial power afforded to him before he fell from the Empyrean shot through the red vapors of rage, its blue flames beating back the hold on his metal. Chest heaving but with his mind clear once more, he called his metallic power back.

No longer being ripped to scrap, the electric vehicle's metal sighed against the asphalt. Mortals flew onto their asses as doors they'd been tugging on finally yawned open. The driver, vermin that he was, scampered away from the car as if the thing was a tampered toy constructed by the laboring class to seek vengeance on the wealthy.

He wasn't terribly far off, but Brass wasn't about to point that out. He had enough problems to worry about. His angel fire extinguished before the next car passed the bus stop. To any mortal driving by, Brass appeared like just another human locked in the infernal cycle of early-morning commutes and miserable day jobs.

Good. Better they think him a mundane misanthrope than a cursed devil.

An insistent ringing filled the interior of Brass's Bluetooth helmet, yanking him away from the mess, both down the road and in his mind. He slapped the button on the side to engage the call. "What."

A grizzled snort echoed against the padding, doing absolutely nothing to ease the headache sprouting behind his eyes.

"Not your usual greeting. Had to check the phone for a second to make sure I didn't call Chrome by mistake."

They both knew that was a trumped-up statement made for no one's benefit. His brother Iron never did anything without purpose.

Including making casual phone calls. The angel wouldn't know casual if it wore a red dress, stripped him naked, engaged in a little wing play, and made him pay for dinner afterward.

Which meant Iron had called with an agenda.

Hell.

Brass sagged onto the bench, biting back the sting of the metal kissing his rear end through his jeans. "Spare me the humor. It doesn't suit you."

"And backhanded comments don't suit you." A grumbling pause invaded the line as several cars drove past. The reprieve was just long enough for Brass's regrettable self-reflection but not so long for him to steel himself against his brother's next attack. "It's happening again, isn't it?"

It.

He and the other sentinels all knew what *it* referred to, along with the unspoken hourglass sifting through his remaining hours until the chains snapped tight and he became a prisoner of his own mind.

The curse.

Brass wrenched his eyes away from the road. The bus stop was perched in front of one of Aurora's many municipal parks. Landscapers had long ago switched out their lawn mowers for leaf blowers, ensuring the manicured fields would stay as such. But the calendar had turned over a new month, and with it came the chilling threat of winter. Out of the corner of his eye, Brass silently marked the edge of green grass, painted a deeper balsam by the shade of his visor.

And speckled with a thin, crisp layer of pearlescent frost. The first of the season and a precursor of what was to come.

The solstice.

Brass peeled his lips away from his teeth, again grateful for the cocoon of the helmet. "Yes."

"How bad was it this time?"

He flicked a concerned gaze down the road, where a tow truck had just arrived on the scene, and the electric vehicle's driver was circling the car, phone to his ear, arms waving like the world owed him penance. "Bad. Could have been worse. I *wanted* it to be worse, but I didn't let it get that far. I managed to control it."

"Managed. Never did like that word. It implies too many out-of-control variables."

"Yeah, well, it's the best I've got at the moment."

"If that's your best, then we're fucked. It's December first, Brass."

"I know!" he snarled. "Don't you think I know that? Don't you think I've spent every last one of these two thousand years searching for a way out of this? Believe me when I tell you there is none. Ragana had made certain that much was . . . *ensured*." Ridicule and disdain floated the word from his distant memories of the goddess's vengeance. "All I can hope for is to command it, master its rule so it can't master me."

Even as he spoke the words, Brass knew they were embers floating on the ocean, something a mighty volcano would sputter out in carefree warning before it erupted into chaos.

"Are you? Have you?" His brother's questions weren't meant to be the attacks they were, and yet they still landed as such.

Brass jolted off the bench, properly parked his bike like a good goddamn samaritan, switched the call from his helmet to his phone, and stormed down the sidewalk in a self-indulgent fit. If the mortal driver with the god complex could be afforded such a tantrum, surely one of the Empyrean's warrior sentinels could be allowed a stomping session or two.

"I'll find a way to handle it," Brass gritted out. "I don't need your censure."

"I'm not giving it. I'm here to help you, brother. We all are." The plea in Iron's tone nearly caused Brass to miss a step. A pervasive silence filled the line, strengthening against the enormity of how few days he had left with his brothers before . . .

A shuddering sigh vibrated through the phone's speakers. "We'll keep looking," Iron assured him. "Always. We'll find a way out of this."

Brass couldn't summon the strength to respond, so he simply grunted his acknowledgment and ended the call.

At some point in his mildly panicked broodfest, he'd managed to wander into the heart of Aurora's downtown. Casual strolls were not indulgences he was accustomed to, but given the events of the morning, he was far more inclined to let himself explore.

Let himself memorize what he stood to lose.

As it was not yet eight o'clock in the morning, many businesses were still locked up tight save for the coffee shops, bakeries, and that one food truck at the end of the cul-de-sac off Spruce Path that always served those churro waffles with the Mexican chocolate dipping sauce he'd enjoy on occasion.

Brass let himself be led by the enticing aromas of cinnamon, cocoa, and chili. Before he made it to the next traffic light, however, his senses drew him in another direction.

A direction he'd tried to train himself, over the past several months, *not* to move toward.

Tried and failed miserably.

The sign that lorded over the corner property no longer boasted the elegant script of the town's most popular fine dining establishment, Serendipity. Instead, hard block letters were displayed prominently, announcing the newest tenant to pander to Aurora's caffeine-fueled clientele.

A throng of people shuffled out the door, hitching overstuffed coat collars high around necks otherwise bared to the frigid New Hampshire elements. Coats that were unzipped, of course, because tourists somehow believed themselves exempt from wind chills.

Move on. Just move on.

Brass urged his legs to hoof a beeline straight for the churro truck, but his damn eyes couldn't resist a peek at a temptation he had no business indulging in.

She wouldn't be there anyway. It was obviously a new restaurant, which meant new employees, new customers, new—

Through the front window, a shock of dark hair shot up from under a table, followed by the swipe of a forearm across a brow that, even from Brass's distance, revealed far more worried creases than when he'd last seen it.

When he'd last seen *her*.

As if he needed more proof of his torturous curse.

In the quiet hours of the evening, when the minerals in the great mountain he and his brothers lived beneath recharged his power and shut out the rest of the terrors plaguing him, new ones would burrow in good and deep for the night. Two, to be exact. Two espresso-rich eyes among elfin features that batted around his bruised brain, soothing away tremors that had only recently begun to surface the closer he inched toward the solstice.

Tremors that would latch onto him with teeth and talons.

He'd only met Molly Resnick a handful of times after guarding his brother Chrome's soul bond, and Molly's roommate, Drea, from demon charmers and later helping Drea move into their den. The visceral reaction to Molly had been the gut punch he hadn't seen coming. Each encounter, though brief, produced a storm that jolted him off his anchor, thrusting him inexplicably toward something he couldn't see.

Or fight.

Brass balled his hands into fists and shifted his weight

behind a lamppost. Curiosity rooted him to the pavement as he observed the woman he'd tried to forget. Her dark waves had been tamed into a stringent bun that sat low on the back of her head and was completely at odds with the flyaway strands of her bangs. A starched denim-colored half-bistro apron was cinched around hips that had shimmied away from him with undue haste the last time he'd seen her at her and Drea's apartment.

When he'd lifted a box containing a Dutch oven from her hands before she could refuse his help and she'd promptly whirled around, shuttled herself down the hall, and slammed a door between her and whatever the hell it was that had him constantly turning his head in her direction.

A crash reverberated from behind the window glass, wrenching his and several customers' attention toward the commotion. Molly was holding a large circular serving tray flat against her body, practically hugging the sodden thing like a shield as liquid and partially melted ice cubes slid down its surface to pool on the floor—a floor now littered with broken ceramic mugs and drinking glasses.

Where the hell was the busser? Or other waitstaff? Brass knew Molly was a chef, and an amazing caliber one at that judging by the write-ups he had *not* made a point of reading shortly after they'd been introduced. When had she taken on serving duties as well? Why? And more to the freaking point, why was no one helping her? Even a hostess or dishwasher would surely have scrambled forward to help with such a mess, especially during prime service hours. Hell, the broken glass alone should have sounded some sort of front-of-house alarm given how many toddlers were hobbling around the place.

But no one moved. Once diners ascertained that the mess was being dealt with, they casually returned to their meals as if the entire fiasco had been no more than another loud noise their brains had lumped into the auditory pile of forks tinkling on plates and knives scraping jam on toast.

One man, a tall, greasy fellow with more hair on his chest sprouting from his V-neck than he had clinging to his scalp, nudged past Molly, bumping into her hip and disrupting the pile of broken glass she'd neatly amassed.

Blood pounded a battle cry against Brass's temples. The cool metal of his gun kissed his palm before he even realized he'd grabbed the thing. Around him, happy families with too many kids and not enough hands to grab them all leaked out onto the sidewalk like newly emancipated prisoners.

Who very much did *not* need to see a six-foot-four-inch guy in a trench coat lose his mages-loving mind while clutching his GLOCK 9mm semiautomatic pistol outside of a pancake joint.

Brass holstered his piece at his back. Once secure, he scanned the crowd—both inside and out—for the man who was about to have his face rearranged. Instead, his eyes snagged on the *Help Wanted* sign perched on the outside of the window. In the background, Molly had popped up from the floor, this time with the serving tray laden with debris hoisted high on a slim shoulder carrying far more than the weight of broken dishes.

Something behind those eyes was broken, her dark brows drooped in obvious exhaustion. With a little hop to redistribute the weight, she was off through the kitchen door, leaving the diners to their own devices.

A sharp tug brushed across Brass's skin, urging him to move with her, toward her. He fought it, tensing against the sensation and the knowledge that he was about as good to be around Molly as a Cat 5 hurricane was for any island in the tropics.

He should run. Fling himself into the street and hope a bus took care of his laundry list of problems if it would keep him away from her.

And yet his boots moved toward the front door anyway. His

insistent strides never faltered, even as his shoulders parted the throngs of people clogging up the pavement.

Before he wrenched open the door, he paused a moment, then yanked the *Help Wanted* sign out of the window and strode in.

CHAPTER 4

Ceramic shards tumbled into the garbage can, along with Molly's will to live, or, at the very least, the desire to show her face to anyone who'd bore witness to her mortified misery. If there had been a heavy, preferably well-hidden surface she could crawl under and hibernate beneath for a good long while, she'd nab her secret stash of Stella D'oros and make a month of it. The little goblin in her brain who wanted to throw itself in front of this particular traumatic situation and warn her away from the embarrassment awaiting her in the dining room had her scanning the kitchen for tight, well-tucked corners.

Of course, there was one hideaway that would always be there for her. Her original den of iniquity turned haven and the place toward which her feet marched out a childish stomping session.

Better to make a racket that way than have the customers hear her sobbing wails of shame.

I can't do this.

It was the single most intrusive thought that had been nipping at her scrambling heels ever since she'd opened her doors and realized far too late that she'd not only bitten off more than she could chew but was at dire risk of choking gruesomely on her bad decisions. Just what the hell had she been thinking?

She hadn't been, not with the appropriate cranial lobe anyway, and that was the grand freaking problem. When stormy emotions and the threat of personal defeat had towered over her in a pillar so high that it warned of pummeling her career into the dust, she'd just reacted. Whatever part of her always bristled at her never-ending karmic bullshit had simply decided, like always, to hike up its pants, throw its shoulders back, and storm the castle.

Except her *castle* was a newly remodeled short-order eatery built on more clouds than support columns.

Molly barely made it over the back office's threshold before she whipped off her apron and collapsed into the blue velvet wingback accent chair she'd scored for a deal from an estate sale a few weeks ago. The thing was about as impractical as they came in terms of office furniture, but then again, so was she.

Impractical. If there had ever been a better word to describe Molly, let alone her situation, it certainly wasn't in a language she was familiar with. As she glanced around the space, a whole boatload of impracticality lined up to throw sucker punches at her kidneys. The basic wood paneling had been replaced with standard drywall papered in teal and gold imagery that depicted a blooming forest with clusters of berries on branches and pinecones nestled among spruce needles. An unnecessary expense, her designer had warned her. It was a restaurant's back office, after all, not a therapist's sitting room. Never mind the fact that these simple four walls had been *her* therapy, much like the scented candles and first-edition cookbooks she'd taken great care to shelve right at eye height on the wall directly across from where her laptop sat.

A laptop she hadn't been able to open as regularly as she

should because she'd been torn in as many directions as there were corners in the building. Even now, the darn thing seemed to take up more space in the little office than it warranted, glowing and growing in her mind with all the orders she needed to place, P and L reports she needed to sift through, and don't even get her started on the tax documents—

"You need help."

If Molly wasn't a thousand percent certain the office didn't have any windows and, therefore, no access to the deep rumblings of semitrucks, she'd have sworn those resonant low-pitched words would have been conjured from her mind. Plucked plum out of there in the way one can recall favorite movie lines or song lyrics.

Or a certain man's unmistakably resonant voice.

The hulking figure in her doorway could have been ripped from any comic book drawn in an age when pencils produced more than just pictures on pages but raw, primal power.

A power that, every single damn time, would leave her slack-jawed and running for the nearest safe space so she could give her body a chance to collect itself. And for her mouth *not* to open up for business and say something that would turn all parties involved into nine shades of beet red.

Molly flattened herself against the chair, wondering whether she could pretend she was part of the furniture if she covertly grabbed her apron and covered herself with it, then stayed still long enough.

Holy butter on a biscuit. Brass was *here*? In *her* restaurant? The man of few words and even fewer body fat percentage points? The most gorgeous, yet oddly nicknamed man she'd ever had the privilege to lock gazes with, only to run and hide from like she was a five-year-old and he was a carrier of the dreaded cooties?

A man who had *distraction* and *destruction* written all over that perfectly chiseled jawline?

Mortification heated her cheeks, and his penetrating amber eyes missed exactly none of it. No hope for pretending to be the furniture, then.

How? How, of *all* people, did *he* get here? And not only *here* but in her private office? They'd only met a few times when Drea's boyfriend enlisted Brass and a few other brothers to keep an eye on their apartment after Drea had been run off the road by an unknown assailant at the time. And then there was the little matter of Drea's moving day, where Molly had tried to stay out of sight while simultaneously making sure Brass's best attributes stayed very much *in* sight. The sum total of all the words they'd spoken to each other could have been iced on a birthday cake.

Not that she'd counted them or anything.

The man had been too beautiful, too stoic, too devastatingly mesmerizing that she'd sooner throw herself into a vat of hot oil than risk the verbal diarrhea that would inevitably fire hose out of her mouth if she tried to talk to him.

So how the heck did he wind up here, crowding out the light from her doorway and robbing her of whatever meager air was left in her lungs?

She needn't look any further for clarification of his presence than the granite shoulders testing the strength of her door-frame's construction.

The restaurant wasn't the only thing solidly built, apparently. Brass's well-toned physique was tucked tightly into a black leather trench coat that skirted past leanly muscled thighs until it just dusted his knees. A high-backed collar swung up and wide, encircling a throat thick with tension, barely kissing the closely cropped auburn hairs around his ears and nape. The only acquiescence to his usual calm demeanor, as far as she could tell, was the thicker and longer hair in the front, which fell haphazardly over a broad forehead. Those amber eyes, again, pinned her to the chair, momentarily dazzling her out of whatever had landed her there in the first place.

Were men allowed to be beguiling? Because he really was beguiling . . . Until he opened his mouth.

"You need help," he said insistently.

Crap. He'd said something already, hadn't he?

Before she could rewind the last few minutes of her meltdown, he smacked a large and painfully familiar *Help Wanted* sign on top of her desk.

Ah, yes. Her call to the universe. Too bad said universe had a twisted sense of humor if it thought Brass should be the one to help with her employee search.

Molly smoothed down the corner of her sign, which had sustained a wrinkle or two during its rough transit from against the window to under her nose. "That's what I hear." She sighed, not at all pumped to be having this conversation *again*, let alone with this particular person. Of all people, *he* didn't need to know her problems.

"Where is the rest of your staff?" he asked, momentarily stepping back into the hall to scan for more employees. When his eagle-sharp eyes landed on Benny, who had just tossed a spatula in the air and completed an annoyingly perfect full spin before gracefully catching the thing, Brass's face fell into a mask of calm, if cautious, reserve. Then he took in the customer-laden yet waitstaff-deprived dining room.

Nope. There will be none of that, thank you very much.

She launched herself out of her chair and lunged for her apron before that discerning gaze had a chance to unnerve her again. "Did Drea send you here? Or Chrome? I adore your brother, but he has no-goodnik written all over him when it comes to minding his own business. I thought the overbearing protective act would go by the wayside once Drea moved in with you guys."

"He didn't send me. No one did. I was walking down the

street and saw the sign." His full lips thinned below flared nostrils, and he slashed his gaze back toward the dining room while addressing her. "Saw how one of your . . . *customers* . . . treated you while you were trying to clean up." That steely jaw of his ticked sharply to the right at the word *customers*, as if he needed to grind down the letters in order to spit the word out. Then he rested an anything-but-casual shoulder against the doorframe. "Didn't know you worked here. Used to be called something else."

"Serendipity. Yes. I bought the place out before the property could be sold at auction. It's been a hell of a few months, let me tell you." Years, really, but who was counting? Molly cinched her apron tighter around her waist to prevent the knot in her stomach from rising.

"You still need help." He nodded toward the sign. "Tell me what to do."

Tell. Me. What. To. Do?

All gears in an eight-block radius ground to a halt in her mind. She could have sworn the din from the dining room lessened, and Benny had turned down his music. Had Brass just asked—

"I'm sorry. Do . . . what?"

"Work." He twisted the sign toward him and leaned in closer to read the words at the bottom. The words she had hastily scrawled on there that encompassed pretty much everything that needed to be done in a restaurant in the impossible embodiment of a single individual.

Christ, she'd become a one-woman corporate greed machine. Yay, capitalism?

"Says here you need a dishwasher and busser, with duties not limited to the back and front of house."

"Yes, but it's not really a job ad."

He raised a brow in question. "Oh?" Then he tilted his lips. "Looks like an ad to me."

"It's an ad," she scrambled to clarify. "Of course, it's an ad. *Obviously.* It's just not really—"

"Filled. Now it is." He pushed off from the doorframe and swiped one of her newly printed menus off her desk. "Besides, dishes are dishes. I've washed plenty, so what's a few more? And I doubt you bought this place so you could nearly get knocked over by some nose-in-the-air mongrel who drives a BMW coupe with a soon-to-be missing spark plug."

Damn. He'd seen that?

Embarrassment flooded her frame. "No, I didn't— Wait, what about his spark plug?"

He waved her question away. "Never mind. The point is, you need the help. I've got the time and skills. Besides, Drea would never let me live it down if I abandoned her best friend to such a cruel and unusual punishment." This he said with a note of levity, though Molly failed to see the humor in the situation, unless, of course, this was all some planned prank.

A prank! Yes!

Any minute now, Drea would come waltzing in, iced coffees for the two of them in hand, and a giant *gotcha!* painted on her face. Molly waited for a heartbeat, then two. After the tenth pounding against her pulse points and her best friend still hadn't appeared, her skin tightened. Breath sawed in and out of her ever-constricting lungs. Was this really happening? "It's not cruel," she added, grateful to have finally found her voice again.

His lips teased one corner of his mouth higher, and everything changed. The tiny office's air thinned to an impossible degree, surely. It was the only explanation for her heart fluttering wildly behind her ribs and definitely *not* the lessening space between them as Brass took a step forward and grabbed her hand. A rough thumb swiped gently over her knuckles before moving down each finger and caressing the multitude of knife scars on each pad.

"What's cruel is hiding these skilled hands away in soapy

water all day." Then he closed his eyes and took a deep breath. A breath they both held.

Brass was touching her. Touching her! And she didn't know whether to lean into it and beg for more or tug her hand free and scramble up the wall like some frightened monkey.

Both sounded like solid choices.

When his eyelids finally swung open, a familiar calm returned to his features, even as he analyzed hers. Whatever tension he'd rode in on had clearly been expelled through several deep-chested breaths. A lightness that hadn't been there before lit his expression and called to mind the intrepid and quiet demeanor he'd always maintained the other few times they'd been around each other.

With the precision of one of the King's Guard, Brass swiped the menu into an inside pocket of his coat and dipped his head. "See you tomorrow morning at five."

Molly hadn't even had time to correct him that the restaurant opened at six, not five, that only *she* ever showed up that early, before the swish of his coat against the doorframe finalized his exit.

CHAPTER 5

Waiting until her phone's display rolled over to four thirty was the kindest form of cruelty Molly could think to inflict on her dearest of dear friends before she called her.

If Molly was truly feeling vindictive, she'd have called Drea at *four* am when she'd first gotten into work. See? Pure kindness.

"Mmm, hello?" The muffled groan tumbling through the receiver was a barely intelligible stretch of syllables that would have been right at home among a herd of pissed-off pachyderms.

Good. It was best Molly's prey didn't see her coming.

"You have five seconds to tell me why the hell Chrome's brother showed up at my restaurant offering to help me wash dishes and relocate asshole customers' spark plugs." She said all this with the phone wedged against her shoulder as she arranged coffee mugs on a rack to ensure all their handles were facing out at the same angle.

Through the line, the phone jostled, and the sound cut out briefly before returning. "Spark plugs? What time is it?" A faint click resounded of what Molly imagined was a lamp's chain being pulled harder than necessary, and Drea's groan progressed from a pained rumble to a shrill bark. "No, no lights!"

"Is that Chrome next to you? Oh, who am I kidding? Of course it is." Molly planted her hand on a hip popped all the way out in indignation. "Good. It'll save me the trouble of cross-interrogation."

"Molly?" Drea attempted to clear some of the morning grogginess from her throat. "It's a little early, love."

"He's going to be here in thirty minutes!"

A sleep-roughened voice a good octave and a half lower than Drea's, and about ten times as alert, planted itself in her ear. "Who?"

"Brass!" Molly shrieked into Chrome's ear, not giving a lick about what her elevated decibels did to his eardrums, seeing as how he was most likely one of the maestros of this fiasco. "Which means you now have"—she drew her phone away from her ear to check the time—"my mistake, *twenty-eight* minutes to tell me which one of you two co-conspirators thought it would be a good idea to volunteer him for dish duty."

Chrome shifted the phone, and low muffled murmurs clouded the line for the eternal length it took her to get all her ceramic soldiers neatly in order. Really, did those two always have to do everything as a couple, even strategize toward what would most likely be a united front while being rattled awake by a predawn ambush? Molly was just about to start refilling the saltshakers, when Drea's voice returned to her ear.

"All right, you're on speaker. We're both here. Now, please, start from the top, and be gentle," Drea pleaded. "You're obviously far more caffeinated than we are, and as much as I love healthy competition, there's no way in hell either of us could catch up to your level of coffee intake this early in the morning, not with your black-market-coffee-bean access."

"Speak for yourself. I always keep some in-case-of-emergency nitro cold brews in our mini-fridge." Chrome's voice drifted closer, as if he had stepped away briefly, and was then punctuated by the classic *tsss* of a well-timed can tab popping open.

"Ignore him." Drea groaned, though Molly didn't miss her friend's whispered, "Give me a sip."

Molly stress-fidgeted with the salt jug's wide-necked lid, wondering why the hell she opted for the seven-pound containers with their dysfunctional pour spouts instead of the twenty-five-pound bulk bags she could just rip open with her knife. She gritted her teeth and gave the lid one more firm yank, only to have salt erupt all over the counter, cascading like sand along the stainless steel. She pinched her eyes closed and pulled her bottom lip into her mouth.

Freaking figures.

"Please tell me you two had something to do with Brass volunteering to wash dishes at my restaurant. And if you could square away your story in"—she peered at her phone again—"twenty-five minutes, that'd be great."

"I haven't spoken to him. Have you?" Drea clarified before questioning the only one of them related to the man in question.

Chrome's voice rose through the shuffle of salt as Molly scooped the mess into a bin. "No. I mean, not about that. Other shit, sure, but I'm not about to pry," Chrome added.

And boy, did she latch onto that nonanswer with the talons of a raptor.

"Pry into what, exactly?" Molly's mental clock ticked off in immeasurably loud intervals, filling the quiet that stretched through the phone. "Chrome? What don't you want to pry into?"

A deep-chested sigh filled her ear. "Winter's not exactly Brass's favorite time of year. He can get a little . . . moody."

Well, this was certainly news to her, though why she was inclined to file it away as something significant she wasn't sure. She knew next to nothing about the man, so anything that offered her a peek behind the curtain seemed like a sort of private treasure. Something she should guard and keep safe. "I get that," she replied. "Seasonal affective disorder can be a real bitch, even for those stalwart New Englanders who brag about wearing their flip-flops through six inches of snow just to grab their morning Dunkin' Donuts."

"Ooh, Boston Kreme! That's what I want!" Drea shrieked.

Molly wrenched the phone away from her ear. After that, she finally had the good sense to put the call on speakerphone. Her overcaffeinated nerves could only handle so much before the sun was up, and she'd just about reached her limit. "Drea, *please* focus. I'm in crisis mode here."

"Yes, of course. Sorry."

Chrome cleared his throat. "Look, Molly, if it'll help any, I have no idea why Brass swung by your place—"

"How? How in the hell would that *help any*?" She curled her fingers in air quotes for no one's benefit but her own.

"*But*," he enunciated, "where's the harm? If he's trying to fill his days with something productive and chooses to do so with you, well, I could think of far worse ways to spend a few hours."

"That's because you don't know me that well, or what he's about to walk into with this place," she countered, cringing when the salt grated like sawdust beneath her pacing stride. "The job I posted is for a *dishwasher*. It's about as far from glamorous as you could get in a kitchen. And we hadn't even talked about the pay yet. That's even less glamorous."

It wasn't glamorous, so much as criminal, a poignant comparison that kept floating to the surface, doing its best to twist her insides into karmic sludge. She wasn't about to volunteer that bit of internal agony, however. She did have standards, or so she imagined.

An audible vibration skittered over her skin, disrupting her salt sweeping. Was that a . . . *laugh?*

She swiped at her bangs with a grouse, if only to give her hands something to do other than throw her phone into the freezer.

If Molly had been standing in front of Chrome, she'd have slapped that chuckle right out of him, no matter how long she'd have to ice her hand afterward. She worked in the restaurant business and had no shortage of the frozen stuff. She'd cheerfully take the hit, regardless of his stupidly stony jaw, so long as her point was made.

"Take the help, woman. Shit, I thought *I* was stubborn."

"Oh, you are," Drea crooned. "Now, shoo. Let me talk to my friend. Molly, you still there?"

"Yeah, technically." She sank down onto a stool beneath one of the counters, but her stupid feet still insisted on tapping out a stupid nervous rhythm against the stupid ceramic nonslip floor painted the stupidest shade of red.

Not red. *Terracotta,* the designer had clarified when Molly had to choose between the cheap red porcelain tile or the cheap red ceramic tile. Apparently, there was a difference between burnt orange and terracotta, and neither of them involved the word red. And Brass was supposed to walk into this kitchen in fewer minutes than it took her to scarf down her bagel from earlier, expecting her to . . . what? Show him how to wash out a pot? How to make sure he bent at the knees when hauling garbage into the dumpster out back?

How the hell was she even supposed to introduce him to this place without sounding like a desperate, naïve, and inappropriately minted business owner who knew more about fennel and radish pairings than finances?

Aaand here's the soap we use, which we keep right next to the sink. Imagine that. Our sinks also have hot and cold water faucets. Isn't that amazing? But don't leave the water running too long, because I'm so far in debt right now, I wouldn't be surprised if the town shuts off the water just as the breakfast rush comes in. So, welcome! Glad you're here! Lunch is on the house. Oh, and by the way, can I pay you in cash? Because Benny's the only W-2 employee I can afford to pay and still spare thirty dollars a week in groceries for myself. Speaking of which, did you know that if you crush up ramen into small pieces before you cook it in the broth, you can sometimes get fuller faster?

"Drea, I can't do this." God, she hated the defeat in her voice, hated that her best friend had to hear her spiral out of control. Again.

"Of course you can. You're, quite literally, the badassiest of badasses out there. But sometimes, even badasses need to take stock of their circumstances and accept help to keep their awesomeness alive. And if Brass is offering, what's the harm?"

The harm is that I don't want him to see the mess underneath. Not him.

"I'm not always this badass at work, though." It was as much of an admission as she'd ever let herself say out loud, and only because it was Drea. "I can . . . struggle, at times."

"Well, yeah, you're human. Der. We have no choice but to experience other basic elements of our natural-born condition as well, like gushing over cute baby animals and being stuck in the rain without an umbrella. All par for the human course."

"Stop trying to make me smile," Molly relented.

"Only if you stop coming up with reasons to refuse perfectly good help when you need it and it's offered to you. Help, I'll add, that comes in the form of someone you know."

"I've met him twice."

"And that's two more times than anyone else who would have responded to your ad."

Molly slouched as far forward as her stool would allow and looked at her phone again. Ten minutes. "I don't like your logic."

"You don't have to like it for it to be correct."

"Now you sound like a scientist arguing with a flat-earther."

"Well, someone's got to." The word *obviously* floated, unspoken, around the periphery of Drea's retort. As if Molly's present and looming situations were both in need of chastisement from an adult wary of using their grown-up voice to make the point.

Was she truly no better than a child prone to impulsive decisions and emotionally charged tantrums?

Molly refused to acknowledge the empty restaurant kitchen she sat in, the one with her name on the deed, or the egregious hour at which she'd maliciously called her best friend.

She was one unwelcome revelation away from sticking her tongue out at the phone, as she'd been in this exact same position with Drea more times than she could count, except with the roles reversed. When her best friend had struggled to keep a job for reasons employers deemed flighty, but Molly always knew to be more altruistic in nature, she'd been there for Drea with a to-go mug full of hot java and a pile of freshly pressed work clothes, encouraging her to attack the day anyway. It wasn't that Molly needed to be needed; it was just that care came easy to her. Far more easily than accepting the same help. It was one thing to shine the spotlight on others, sweep up the dirt around them, and fill in the neglected spaces with what was missing.

It was quite another thing to have that light glaring on her, illuminating holes far larger than any she'd managed to patch for those she loved. Holes that, if one looked too closely at, would reveal decrepit parts of herself she'd managed to successfully wall off and keep from doing irreparable damage.

The irony of all that could go crawl into the grease traps and choke on a petrified cheddar cheese biscuit.

"I should go," Molly said, scraping circles into the spilled salt with her toes. "Made a bit of a mess. Benny'll call the health department himself if he doesn't find his kitchen the way he left it."

"Mmm, but his lemon ricotta pancakes are amazing. Kind of worth the violation, in my opinion."

"You would say that."

"I'd say a lot of things for the right amount of carbs and sugar."

Molly nodded, finding little fault in the statement. "Fair."

Once she'd hung up and the impending sunrise blanketed the kitchen with a preternatural stillness, Molly sat there, wishing like hell all the stainless steel around her would stop reflecting so damn much of herself back at her.

CHAPTER 6

Brass could count on zero hands the number of times his nerves had rattled so violently within his frame. Oh, fear had certainly been an inevitable companion, ruthlessly popping up throughout his existence like a rabid wolf. Over the eons, however, he'd learned to temper that darling emotion into something useful: inscrutable and merciless battle tactics, the thrum and pump of terror fueling each blow, even a well-timed display of destruction born of desperation.

Nerves, on the other hand? The kind that altered one's gait and tossed logical thoughts to the wind like so much dandelion fluff?

They were as foreign as a fish attempting to live topside, yet there he stood, hand gripping the cool brass of the door handle and boots frozen to the sidewalk, waiting for the precise moment when his internal clock would throw up its skirts and announce the top of the early-morning hour.

Apparently, his nerves manifested as a French cancan dancer. Lovely. What a comfort to know that his circumstances not only lured the madness and rage closer but a maniacal delirium as well.

He truly was in the weeds.

What other reason could there be for him standing outside a not-yet-open-for-business breakfast spot at five in the morning, freezing his balls way the hell off, all while shifting his boots against the pavement so as not to appear too eager?

Eager. A derisive snort colored the air before him, clouding his vision with the white mist of his impatient breath. The memory of Molly on her knees scooping up ceramic shards beneath the feet of a greasy giant was strong enough to obliterate any semblance of nervous energy or unanswered queries. Oh, he was *eager*, all right, for more things than the honorable part of him cared to admit. And yet . . .

He jerked his hand away from the door handle and forced his feet to retreat a step. Was he really about to bring this to her doorstep? This blinding haze of berserker-like fury that he risked setting off like a shot whenever a customer behaved as entitled mortals were wont to do?

No. No, he couldn't do this to her. He already had a regrettably long list of lost souls he'd been responsible for, but he'd sooner carve his own heart out and feed it to Cyro, the ruler of the demon charmers, than add her to the list.

He made to go, but a sharp wind stirred at his back, pressing against the high collar of his trench coat, urging him with a strange serene calmness to take that final step across the threshold.

There was no fighting it, no turning away, and to his lamentable shock, the beast within didn't want him to. The damn thing practically preened as Brass's choice solidified into action. How strange. Though, did he ever really have a choice?

As if that woman's relentless brilliance and inviting warmth hadn't lured him to her with some invisible magnetism. Along with something . . . *more.*

He wrenched the door open. Crisp, chilly air subtly scented with dried maple and the mustiness of wet leaves followed his footsteps into the restaurant. The dining room was dark as the door shut slowly behind him. The only source of illumination was the faint light peeking through the two rectangular panels on the swinging door that led to the kitchen. It was enough to afford him a proper look at the space, one unmarred by boisterous diners, clanking dishes, and far too many bodies for his taste but still well within the limits of the room's legal occupancy.

If there had ever been a more devoted love letter to New England, he'd not seen it. Rather than hitting diners over the head with effusive log cabin décor and belching out dark wood paneling, the walls were adorned with a textured granite-colored wallpaper made to look like wood grain but more elevated. The effect was rustic and immersive and a wonderful backdrop to the cozy environs of the dining space. Outlining the room's perimeter, in the center of the wall, was an endless banner of lilacs sporadically dotting a snaking evergreen vine that encircled the entirety of the restaurant.

As he stepped farther into the room, a delicate smell greeted him. He dipped his head toward the wall to his right, following the fragrance until his nose met the nearest bundle of painted lilacs. To his surprise, the flowers were not painted at all but dried and pressed. A quick test with his finger revealed textured petals beneath the translucent overlay, and he caught himself almost smiling at the utter humanness of the decoration.

In a world of digital devices and whatever the hell cryptocurrency was, did appreciation for something so simple as lilacs truly still exist as a part of the mortal condition, or just Molly's?

Brass marked the floral scent and how it mingled with her lingering essence, the one that always had his head snapping in her direction no matter where he was. Had she pressed these flowers herself? He lifted that intoxicating fragrance from the wall and deposited it directly into his lungs, battening it down into that secret protective part of him his curse had not yet managed to mangle, and resumed his quiet inspection.

Fifteen wooden tables of various sizes, adorned with russet-brown and hunter-green table runners, filled out the floor, while wicker baskets of winter wood sat huddled around a small stone fireplace. Judging by the clean hearth and even cleaner air surrounding it, the thing served more as decoration than a decided source of heat. Not surprising, given the perilous purview of building inspectors tasked with ensuring the welfare and safety of occupants in structures older than the majority of roads in the town.

Shelves interspersed throughout were all decorated with regional mementos, while tabletops featured baskets of local maple syrup, small stuffed ornaments stitched with balsam fir needles, and satchels of cinnamon sticks tied together with dried apple peels.

It was as cozy a New England dining experience as one could ask for. Perfect for the tourists, as well as the locals, right down to the plump tufted cushions atop each chair.

A brilliant bit of business all around. Amid the hazy shadows that followed him through the small space, Brass couldn't help but be impressed, especially when very few things could claim the distinction.

"Oh, you're here! I thought I heard the door." Wall sconces burnished in gold and decorated with acanthus leaves flared to life, putting an end to his silent perusal.

Molly was just as he'd left her, though, judging by the rich, roasted aroma she brought with her into the dining room, the brightness in her eyes hailed not from stress and adrenaline but from—he sniffed again—what he'd guess were several shots of ristretto. A light flush tinted the pale skin of her cheeks a peachy hue and was nearly kissed by two tendrils of dark hair at her temples, which hung lower than the rest of her clipped bangs. It was almost as if the brackets of brunette had been called into service, perpetually lifting the apples of her cheeks to ensure she always had a smile on her face.

"I made a list." She produced a folded piece of paper from within her apron and unpeeled it before jabbing it under his nose with a force better used for pounding meat. "It outlines the important stuff, basic hours of operation, expected duties, all subject to change as needed, of course, general building and seating layouts, and the types of equipment we use here. Oh!" She stepped forward, using the pause in her barrage of information to take a breath and point a finger at some of the text on the bottom she hadn't read yet. "And here I list out all our delivery days and inventory procedures. Most of the food we get delivered, obviously, but some specialty items we have to pick up, like our breads and desserts. Also, there's the garbage schedule and recycling regulations. The sanitation department has a *whole* list of their own rules, but despite my, *ahem*, frequent requests, I've never actually seen them. Probably because they know their recycling dumpster isn't fully seated on the cement pad in the back alley as it's supposed to be and is a *major* hazard, but do you think they've returned my calls? Nope." Her resounding pop of the P jerked any nerve in his body that hadn't given her mouth its full attention and yanked it front and center.

How, of all the creatures in the mortal realm, did one manage to cram so much into so few breaths? It was as if her mind and mouth were in concert, having trained for years in a 2x100 relay race that they were just now being called upon to win lest they let down an entire nation of fans.

Brass tried to hide his smirk of amusement as her verbal tumult continued, seemingly unimpeded by her tangential storytelling.

"Oh, and just so there's absolutely nothing weird about any

of this," she said, taking a step back and swiping her hands to the side to encompass all of the aforementioned invisible weirdness, "I talked to Chrome and Drea this morning. Your brother might have mentioned that this isn't exactly your favorite time of year, and I completely hear you on that one, though maybe only a little bit because I do really love the winter, especially in New Hampshire. The White Mountains are so stunning when everything's snowcapped."

"You spoke to my brother? At five in the morning?" he snapped. Before the Fall, Chrome had served as the Empyrean's intelligence master, and some habits died hard in that regard. Chiefly, his bigmouthed brother's ability to peddle secrets like silver, especially when that angel's soul bond was involved. "And what, pray tell, did the two of them have to share?" Brass fought to keep the snarl off his lips, though based on the war Molly's features were engaged in, he'd done a piss-poor job of it. With a furtive swallow of self-restraint, he wrestled back the rage heating his blood.

"I just meant that he and Drea were checking in, like they usually do, although I *did* call *them* this time, admittedly, and I may have let slip that you'll be working here. It was totally a casual thing, not any sort of behind-your-back gossip." Molly retreated from her original topic, tripping over her words the way a rabbit would scamper out of a fox's hole knowing full well it had just gotten itself into nine kinds of trouble.

Behind-his-back gossip. Was that what his brothers thought of him? That he was such a lost cause, it would have been better to keep their counsel than have him know the truth depths of his helplessness?

"It's no matter, really," he replied, marshaling the bleakness from his tone.

It wasn't until Molly relaxed against the kitchen door that Brass noticed a blue and white flier adorning a corkboard on the wall next to it. She followed his gaze, and as if relieved to steer the conversation anywhere but off the cliff they were careening toward, she snatched the thing from its tack.

"This was why Chrome was giving me the heads-up about your aversion to the season, I suppose." She offered the paper to him.

In a single stride, he was in front of her, fingers grazing the warm spots of the paper where she'd touched it. Though hardly a caress, their almost-connection leveled a softness over his frame that calmed the final ripples of rage he'd been struggling to tamp down. This unburdened weightlessness was a new torture, however, a distinctly honed infliction that made his soul sigh instead of scream and only came upon him when he was near her. Was this another trick? A different punishment manifested by the curse, one that teased him with relief on the eve of his demise?

It was a trouble he'd have to examine later. For now, the comfort was too great to dismiss, allowing him to lean into what he'd come there to do startlingly unencumbered. Glancing down at the paper, Brass tried to focus on the whorls of snowflakes, pudgy bubble letters, and two types of glitter used to convey a message that, if it were up to him, would have been just as fine scrawled in ballpoint pen on the back of a crumpled cocktail napkin.

"It's the Aurora Winter Whimsy Festival. The town holds it on the winter solstice every year, and this year, Suerte and Honeysuckles is going to have a vendor booth." More resignation than excitement tinged Molly's voice, especially given the milligrams of caffeine no doubt bouncing around her nervous system.

"You don't sound excited," Brass observed.

"I'm excited," she confirmed, brightening with false assuredness before her voice betrayed her. "I'm also terrified, ill-prepared, and worried about impressing the right people."

Molly settled her weight against the swinging door behind

her, mistaking it for an immobile surface. Before Brass could catch her, she righted herself. After covering the gaffe with an adorable hop, she tested the counter next to her and, seemingly satisfied, rested her hip against it.

Brass didn't even bother fighting back his smile that time. The once-playful part of him had the desire to use his power and melt away every screw securing the counter to the wall just to have her lose her balance all over again so *he* could be the one to catch her, to feel her softness writhing and wriggling in his grasp.

Would he feel the heat of her skin beneath her flannel button-down shirt? Did she run hotter because of her natural exuberance? Then his mind sank into other depths, wondering what it would take to cause other parts of her to flush the same high color currently painting her cheeks.

Mages, it had been so long, so infuriatingly long since he'd even had the desire to tease and tempt, let alone allow himself to indulge in a woman. And with Molly, it would be the ultimate indulgence, one a male like him didn't simply sip but savor, if his time were his own.

If all the days before him weren't measured in hours but eons.

He cleared his throat against a host of alternate realities that did *not* have his name on them and did his best to rejoin her regrettably one-sided conversation.

"The festival always has a good turnout, not only of the town's residents and tourists but also of business investors, restaurant groups, catering companies, and local food industry professionals. Lots of the right people to rub elbows with and tempt into financing my venture with a huge influx of cash. Many of the region's well-beloved restaurants either got their seed money or expansion investments from being noticed at the festival." It was easy to catch her excitement, enthusiastic as she was about everything pertaining to her profession, until her gaze slid away and some of that spark dimmed. "It's a really important date on the calendar, and we've only got three weeks to pull it all together."

Then the gears abruptly clicked into place. That was when her words from earlier broke through Brass's fog of euphoria. "It's on the solstice?"

"Yup. December twenty-first. It's a snow or shine event, too. The only thing that shuts it down is a blizzard, and that's only happened, like, twice since the town's been running it the last thirty years or so."

Brass slid the paper onto the counter, putting as much distance as possible between him and that date. The chilling bite of the wind outside had somehow found its way to his skin, nipping and pricking its little agonies along every nerve ending.

"Are you all right?" Molly asked, and damn how he wanted to rip out the concern lacing her words. If he'd wanted concerned eyes and remorseful pleas, he'd have stayed home. But here, with the one woman who could somehow calm his curse while he offered to help with her business on *that* day? A day that should enrage him?

She stepped closer then, her fingertips hovering and her chocolate doe eyes unsure where to land, trying to decipher what about him needed the most aid.

Everything.

Before he could shutter his eyes and lean into whatever it was about her that soothed his seething, he flung himself away. Only once he'd placed no fewer than two tables between them did he trust his voice enough to speak.

"Yes, I'm fine. All this is fine." He swept an arm out to encompass the restaurant as a whole, as well as the contents of the flier. "Now," he said, shrugging out of his coat and walking past her toward the kitchen. "Show me what you need done. I imagine your line cook will be here any moment, correct?"

Because if he didn't throw himself into some manual labor soon, the restaurant's front windows would be next.

CHAPTER 7

For the third time in as many hours as the restaurant had been open, Molly wondered just how the hell servers did this job without a tub of pain relief cream at the ready and a one-ounce bottle of the holiday cheer du jour tucked in their back pocket.

Relishing a blessed break in the breakfast action, she dragged herself to the corner of the dining room and unceremoniously arched her back, pressing out the kinks at the base. Molly had spent the better part of her adult life on her feet with her face hovering dangerously close to high-octane commercial kitchen flames. While it was literally hotter than the hell some people believed in, she'd take that any day and twice on Sundays if it meant, for one goddamn moment, she didn't have to lean over a table anymore to clarify which menu items were gluten-free, dairy-free, and nut-free, despite the helpful key she'd specifically designed in the menu's corner outlining all of this.

For every year she spent perfecting her signature black truffle and Gruyère cheese souffle, she'd give each one of them back if she never had another guest ask her whether the chicken the restaurant sourced was gluten-free. When in the holy hell had restaurant service come to this? All she wanted to do, all she *ever* wanted to do, was cook, dammit. If she'd known running her own eatery would require her to answer more asinine questions than there were hours in the day, she'd have more strongly considered her mother's suggestion to go into veterinary school.

Not much more strongly but definitely more so than the eye roll she'd originally answered with.

"I got eggs Benny and sweet potato corn cakes for table two." Benny dropped the plates onto the service window's counter and tapped the bell in time with the beat of his music, more out of his flair for excitement, she wagered, than his expectation for expediency. Lord help the man if Marisol ever caught him rushing Molly.

With another pop on the bell's tiny tip, the shrill thing rang out, causing Molly's back teeth to meet in a jarring clash. "Nope! No more. We're having none of that." She stormed over to the window and swiped the bell out of Benny's reach, narrowly avoiding the jab of his tongs. "I told you, we don't need a bell. It's only me, and I can hear you just fine." She hissed the last words and deposited the bell next to the extra stash of napkins on the counter by the register.

Far away from prying tongs.

"Do we need to have a vocabulary lesson on the definition of *only*? Because last I checked, that fella you dragged up and threw into my kitchen doesn't fit that bill." Benny briefly shifted away from her to throw a sizzling pan of browned-butter french toast into the oven. "Man moves so fast, I hardly see him. Where'd you find him, anyway?"

That *him* was the Adonis-shaped elephant in the room she'd been avoiding all morning.

Molly collapsed against the counter, letting her head relax backward on her neck and forcing her shoulders to drop away from her ears. "He answered the ad," she replied quickly, keeping the precise details of their prior acquaintances to herself. "And as long as we're on the subject of definitions . . ." She turned around and braced her elbows on the counter, then leaned in conspiratorially. "The woman over at table three asked whether the corned beef was grass fed."

Benny snorted. "I can roll it around in the grass for her if she likes."

Molly tossed her hands in the air but still kept her voice low. "I can't. I just can't. If I had started my career off as a server, I can tell you right now I'd never have bothered stepping foot into a professional kitchen."

"My dear, I hate to break this to you, but . . ." His mouth quirked on a wry smile. "You're about as personable as a potato."

She gasped, not only for herself but on behalf of all maligned spuds everywhere. "I am not!" Several pairs of eyes looked up from their breakfasts, and Molly curved her back away from them in an attempt to shield her and Benny's conversation. "I'm perfectly lovely."

"Sure, with people you like or you have to work with. But until someone sprinkles some salt on you and fluffs you up a bit, you're not the easiest thing to choke down. That's why you're such an amazing chef. Customer service isn't necessarily a prerequisite for the job most of the time, especially for closed-off folks who don't prioritize people skills."

Closed-off folks? If that wasn't the most infuriatingly tone-deaf, hurtful, shortsighted . . . and potentially accurate way to describe her, well . . .

"I can't believe you just compared me to a potato," Molly whispered through gritted teeth.

"And I can't believe the itemized instructions you gave that poor guy. You made three pages of lists for the man and scheduled everything for him except when he should hit the head. This is a pretty straightforward gig, and he's picked it up faster than anyone else I've seen. No reason all of his duties couldn't have been conveyed in a four-sentence conversation." Benny held out his fingers and ticked off said sentences. "Wash the dishes. Bus the tables. Empty the garbage. Repeat until closing. Unless there's a reason you don't want to talk to him?"

God save her from meddling men who prioritized her personal business as *their* personal business and thought to impart upon her a hard-learned thing or two. Though she loved Benny and owed him more than she worried she could ever repay, she was certainly not above dropping a laxative or two into his coffee. Nothing permanent or even particularly harmful, but just enough to hammer home the ethos of her entire cooking career: Molly didn't take shit.

At least then she'd get a day or so back in the kitchen to experiment and—

The steam curling above the two dishes Benny prepared lifted and pulled away as Brass snatched the plates up with brisk efficiency. Where most creatures possessing two hands would simply carry one plate in each, it was abundantly clear that her newest hire was not like most creatures. Shucked of his familiar trench coat, Brass wore a long-sleeve dusty-blue Henley shirt that served as the landing pad for every single dish he'd grabbed. The plate of eggs, which Molly knew to be skin-scorching hot, rested neatly in the crux of his elbow, while the sweet potato corn cakes made their home stretched along a toned forearm that might as well have been armor-plated. Beneath his spare arm, he tucked a large serving tray while also carrying a small rack to accompany it.

All morning, he had moved through the restaurant like a dancer proficient in an entire company's choreography. He took no extra steps, never stumbled, and generally maneuvered with martial arts proficiency. Molly swallowed around a dry tongue as Brass, literally single-handedly, placed the meals in front of the diners, arranged his rack and tray, cleared the table of finished dishes, and then hoisted the laden tray high on one shoulder. The light blue fabric pulled taut over a flexed bicep, the strain of which caused the hem of his shirt to rise ever so slightly when he turned, occasionally offering a flash of hip bone or a peek at a stomach rippled with just the right amount of muscle.

Around the dining tables, women of every conceivable (and some inconceivable) age sat up and took notice as well. One woman, a grandmother still in the early years of the distinction, scooted her chair away from her toddler granddaughter and rowdy family when Brass stepped by, even going so far as to drop her napkin and place a manicured hand on his arm before asking him to retrieve it. The syrup in the woman's voice caused Molly to cringe. The stuff was so sugary and thick, it would have been better served on the plate than as a parlor trick.

A well-practiced cougar tactical plan if Molly had ever seen one, though it was obvious the woman's silver-haired husband, who was still trying to arrange his scrambled eggs on his fork for the third time, hadn't.

All that was missing from the scene was for Brass to turn around and gift the grandmother with some sort of teasing smile, something to encourage and reward.

Something Molly had fortified herself against, battening down her responses with years of diligent training and painful preparation.

And running. A boatload of running.

Molly pinched her eyes shut, blocking out the inevitable, and grabbed the bell off the counter. "No more bells, Benny. Message received."

Her nonslip soles carried her with record speed through the rear hall until she punched through the door and was tossed out in the back alley next to the dumpster. She'd never been more grateful for the hideously ugly footwear and had immediate plans to make amends for all the comments she'd made over the years berating her industry's fashion crimes.

Though the alley behind her restaurant was cleaner than most, it still held some hallmark signs of putridity. General animal funk painted the buildings where the pavement met the brick facades, crusting over into unfortunate icy sheens under the weight of the impending winter's wind chills. Frozen discarded soda bottles met their fate alongside abandoned bags of empty potato chips, some of which had their corners and seams plastered beneath iced-over puddles of dubious color and even more dubious origin.

Perhaps the deep cleansing breath she'd banked on wasn't the most advisable course of action. As the heavy metal door slammed shut behind her, taking the restaurant's subtle sweetness with it, Molly clutched the bell harder and stomped over to the dumpster before stopping short. To her surprise, the lid had been left open, propped up by the two-by-four she always left next to the cement pad for when she needed to throw in several bags of garbage at once.

She'd be sure to thank Benny for his thoughtfulness later with an obscenely large aged prime rib roast. Honestly, it was so easy to shop for a man with meat as a love language.

Molly scuttled back a few steps for good measure, then with her best pitcher's impersonation, she heaved the bell into the dumpster. The poor thing thwacked against the green metal lid but still had the courtesy to tumble inside the bin and land with a satisfying thud. What was *not* satisfying was the startling yelp that rose up in an answering echo.

"What the hell was that?" Molly spun around the alley, but nothing struck her notice until four russet paws peeked out from behind the dumpster.

A squeal erupted from her chest, bouncing off the bricks and nearly startling the little dog back into whatever grimy hole it had been hiding in.

"Oh, look at you! Come on out. I won't hurt you. Oh my

gosh, you poor thing. Please don't tell me those are your ribs. I'm going to lose it in a puddle of tears if I see your ribs."

The small hound dog meekly trotted out from behind the dumpster, hesitantly poking its black nose in her direction. The red coloring on its paws gave way to a short sleek ebony coat, which largely covered the rest of its body save for the muzzle and underbelly. Curious brown eyes darted around and eventually settled on Molly's hands when she held them out. Apparently surmising that her human scent was more than agreeable and what Molly hoped was a fair amount better than the frozen urine puddles, the pup followed up its sniffs with playful licks.

While there were no ribs on display yet—a serious thanks to all the heavy-hitting deities that usually ensured against that kind of animal suffering—Molly worried about that changing as winter kept moving up its timeline with the frigid weather. Seriously, there was a special place in hell reserved for people who abandoned and harmed animals, one where humans were the ones kept in cages and left to the mercies of all the animals they'd wronged. Preferably with shock collars.

A girl could dream.

"Would you like some treats? I've got all sorts of breakfast foods. Any kind of meat you could think of, really. Let's see, there's maple-smoked bacon, apple sausage, corned beef hash, ham steaks with red-eye gravy . . ."

The dog's floppy ears swung like a pendulum with each choice, its relaxed tongue lolling from side to side.

Molly sat back on her heels and welcomed the dog farther into her lap. To her surprised delight, the little pup accepted the invitation. "Hmm . . . No collar." She palpated around its shoulder blades, feeling for the rice-sized lump indicating a microchip beneath the skin. "Nothing there." Her chilly fingers prodded some more but came away empty. "One last thing I'd like to check, if you don't mind. I recognize it's a bit insensitive, but I'd like to become more properly acquainted if we're to share a meal." With a flash of an apology, Molly gently lifted the dog's leg. After a brief, strained bit of eye contact between the two, she swiftly righted the dog. "There, ma'am. You're all done."

The dog scooted back a bit and quickly sniffed its undercarriage, so to speak, no doubt ensuring that everything was as it should be. Once satisfied, she settled on her haunches and mirrored Molly's position while leaning into all the ear scratches offered up. If Molly's heart hadn't been thoroughly melted, then the pup's cheerful mewls evened her out into the most homogenous goo of warmth. The last time she'd been so stupidly giddy was when a company breeding Seeing Eye dogs brought the puppies into town to do crosswalk training.

She'd spent the day with her butt parked on a bench, asked Benny to keep an eye on the dining room for a bit, and cheerfully watched young balls of happy fluff pounce through downtown Aurora.

It had only cost her a whole tenderloin in recompense. Totally worth it.

Molly worked her slowly warming fingers over one spot along the dog's flank with extra enthusiasm, which seemed to increase butt waggles exponentially. "If only people were as eager to please." She chuckled softly, before remembering what had dragged her outside in the first place. "Well, maybe not *so* eager. At least your smiles are genuine. You'd be surprised at how much of an anomaly that is, especially among our opposite sex."

Creaking hinges drew the dog's attention, causing it to step out of Molly's grasp with a yelp. When Molly turned around, the restaurant's back door slammed shut with a reverberation she nearly felt in her teeth. In front of the door stood Brass, with a bag of garbage at his feet, and a hard expression on his face that would have scorched the earth beneath them.

Molly sucked in a sharp breath and froze.

Because he leveled that threatening gaze right at her.

CHAPTER 8

At least your smiles are genuine.

There weren't enough hours in the day for Brass to codify all the ways in which those six little words urged his curse that much closer to the surface. And he'd been doing such an admirable job that morning keeping it at bay, in his very humble damn opinion.

He'd had to, at first, resist the temptation to upend every table in that place each time a woman had asked him to pick up another napkin or when one would brush against his ass with a murmured "Excuse me" on their way to precisely nowhere. Given how quickly he'd calculated the trajectory needed to hurl his serving tray through the window, and he *still* hadn't wound up cranking that oversized frisbee yet, he figured he deserved far more than that Medal of Honor pinned on those homespun mortal military heroes.

An act of freaking valor, to be sure, which was why Molly's words hadn't simply plucked at his too-short tether but nearly snapped it.

Before he offered to help her, no one would have ever dared

touch him, let alone *accidentally* bump into him, had they known his true nature—the one born of celestial fire and wings he was forced to hide in the mortal realm. In the dining room, however, every inadvertent flex or grunt on his part seemed to invite any human with two X chromosomes and, based on some lascivious glances, a few with Y chromosomes as well, to lose their ever-loving minds.

Ironically, he could relate.

When a—well, he'd go with *mature*—woman at one table placed her hand on his forearm, even going so far as to squeeze the muscles there, he'd had to swallow down his urge to flay off his skin. Worse yet, Molly had left the dining room several minutes earlier and hadn't returned to cajole and schmooze with the patrons, though there were times when he suspected she enjoyed it about as much as he did: not one damned bit.

He'd killed for far less, and boy, did it chafe that he couldn't do so now.

How, by all the mages, did mortal women in general, let alone those in the service industry, make it through a single shift without impaling no fewer than fifteen customers who got too handsy? For every coy glance or soft smirk thrown his way, there were two more bolder, more appreciative, though equally as flagrant maneuvers from women waiting in the wings.

Once he noticed Molly hadn't returned with her usual efficiency, his trapezius muscles had begun to bunch with strain beneath his collar, and unease prickled his spine. Her proximity had been the only thing luring him away from what he *might* do to her fine restaurant had his hairpin trigger been pulled just a little bit harder. Whatever thrall her presence had over him wasn't only noticeable but needed. It was a mysterious circumstance he vowed to uncover, just as soon as he could breathe again without the red haze threatening to snuff out his humanity over eggs and hash browns.

Eventually, faced with a desperate choice and having lost sight of the very reason he'd offered himself up for this ordeal in the first place, Brass had decided to choose the only option that would most assuredly put off his admirers.

Garbage duty.

What he hadn't been prepared for was the sight of Molly, knees near a puddle and her shapely backside separated from the foul ground by the cradle of her shoes, loving on a random hound dog while confessing that, somehow, somewhere, there lived a male who had used his affection toward her to . . . deceive her?

"Who?" he asked, grinding out the word to deliver it with all the punch his fists could not.

Yet another regret.

Molly shot to her feet, her espresso eyes widening with shock that quickly masked the bleakness he'd briefly glimpsed there. "Who, what?"

"Who was disingenuous to you?" And mages, did he hope that was the mildest word to describe whatever he'd caught her reminiscing about.

"No one," she replied, wrapping her arms over her chest, but not before his heightened celestial senses caught a glimpse of her nipples pressed against her thick flannel shirt. At the sight of it, his angel fire writhed within his core, flexing and tensing against the wall of his muscles. Brass swallowed around a dry throat and filled his lungs with frigid air, doing his best to douse the flames.

She was cold, dammit, and he was on a thousand kinds of fire just staring at her, breathing her into the cells of his body. Each inhale within her proximity pummeled his fury further back into its recesses, where he could finally form a goddamn thought without worrying whether his next emotion would either spark or snap the tether to his rage.

An inexplicable lightness filled his chest, once again catching him off guard, so he pressed on about what had still managed to hold his focus. Brass lifted his chin toward the dog. "Is he the only one who gets to know your secrets?"

Molly blanched, and even the dog stopped its fidgeting to cast a reproachful glare in his direction, as if it had spent far too much time around alley cats and had mastered their apathetic lingo. "*She* doesn't know anything. She's just a stray I found when I came out here to get some air."

A little black nose reached higher, sniffing in Brass's direction. After a few good whiffs, the dog sneezed, shook out its head, and retreated behind the protection of Molly's ankles. Of course the mutt would be a female.

Preferring to only engage with one member of that particular sex at the moment, Brass chucked the bag of garbage into the open dumpster, wiped his hands on the apron around his waist, and tossed his head back toward the restaurant's door. "Why do you need air? Did one of the diners say something to you? Do something?"

"What? No!" She scoffed, then dismissed the idea with a wave of her hand.

"I've seen it before." At that, she tensed, and a small crack in the bravado of her proprietress demeanor began to form. "Haven't seen that guy since, have you?"

Molly tensed, then folded her arms over her chest and darted her eyes from the dog to somewhere just below Brass's chin. His collar, maybe?

There was no need to clarify which guy he was referring to, nor did Molly need to know the particular dimensions of compact crusher cube Brass had turned the asshole's car into later that evening.

Though he *did* take the spark plug out first, as promised.

"No, no I haven't."

"Good. Then who was it?"

The dog chose that precise moment to jump up on Molly's thighs, wagging its slender tail with an enthusiasm that belied its bedraggled state. If the thing wanted food, there was an entire dumpster full of slightly-below-excellent dine-out options not ten feet from them.

And yet, as predicted, Molly took the adorable bait, crouching down to resume their little love fest. "Poor little dear. Don't worry, I've got you. I'm sure Uncle Benny has some delicious scraps to share, though don't let him hear you call them scraps. He's more of a nose-to-tail kind of guy, so anything in between is fair game."

"Molly." Her name skittered out on a growl he hadn't meant to unleash. Regardless of the delivery, it still had the desired effect. Her head shot up, and for the first time, apprehension clouded her gaze. The expression wasn't the shy, coy glance she'd give him when she thought he wasn't looking or the sweet and amenable manner she adopted when working out a customer complaint. No, this was something entirely foreign, something that spoke of sinister motives and deep, soul-crushing regret.

Uncertainty. Betrayal. Shame.

A thunderous pop resounded behind him, followed by the distinctive smell of sulfur and smoke. The dog began barking, erupting at Molly's feet and prancing around her in a circle of defensive energy.

"Oh my God! There's a fire!" Molly screamed, trying to corral the frantic beast.

Brass spun around and caught the tendrils of black fumes trickling out from beneath the open lid of the dumpster. He vaulted toward the metal container and gripped the edges to peer in. A small fire had ignited, sputtering among a bundle of copper wires protruding from some discarded kitchen appliances nestled on a bed of every crumpled paper product the restaurant was capable of producing. The flames were, thankfully, slow-moving and contained, though the wind was picking up and tended to grow fiercer when funneled through alleys. With so many electrical lines nearby, all it would take was a good spark to catch flight on a stiff breeze and they'd be in real trouble.

"Something must have ignited in here," Brass called over his shoulder. "Grab a fire extinguisher."

"There's one in the hall right by the kitchen." Molly left the dog and hurried back into the restaurant.

With Molly gone, Brass sent ribbons of his metallic power into every copper molecule until they were no more than molten puddles splattered over kitchen refuse. With the matter melted into its liquid form, the flames had no choice but to shift as well.

Except they didn't.

Where Brass had expected the fire to smother and sputter out once robbed of its ignition source, instead it licked across the smooth metal with renewed vigor. Barely simmering oranges erupted into blazing blues that fiercely raced through the entire contents of the dumpster with the voracity of a swarm.

What the hell?

Amid the roar of the growing flames, Brass recalled what he'd first found at the base of the fire. Copper wires. Metal machinery. It would take heat far hotter than a simple carelessly tossed match to ignite and smelt copper into its liquid state.

Only angel fire could do such a thing so quickly—specifically *his* fire, as his alloy commanded the copper element, among others.

Before Molly could come back through the door, Brass released a pulse of his celestial power into the flames, matching that of the fire. The electric blue infernos clashed with a resounding roar, then melded together under Brass's sole command. Once controlled, the flames extinguished with a deafening hiss, leaving behind a thick plume of black smoke.

Just as the last of his flames extinguished, Molly burst through the alley door, holding a red fire extinguisher in the air like it was a forty-pound sandbag and she'd just crossed the finish line at a Spartan Race. Her eyes widened as they took in the smoke. "Here!"

She tossed the thing at him, and he made a show of dousing everything in the dumpster. His power had taken care of the flames, but the smoke still lingered. The extinguisher was the wet chemical kind, primarily used to fight cooking oil fires and not so much live electrical equipment, but its cloud of chemicals concealed exactly what he needed them to.

At the base of the alley, where the pavement spilled out onto the main drag, a few holiday shoppers had stopped to gawk at the commotion. Phones were held to ears, and worried parents pressed insistent hands on the backs of their children, urging them not to dawdle.

Of all the times to have a damn audience.

"It's done," he said loudly. "Fire's out."

Brass climbed down off the dumpster and wiped his sooty palms on his apron. When he glanced up, he noticed that, for the first time since the outbreak, the dog had grown quiet. Molly had run over to a group of worried diners to hastily reassure them that all was well after they'd probably smelled the smoke. The dog, however, sat patiently next to the back door, its brown eyes fixed on Molly as she used her hands to recount the details of what had happened.

Details he'd like to know as well. One thing was for damn sure: there had been nothing electrical in nature about that fire.

He stared at Molly more intently, and the pleasant smile she tossed out for her customers' benefit reminded him of the words she'd spoken earlier.

At least your smiles are genuine.

A tremulous awareness vibrated through him at the conclusion his mind was drawing, one that began to unravel all he thought he knew of the alluring Molly Resnick.

Those flames had been his all right, but they had been ignited by magic most definitely not his own.

CHAPTER 9

Though the fire had started in the middle of the breakfast service, the shitstorm that followed lasted well into the evening. It was almost five thirty before Molly was finally able to collapse into her office chair, deeply lamenting that it wasn't a proper fainting couch like the situation called for.

Because when one's nerves got you up at three a.m. to prepare for a new employee who was heavy on the breathtaking and light on the actual legal requirements of employment, it made for a very long day.

Molly's head sank back, and for a brief moment, she let the brushed blue velvet hairs of the chair soothe away the knot of tension forming at the base of her neck.

After word got around about the fire in her restaurant's dumpster, tables cleared out mass-exodus style just in time to effectively deter any future diners that may have come her way for the lunchtime meal service. Several elderly patrons, who never did anything quickly, had somehow managed to toss their cash onto the table with such brisk efficiency it made Molly wonder whether the *slower-with-age* concept was all an act just so the blue-hairs could still do whatever the hell they wanted without having to answer for it. Likewise, the preschool moms, who always breakfasted there every Tuesday morning for the entire two and a half hours their kids were in the half-day program, cut their girl time short as soon as the fire trucks rolled up. Well, maybe not *super* short, as there had definitely been some lingering when the firefighters jumped on scene.

None of that held a candle to the complaints, however. *Those* stuck around for-freaking-ever. One particularly memorable objection had been made over the phone by a regular retired customer who had thrown just as much heat into his ire as the extra hot sauce he always asked for on his morning soft veggie scramble.

That conversation, strangely enough, occurred while the man stood across the street—a safe distance away, according to him—but maintained his eye leer at Molly through the restaurant's window regardless.

"Mr. Campbell, everything's fine. The fire department's here. They reported no damage to the building and said we were safe to resume normal business operations. You're welcome to come back and finish your breakfast. You won't be charged for today's meal," Molly assured him, already hating the placating tone she'd adopted while delivering her fifth variation of this exact conversation in the same hour.

"Like hell I'll come back there! Look, I don't know what kind of establishment you're running, my dear, but I heard that one of the other guests saw your employee rummaging around in the dumpster before the blaze ignited. The fool probably tossed his cigarette in there and put us all at risk. Smoking is a deplorable practice and has no place in food service." The jowly response was heaped high with indignation and just the right amount of judgment coming from a generation that was raised without seatbelts, screens, or sympathy. Plenty of nicotine, though, but even Molly knew better than to aim that particular irony missile back at the man.

There were only so many times she could offer up a "Sir, let me explain" or "That's not what happened, and I can assure you . . ." before the words all strung together into one long sigh of exasperation.

Eventually, concern about the cause of the fire gave way to questions about her business's integrity, her hiring process, and —most infuriating of all—whether her building's safety certificates had been fabricated.

Had I a penis, these would be far different conversations.

It hadn't escaped her notice that all the accusations being flung at her and calling her business prowess onto the carpet to stand trial had been made by men.

Story of her fucking life.

If she had to hear the phrase *my dear* one more time, she was liable to take her favorite Japanese cleaver and start hacking off things those men found very *dear*, indeed.

"Knock knock, Molly girl." Benny's sad smile poked around the lip of her office doorway. "Why the hell are you still here?"

"Why the hell are *you* still here?"

"Uh-uh. Don't play that game. I'm here because the light lunch service gave me extra time to dry-brine the ducks for tomorrow."

"Oh, right. The duck confit hash." Molly nodded woodenly, completely forgetting she had bought the poultry to begin with.

"And the spicy duck tacos at lunch."

"Yes. Of course."

"I hear they're going to be on *fire!*"

Molly leveled a glare at him. "You did *not* just go there."

"Oh, I did," he said with a satisfied smirk, then rubbed his chest. "Couldn't help myself. With everyone losing their minds over a smoking dumpster, not knowing how many times us cooks have literally seared off our fingertips or eyebrows, I figured I deserved some of the comedic irony as well. Those people have probably been chomping on my scorched skin cells all morning without even knowing it, and yet they freak out over a barely there fire that was completely controlled, contained, and in no way threatened their safety."

A slight chuckle lifted her shoulders briefly before they sagged right back down under the weight of the day. "You're not wrong, but they don't care."

And wasn't that the freaking truth? It was yet another stark reality of the restaurant industry that she hadn't considered when she bartered her good credit in exchange for her dream.

Being right didn't matter, she was coming to learn. Not nearly as much as perception, anyhow. Others' perceptions. And, God, she did *not* want to peel back that particular curtain just yet.

Molly leaned forward, clasped her fists together, and stretched out her arms in front of her. "Good night, Benny. Oh, and just make sure you temp the duck thoroughly tomorrow."

The outrage on his face was enough to incite a Senate fili-buster. "I know you did not just imply that I don't know the proper doneness temperature for a duck."

She held her palm to her chest. "*I* would never, but I got a call from a guest earlier. She ate here a few days ago and got sick. Something parasitic, which just skeeves me out in all the ways." Molly shuddered. "She wasn't entirely sure it was our food that did it, but her doctor told her to make the rounds and notify any places she ate at over the past five days in case there were others. Lucky us, we made the list."

"Yeah, I'm going to pretend I didn't hear any of that," he said before pumping his fist on the doorframe by way of goodbye and turning to go.

"Wish I could, too," she muttered to herself.

Outside in the dining room, a concerto of chairs being softly stacked reminded her she wasn't alone. Not so much reminded her, really, as poked at an uneasy awareness she'd been skirting around ever since the fire.

God, what did Brass think of her? Of this whole insane situation? He'd been here one day, and already he had to deal with emergency services, irate customers, and a spastic businesswoman whose only redeeming quality as a property owner was that she knew where the fire extinguisher was. She didn't want to think about what would have happened if he hadn't been there to put the fire out. Did he think she was an unsafe employer? That not only did she suck at putting out proverbial fires with customers but now real ones followed her around like she had some cartoon fuse attached to the bottom of her butt?

Through the whole ordeal, Brass had been . . . Well, she didn't have the words to describe him, at least not any that did him justice. The phrase *godsend* had briefly popped into her mind, but it had been quickly shoved out by the mob of customers and bystanders who had started to batter her incessantly with questions.

Questions that kept including *her* restaurant's name, and not in a good way.

Did Suerte and Honeysuckles not dispose of something correctly?

What did your employee drop in the dumpster?

Was something not up to code?

They'd grabbed her by the elbow and huddled her into a circle of concern and accusations before she'd been able to come up for air. By the time she did, the literal smoke had settled, and she braced herself for yet more questions from the fire department . . .

Except there weren't any, because Brass had already spoken to them. Somehow, he'd engaged every fire official and answered any question they'd thrown at him, even providing details about the combustible contents of the dumpster and when the thing had been emptied last. At one point, Brass had retreated into the restaurant, only to return with the proper business receipts for their garbage and recycling disposal contract, along with the numerous complaints Molly had filed about the dumpster not lying correctly on the cement pad. She hadn't even realized he knew where those documents were, yet he handed them over with calm authority.

Every time she tried to pull away from whoever commanded her attention, Brass had been there, talking to another firefighter or issuing a sharp glare to onlookers who dared to get too close to the scene in question. A handful of times, when her back started to ache and she found herself answering the same question for the fourth time in a row, she'd cast a worried gaze out for him without even realizing it.

Always, his amber eyes had found hers but not in the way one searched for a friend in a crowd. It was different. Every time, his connection hadn't just been a beacon in a storm but an anchor, one that had him immediately pulling her out of the crowd and rescuing her to the safe shores of her quiet office.

And then, once he settled her with water and a few chocolate rugelach from her hidden stash below the register, he'd be off to put himself in front of whoever was looking for her.

She'd be lying if she said she didn't appreciate it, and lying even more if she confessed that the acts didn't make her want to stay close to him in other ways.

They'd hardly spoken throughout the day, and yet there was a natural rhythm to their strange dance, if she could even call it that. It was as if he knew exactly when she needed to take the lead in certain circumstances but also when it wasn't necessary and he'd step in. It reminded her of being on the line in the kitchen, where all the chefs came together to get the dishes out, whether through prep done hours before or a sharp sear achieved at the last second.

It was all a concert, a seamless masterpiece, and one she missed terribly but had been too overrun to get back to since she took over the place. The relief and joy at having found that flow again, especially with a new person, was the only silver lining to her black cloud of a day.

All those subtle things and behaviors gave Molly the impression that Brass wasn't just working here out of pity or boredom, and perhaps there was more to his motivations than simply going through the motions of being charitable.

They worked well together, and that realization didn't just come with warning bells but emergency sirens and doomsday broadcasts. Alerts she'd learned to pay extra close attention to.

Molly pried herself out of her blue velvet cocoon and drifted toward the dining room. At the very least, she needed to thank him and, she supposed, ascertain whether he planned on sticking around. Men like him, whose natural sex appeal and charming magnetism attracted no shortage of good fortune, didn't need whatever sort of trouble she had brought into his orbit.

When she rounded the corner, she expected to see Brass standing in front of the door, shrugging on his trench coat before nodding toward his discarded apron on the table with an unspoken expression of *I'm done* blanketing his features. What she got, however, was a sensory assault of rich roasted coffee and—dear God, please let it be—

"Is that cardamom?"

Brass, with his lean hips resting against a table, pushed away from it and extended the to-go cup out to her. It might as well have been manna from heaven. "Sure is. Mixed it into the grounds before I brewed the coffee."

Molly ran to the proffered cup like it was the Holy Grail capable of healing everything wrong in her life and took the thing from him with no thought to the contrary. "You have no idea how badly I needed this."

"I had some idea."

The bracing brew hit her lips and, saucy minx that it was, managed to singe and still coax out a moan of pleasure so powerful, she'd have been embarrassed if she hadn't also been completely depleted of any fucks to give. Molly licked her lips, then greedily took another pull of coffee. Damn, it was good. Hot, sweet, and invigorating in all the ways her soul needed. Did she burn her mouth again? Yes. Was it worth it? Also, yes. Once the steam cleared and she refocused on the man in front of her to thank him, however, she immediately wished she hadn't.

The same honeyed amber eyes that had tracked her throughout the day now lingered on her mouth, which was still slick and plump from the hot coffee. Molly's heart beat out a gallop, warming every inch of her. As much as she itched to look away, squirming under his scrutiny, she was also painfully aware that her perusal of him made her no better. Looking away from Brass, when the sun had nearly fallen and lazy golden rays poked through the windows and streaked across the exposed skin beneath his open collar, was like tearing your gaze from a shooting star. Impossible. The man belonged on a magazine cover, not in her New England shabby-chic tourist trap mopping up spilled apple juice, and yet here he was.

The part of her that had been honed into a chef, with skills forged in roaring fires and tenacity sculpted by brutal critics, wanted to question everything about him, demanding he declare his true motives so they could go their separate ways before her protective bubble burst so spectacularly. Another part of her, one that was growing increasingly louder by the hour, wanted to ask him a whole different set of questions, questions that had been plaguing her ever since he'd walked into her restaurant that first time.

Why me? Why have you stayed? Why—

"Why are you holding my car keys?" Molly's small sundial keychain winked at her as it dangled from Brass's closed fist.

The corner of his lips lifted, and as fast as the electric moment between them took hold, it was ushered out just as quickly. All that remained was a cloud of confusion on her part that, judging by the soft chuckle lifting his chest, gave him more delight than delusion.

Well, didn't that just freaking figure?

Brass lifted his arm, draped over which was her coat, and with his epic flair for short conversations and getting his point across in as few words as possible, he answered her question. "Because I'm driving you home tonight."

CHAPTER 10

The sun made its final descent below the horizon, casting Aurora into an unseasonably cold twilight and dragging Brass's thoughts down along with it. Maybe he should have been grateful that they caught the third damn traffic light in a row. It certainly gave him more time to think through the clusterfuck of events that had steamrolled over them the past several hours.

He stole a subtle glance at Molly over the high collar of his coat. Exhaustion had pushed her head against the passenger window. Hooded eyes, more distant than dazed, stared out at the passing cars. Her proud shoulders, which Brass hadn't thought were capable of slouching, supported what remained of her usually strong frame.

His jaw ticked in frustration, and the leather steering wheel groaned beneath his tightening grip. Despite his best hopes, worried suspicions began laying their damn stones, crafting a framework for an uncertain reality that heightened Brass's concerns. It was why, he told himself, he'd never strayed too far from her side all day. Why, even in the chaotic crowds, he'd watched her with the intent focus of a man eyeing a mirage.

Or a wolf eyeing another apex predator.

Magic.

Of course that had been the reason. The enigmatic pull that had constantly tugged him into her sphere had finally begun to make sense, if anything born of unknown powers could claim to do so. Though he was certain of Molly's mortality, he'd been alive long enough to know that the allure of magic had no preference for a being's longevity. Was that why, even among the throngs of people in the alley, she always searched for him?

And, mages damn him, she'd always found him, hadn't she?

Why? Had she really had something to do with the fire? He'd tossed that grating thought around incessantly throughout the day, and every single time it boomeranged back to him, he'd stare at her with equal parts disbelief, skepticism, and mesmerism.

Red light shone through the windshield, casting a garish tint across Molly's face, still tight with unease. Clouded puffs of breath fogged up the glass beneath where her open lips rested. Her bottom lip, only slightly fuller than the top and painted a sultry crimson beneath the light, hung slack against the glass.

Brass should have kept his eye on the road. Since they were at the mercy of the traffic light, however, he allowed himself one last look at her.

Big mistake.

Painful urges raked claws down his skin as images of that mouth flooded his mind, taking hold of his senses. Again, the voice of his curse pierced his temples, singing its tempting torment in trills of shrieks and sin. Blood coursed through him, flooding his muscles with the strength to act on heated hungers.

Brass silently fought for control, flexing against the dark demands of his rage. Every time he tried to blink it away, however, temptation would flare up in the form of Molly's mouth molding to the coffee cup he'd offered her at the restaurant. Thoughts pummeled him, needs that were not his own and never had been. Temptations surged to the surface with the memory of each of her swallows. Earlier, his angel fire had responded, giving strength to his remaining shards of humanity. Celestial powers born of the Eternal Flame, the source of all light and life in existence, had surged through his system, helping him beat back the devious desires of his curse.

Molly's perfect lips stretched wide over his cock.

His fingers entangled in her silken hair knotted at the nape as he fed her more and more of him.

Hips brutally thrusting into the warm cavern of her mouth.

It hadn't just been a battle to suppress it all but a fucking crusade, and it had cost him every ounce of willpower he had. It was only by some miracle of the mages that he'd kept his fire from his eyes earlier, especially under her timid perusal of him. Yes, he'd seen her watching and cataloged every eyelash flutter as she'd tried to steal her shy glimpses. If he'd had the strength, he'd have dived headfirst into the examination of her assessment. Studied whether her pupils dilated when her gaze touched upon his body and for how long. Analyzed the bright flush of her cheeks when he couldn't help but move closer.

Now, however, his energy was more than spent, and trapped alone in the car with her was the absolute last place he could afford to be.

He needed to be underground beneath the mountains while the minerals and elements soaked into his spirit, strengthening his soul and recharging his celestial power. Not here, not with her and that gorgeous, sinful, fucking devious little mouth . . .

She doesn't smile for you, but others smile for her. Many others.

Veins throbbed in Brass's temple, and he whipped his head away from her, burying it against his collar as he quietly beat back his torrential temper.

Others have smiled at her. Kissed her. Touched her. Fucked her.

Sweat slicked his palms as he fought to hang on to the steering wheel while his mind spun out of control.

How many males? One? Several?

"No," he breathed, shaking.

Males. Many many males. Kissing her. Touching her. Taking her.

Flames of rage erupted in Brass's eyes. His lips peeled back against the onslaught, and he snarled, roaring into the windshield in an unrecognizable sound.

A horn blared long and low.

Molly gasped and threw her hands against the dashboard. "Brass!"

Her cry of fear, combined with her sudden movement in his periphery, slammed into his consciousness. The red haze of rage subsided, and the luminescent glow of the red traffic light before them once again filled his vision, along with the car that was careening toward them from the left.

"Shit!" Brass's foot found the brake pedal while he braced his arm in front of Molly, securing her to the seat. Tires screeched, and Brass spun the wheel at the last moment to narrowly avoid clipping the hood of the other car as it sped past.

Once their car slowed to a stop, Molly sucked in several ragged breaths. "What the hell was that?"

"I . . . I thought the light had changed," Brass admitted quickly. Only after her breaths had returned to a more regular rhythm against the cage of his arm did he pull away from her and slowly maneuver her car through the traffic as if he hadn't just almost killed them. "Are you hurt?"

"No, no I'm fine. Just spooked."

"I'm sorry. I've never— That is, my mind was elsewhere for a moment. It was inexcusable." He tried to keep the venom out of the woefully inadequate words.

An ominous chill seeped into his bones through the silence, amplifying the severity of what his loss of control meant. One minute, he was idly admiring Molly; the next, he was somewhere else entirely, trapped through eyes that were both his and not his. His soul's fire had thrashed wildly in alert against the prison of his body, but not even his celestial power could crack the facade. Every Empyrean power had been lashed down tight, tethered to his humanity in the same fashion his curse's rage had been originally contained.

Originally contained, yes, but soon no longer.

For those few horrid moments, Brass had truly glimpsed what was in store for him if he couldn't find a cure.

Eternal consciousness through brutal imprisonment.

"This is all my fault!" Molly's desperate cry pulled him free of his wretched internal analysis.

He blinked. Surely, he hadn't heard her right. "Molly, I almost ran a red light. The fault is entirely—"

"No!" Her terrorized scream punched through his thoughts, spiking a new fear in his belly. "You see, this is exactly what happens!"

"What? What happens?" Her frantic pitch eclipsed all prior worries. "Molly, speak to me. Are you sure you're not hurt? I'll take you to a hospital right now."

"No, I don't need a hospital," she whined, despair replacing the anxiety from a breath ago. Her head fell back against the headrest. "I need about a thousand rabbits' feet, a football field of four-leaf clovers, and a few dozen of those evil eye bracelets my superstitious mother always seems to buy in bulk."

Brass blinked again, then peered at her over his collar. "I'm sorry?"

Molly let out a weighty sigh. "My whole life, I've had the shittiest end of the shit stick when it comes to luck and good fortune."

Brass shook his head, struggling to see how good luck had anything to do with him almost killing them but unwilling to drag her focus back to the near wreck. "I don't understand. You're very fortunate. You're one of the most sought-after chefs in the region. People would kill to have that kind of prowess in your profession, no?"

"That's exactly it. Luck had nothing to do with it. Every ladder rung I've climbed up has only supported me because I've built legs that have had to withstand far more falls than one person should ever have had to endure." She turned her head to the window again, and Brass immediately hated the dejected look in her eyes.

"Hey, look at me." With one hand, he reached for her chin, guided it toward him, and was pierced with a desperate sadness he'd give his shooting arm to never see darken her gaze again.

With one hand on the wheel and the other dropping from her chin to snatch up her cold hand, Brass expertly turned into the parking lot of Molly's apartment complex and killed the engine. Ironically, there was no shortage of other things he'd rather kill at that moment, because looking into her eyes as she blinked back hidden troubles, he *knew*. Without another word from her or even another exchanged glance, he damn well knew what he was about to hear.

Without meaning to, Brass pulled on that tight tether of his curse. Instead of roaring to the surface, however, his rage simmered, controlled by Brass's command and tempered by the worried insecurities he read in the chocolate pools of her eyes.

"What was his name?" he growled out.

CHAPTER 11

Molly took longer than strictly necessary to hang up their coats in the hallway closet. For one thing, the open door gave her the added benefit of a good, sturdy thing to hide behind. And second, it allowed her compulsive urges to funnel some of her nervous energy into ensuring the high collar on Brass's trench coat popped just right against the hanger. She took another borrowed moment away from the unsettled man down the hall to swipe her finger along the garment's shoulder seam. Tactile abrasion was one of her preferred avoidance tactics whenever her nerves threatened to flare up, and she currently had the mother of all threats wearing a hole in her linoleum floor down the hall.

After she'd flung forward against Brass's outstretched arm during their near miss on the road, something more than just fear and adrenaline had been knocked into her. It was almost as if his strength, while keeping her safe, had also rattled something loose. A somber realization of her life's strikeouts had fallen off the top shelf of her mind and landed with a meteor's intensity.

Hell if she knew the why and how of it, but in that strange

transference, something within her had just snapped, and she'd blurted out the first words her startled body could no longer contain. Why, oh why, did those words have to be a confession, and *that* confession no less? To him, of all people?

Molly risked one more peek around the door. When she couldn't see Brass bounding into the hall before pacing back into the kitchen, she took it as a sign that maybe he'd taken a seat on the couch in the living room. That was a good thing, right? Calm people sat on couches, and she desperately needed a calm Brass, especially after what she'd witnessed when they'd pulled up in the parking lot of her building.

When she let her little outburst slip regarding her perpetual bad luck in life, it was almost like a switch had flipped and something ominous arced within the small space between them. Brass had parked under a streetlight that took its job as seriously as an overworked and underpaid employee being asked to pick up another shift. The starved thing threw off more shadows than light patterns. If it wasn't for that lack of light, however, she'd never have noticed the blazing ochre swirling in Brass's eyes when his warm fingers cradled her chin and he told her to look at him. By the time she realized what she was seeing, he'd blinked away whatever storm she thought she imagined, exited the car, and walked over to her side to open her door for her.

And because he still had her keys, he'd promptly stormed ahead, unlocked her apartment, and threw off the covers on a world she had managed to navigate just fine in the dark.

Or so she'd thought.

That had been several minutes ago, and he still hadn't spoken to her, which left his final words reverberating around her nervous system like a poorly weighted pinball.

What was his name?

The way he'd said those words, with each intonation dripping the same dark devotion reserved for vengeful villains, had frozen her to her seat. And the real kicker to her reaction wasn't that she was terrified of him but oddly thrilled. In the privacy of her car, with no onlookers to judge her save him, and illuminated by the candlepower equivalent of an incandescent nightlight, well, was his reaction such a bad thing? The way he looked at her, with shadows carving war paint slashes across his handsome face and eyes that seemed to glow when met with hers, was the kind of thing that, had life turned out differently, she'd have fantasized about for more than a few happy sleeps.

Because up until ten minutes ago, the words *man* and *fantasy* had been mutually exclusive.

With one final assessment of the closet's hiding capacity, the outlook of which was decidedly not so good, Molly slowly closed the door and walked out into the living room. However, when she got there, she was promptly greeted by a very empty sofa and loveseat. Confused, she turned around toward the kitchen, where Brass already had her stockpot and straight-sided sauté pan heating on the stove.

"What are you doing?"

"Feeding you."

"Oh. You don't have to do that. I'll make something later—"

The soft *shhh* of salt pouring out of her saltbox masked any further protest. Brass held the stuff high above the pot of boiling water, creating a cascade of little white crystals that settled with a hiss upon impact.

"Wait, how did you already get the water to boil? That stove is about as ancient as the building codes governing the complex. On a good day, it takes about forty-five minutes for any water to come up to speed."

And that was when she took stock of all the ingredients he'd somehow scouted and set out on the counter. A box of spaghetti, garlic, her good olive oil, crushed red pepper flakes, some past-its-prime parsley, though there were still a few decent leaves if one was an industrious picker, and—she gasped

—her last hunk of sell-her-soul-worthy Parmesan cheese. The pieces knitted together faster than a competition Rubik's cube. "Oh my God, you're making spaghetti aglio e olio, aren't you?"

Brass moved to the cutting board but still didn't look at her. "Chef's pasta. Figured it was fitting, and you haven't eaten dinner yet."

"Oh, it's more than fitting, though I do have a bone to pick with whoever coined the term. I know the idea is supposed to be an easy, simple meal for cooks to whip up after a long night on the line, but honestly, even turning on the stove is too much most nights. I'm perfectly content with a bowl of cereal." She hefted some well-honed customer-service cheer into her state-ments, hoping it would cut through some of the tension. When Brass simply plucked her chef's knife out of her worn knife block and got to work slicing up the garlic, she wasn't sure whether it was better to fall back into the silence or run and hide in her bedroom.

Was he angry at her, and why the hell did that bother her so much? If anything, she should be miffed at him after he almost ran that red light. Molly tried to hold on to that small flicker of displeasure and willed the stuff to fan into anything remotely related to a good angry tantrum. No dice. The best she could muster was mild indignation, and even that was forced.

Revisiting her original tried-and-true method of running from her problems, she eyed her bedroom door down the hall. Perhaps he wouldn't mind if she stepped away for a few—

"I don't like the idea of you hurting. It doesn't . . . sit well with me," Brass remarked after setting the knife down and turning to face her. "And the longer you go without saying anything, the more time my mind has to spin stories that all result in a body count. I've been around you all day and have yet to see anything that would suggest that, by virtue of being you, you're somehow worse off by default. So, unless you tell me otherwise, and based on your confession about men to a damn stray animal who can't understand you, that leads me to believe someone must have hurt you." He slashed the air in front of him in frustration with the knife in his hand, and she winced at the proximity of the sharp blade to her curtains above the window. "I've tried to wash the notion away, tried to mind my own business and help in the ways I promised, but it's gnawed at me like a rail pike in my skull."

Then he lifted his face, and Molly saw something that made her rethink ever running away from the man. It was almost as if he'd become . . . unraveled, as if whatever spool he'd been accustomed to drawing from had spun out of control and he had no idea how to gather things back into a tight order again. His eyes searched hers, and something in those amber depths persuaded her that this confession would be safe with him and that maybe, just maybe, he wouldn't pull it out and whip her with it.

With a deep, shuddering breath and one last look toward her bedroom, she unearthed what she'd always sworn would stay good and buried.

Please don't let me regret this.

"Braden," she said through tight vocal cords. "His name was Braden. We used to work together, back when I was still just starting out in the culinary world. And if you want to hear more, you'd better drop the pasta in the water and grab that bottle of wine from the top cabinet." She gestured toward the panel above the stove.

Fifteen minutes later, with the two of them settled catty-corner to each other at her vintage dining room table and their plates and glasses filled high with the most uncomplex of carbs, Molly ripped open a bandage that hadn't just been adhered over wounds but cemented.

"Five years after culinary school, I got a job working for a modest catering company. We did all of your standard fare, small-scale weddings, graduations, bar and bat mitzvahs, even private parties. It was a newer operation in its own right but was quickly gaining steam. I think that was largely because the chef and owner offered a decent mix of the usual suspects but were also trying out some farm-to-table fusion concepts that were really popular at the time. That popularity gave way to more expansion, and additional cooks were brought in six months later. Braden joined the company in that wave."

Molly idly twirled her spaghetti around her fork tines, desperate for her fingers to be occupied lest she allow her nerves to nibble her nails away. "I was on cold apps, and he was on pastries, which meant our schedules had a lot of common hours. Most of the prep for our food was done in advance, so we wound up spending a lot of time together during plating sessions." She lifted her fork toward Brass to aid in the story-telling. "Let me tell you, *nobody* wanted to plate. It was grunt work at its finest. Lots of tiny little cups and ramekins, with finicky garnishes that were technically edible but didn't add any real value to what they were sprucing up. Literal window dressings. Most of the other cooks weren't focused on presentation like Braden and I were, so we found ourselves connecting on a lot of things. After a month or so, those connections got a lot stronger and we wound up connecting out of the kitchen as well."

A low grunt rumbled from Brass's chest as he took several large gulps from his wine glass.

"For about six months, things were going great. The catering company was booking bigger gigs, and at one point, we'd been hired to cater a Christmas wedding down in Boston for a well-known football player at the time. Well, well-known to football fans. You could tell me that guy's name until you're blue in the face and I'd still have no recollection of him, but the holiday bonus that year was phenomenal. It was right around then that some of the cooks started spreading their wings a bit and used the pseudo-fame of our more high-profile clients to explore other opportunities, so I did the same, after a fashion."

"What did you do?"

No matter how wretchedly past events had soured the memory for her, Molly could never fully tamp down her pride at the brainchild she'd birthed. "For a couple of months, since there were fewer on-staff cooks and we were mainly working with temps, there was less competition. I wanted to impress the head chef, so I tried something that had been lurking in my mind for a bit, but I hadn't had the chance to ever present it to the higher-ups before."

Brass lounged back in his chair, leaving the muscles of his chest on resplendent display against the tight waffle knit of his Henley shirt. "Clever girl," he said with a hint of pride in his voice.

Molly's cheeks heated, and she took a quick sip of her wine before continuing. "There was a Cinco de Mayo event that had been scheduled the following month. One night, after the rest of the staff went home and Braden and I were getting everything ready for the following day's event, I went into the walk-in fridge and pulled out a tray of tacos I had secretly been working on. They were all single bites of puffy fried tortillas folded around minced jicama, mahi-mahi, jalapeños, and pineapple with a chilled dollop of avocado crema that would melt into a sauce at room temperature. But the real kicker was what held up the tacos."

Molly leaned forward, still unable to curb her enthusiasm after all this time. "Each taco had been skewered to sit on top of a halved lime. Almost like a pedestal of sorts. These made for easy and stable handles as well as stands. Then guests would pluck the taco off the lime and squeeze the lime juice on it before popping the whole thing into their mouth in one bite. It solved so many problems, both from the catering side and the consumer side. Tacos are notoriously hard to serve without taco stands, which are single-use items that take up a lot of inventory space physically, as well as in the budget, especially when you're traveling. The good ones don't exactly fold down neatly. And everybody loves tacos, but they can be messy as hell. Braden had been so impressed, he picked me up and twirled me around the kitchen, saying how the world wasn't ready for me, but he sure as hell was, and everyone better look out."

If only the memory had stopped there, Molly might have been able to carry on without her stomach revolting against what little spaghetti she'd managed to eat. She took a deep shoring breath and dropped her head into her hands. "I'm not sure I can do this."

From beyond the cage of her fingers, she could sense Brass's warm presence moving closer. With gentle encouragement, he placed a soothing hand on the back of her neck and rubbed away the strain she'd amassed from holding everything in for so long. She didn't bother to dwell on how he knew it was the exact touch she needed at that moment.

"You don't have to," he whispered, dangling the out in front of her while the warm caress of his breath tickled her ear. "It's just a memory, Molly. Your brain's trying to protect you from pain by making it easier and more desirable to keep the hard stuff buried. But it can't hurt you, not truly."

One pervasive thought pounded through her mind as his firm touch began dissolving her long-built defenses.

But you can.

CHAPTER 12

But *you can.*

Molly's subconscious flung that hard truth against her prefrontal cortex faster than she could conjure all the reasons to believe him. Logically, she knew it served no benefit to sit in the suck of her misfortunes, but when those strings of bad luck went from manageable curve balls to four-seam fastballs and just kept coming, it was hard to see things clearly.

Molly's hands fell away from her face, and she braced herself for the pitiful sad eyes and slanted brows that always came her way whenever she shared the grimier parts of her life with unsuspecting well-wishers. What she got instead took her breath away.

Brass's sharp features were carved into a mask of dogged determination. That amber gaze bore into her with fierce precision, until Molly was certain she didn't need to tell him anything more, for surely he could see every hidden part of her. It was unnerving, not because of what she felt but because of what it promised.

"It's okay if you hate me for this," he added, still massaging the back of her neck in short, calming strokes. "I'd rather you hate me for dredging up past pain than look at me the same way you look at every other man."

"H-how do I look at other men?" she stammered.

His lips thinned, and his expression changed into something darker and dangerous. "Like a storm to be avoided."

Was he right? Did she view every man as an inevitable disaster that could only be circumvented through forti-fication?

"It's not unwise, you know, to protect yourself against the elements," she replied.

"You don't need to protect yourself from me." Brass's declaration was as bold as it was tempting, especially as the very mouth that proclaimed it hovered inches from her own trembling lips. She didn't want to think about the wiggle room in his words or how his slight touch on her skin settled more than just her nerves. The longer he sat with her, kneading her tension away with soft sensuality, the more his shoulders seemed to relax. Whatever had gripped him in the car right before they spun out had fled just as thoroughly as any lingering doubt she had about this man.

And then, like frickin' clockwork, she said the first thing that popped into her mind. "You're like a cat, you know that?"

The energy between them didn't diminish but lightened to a comfortable flutter. "A cat?" Brass lifted a brow.

Well, since she couldn't call her embarrassment back into the bag, along with the damn cat, she had no choice but to commit and give further voice to her thoughts. "It's how I think of you sometimes. Like a stray cat who follows a deli worker around because they always smell like tuna."

Those big shoulders lifted on a merry chuckle, which was adorably endearing for a man so serious. "I don't know if that paints you in the most savory light, but continue."

"I just mean you're always around, even when I need the

space to deal with whatever I need to, you're kind of just there, lurking."

"Lurking," he said, testing the word while he scratched beneath his chin. "I don't think I like the sound of that. Makes me sound like a predator."

"Okay, maybe not lurking so much as . . . hovering? Or, maybe like a stand-in for an athlete or an actor. Prepared, poised to move if need be, but always just . . . there."

The wine she'd had was clearly winning the evening, and damn if the hits didn't keep on coming. Her mind and tongue had been thoroughly loosened, and there was very little to hold her frenzied thoughts back.

"This is going to sound crazy," she said, leaning close enough to take him into her lungs, "but sometimes I get the impression I *do* reek of tuna, not literally, obviously, but like there's some lure swirling around us." Molly searched his eyes for confirmation. "Is that— That's nuts, right? I mean, this is just—"

"What happened with Braden?"

And just like that, he'd thrown out the one name that could shut down her alcohol-addled spiraling theory. Brass dropped his hand from her neck and shifted uncomfortably, as if her words had stung him.

His reaction was a slap to the face, more due to her confusion than obvious rejection. Had she said something out of line? Was she way out of left field with her assessment of their chemistry? Because, surely, there was something there, right? Men didn't just offer to pry a woman's pain out of her if there wasn't a vested interest in being a part of the healing journey.

Or, like always, she reminded herself, maybe other motives lurked beneath the surface that told more of the story.

And there was always more to the story.

Molly recoiled, did her best to don the mantle of indifference that had gotten her so far in her career, and drained her wine glass before giving him the courtesy to finish what she'd started.

Not that she was entirely sure he deserved it.

"Not much to tell. We worked closely together on the Cinco de Mayo event for weeks. He encouraged me to incorporate more of my ideas into the spread, all the off-the-wall creations that I normally didn't get a chance to express, and I even sketched out some future concepts in my notebook to help him visualize things when I didn't have the materials to bring them to life. Then, a week before the event, Braden took a tasting menu of my dishes, along with my notes, to the head chef. When he came back, chef raved about them—along with the rest of *Braden's* menu ideas."

Brass's eyes darkened. "He took the credit."

"Not only did he take the credit," she sneered, "but he didn't even look at me when chef lauded him for his originality and ingenious problem-solving in front of the entire catering staff." Molly sat back and braced herself for the boulder to the chest that always hit her whenever she thought back to those years. "A few months after Cinco de Mayo, Braden was promoted while I was let go in a round of layoffs once the bustle of the wedding season died down." She lifted misty eyes to Brass and didn't even try to tame the hurt in her voice. "Did you know he went on to work for a Michelin-starred restaurant in Paris? Asshole didn't even know how to spell the damn word until I told him how I'd love to work under a Michelin chef one day."

She sniffed away the clog of emotion and forced herself to continue. "And that was just one bump of many in the long road of shit luck that's always followed me around. Before that, it was not graduating on time because even though I studied abroad for a semester and triple-checked that all my credits would transfer, there had been an administrative error and I had to redo the entire semester. Oh, and then there was the time my car broke down on my way to a major job interview, my very first one out of school. I was forty-five minutes late and was told I should have anticipated the delay and figured out how to show up on time regardless." The memories kept railroading her, and the only way she could survive their onslaught was to name each and every painful one.

Molly counted off on her fingers. "Age sixteen, meningitis the week of junior prom; age eight, my father lands the best job of his career, only to be diagnosed with stage 1 lung cancer two weeks into his new health insurance's waiting period, so nothing was covered." She let the rest of her breath out, only to make enough room for the largest tsunami to crest over any remaining good thoughts Brass may have had about her. "And the pièce de résistance," she said quietly into the belly of her wine glass, "age eighteen months, birth parents are killed in a car accident, and for reasons that were lost with them, they never recorded my birth with the national hospital. Because of my lack of identity and health information, I spent a full year in a Latvian orphanage as a toddler before I was able to formally be added into the adoption data banks, adopted by my new parents, and brought here."

Before her, Brass had already cleared her plate away, leaving just the right amount of room for her to brace her arms across the table lest she fall over from being scooped out hollow. "I've learned to make my own luck, because no one has ever handed it to me. I wasn't just born under a bad star but followed around by some trickster with a sick sense of humor. I've stumbled more times than I can count and learned how to stitch up more wounds because of it. Everything I've earned has come on the backs of countless late nights and even more early mornings, while the men in my industry get to sleep late and watch others climb the ladder for them, holding their place until they can find a way to tag in and capture the flag on someone else's merit. So forgive me if self-preservation is more important than the egos of others, especially those I work with. Excuse me."

Before Brass could say anything else, Molly made her long-overdue retreat and shut herself inside her bedroom. Once huddled against the door, vibrating from the torrent of all she'd confessed, she squeezed her eyes shut and tried to erase the look on Brass's face when she'd dared mention whatever energy seemed to curl around them.

Revulsion. Rejection.

He was right, she concluded after the shaking finally stopped. Maybe she did look at him like a storm to be avoided and fortified against.

And what better way to do that than by walling up her most fragile parts?

CHAPTER 13

The stockpot had been cleaned, dried, and buffed to a shine so brilliant that Brass couldn't ignore his shame staring back at him. And because it wasn't a day that ended in Y if some form of torture wasn't on the menu, he'd had to marinate in Molly's parting shot while he gave her the space she needed and worked on cleaning up at least one of his messes.

Brass slapped the kitchen towel onto the counter as he mentally corrected yet another foolish gaffe.

He didn't *give* her anything. That was just it. After she verbally smacked him across the face with his own dick—an obviously oft-used skill set on her part—she'd stormed away, taking every inch of space she'd needed, most likely knowing he'd be reluctant to give it. She hadn't asked, nor did she wait for him to reply with words she had no interest in hearing.

Because whatever he might have said would have had exactly zero bearing on her lived experiences. She had no room or use for his pleas—for there definitely would have been a few of those in there—had she stuck around to hear them.

She had, in one sentence and a flourish of fervent retreating steps, clearly depicted what self-preservation looked like for her, and not just on the surface, but in anguished action and repressed emotion. The pinched brows, the squared shoulders, even her reluctance to push one of the elongated tendrils of hair out of her eyes when she delivered her blow, it had all been intentional.

Molly had *wanted* him to see how quickly she could don her stone skin, and how, just as quickly, he could be dismissed like the piece of shit he was.

Brass glared at the stockpot again, as if he could frighten his reflection into not revealing more about himself than he was willing to see. The visage sneering back at him matched his anger beautifully and infuriatingly called to light other elements he'd been avoiding.

How damn wonderful.

The hair around his ears had grown shaggier than customary, contrary to his normal fastidious upkeep. Shadows pooled in harsher grooves along his cheeks and jaw, which had grown gaunt over the last month or so. His usually clean-shaven chin twitched beneath a fine spray of auburn stubble, which traveled farther down his neck than he'd ever allowed before.

Mages damn him. When the hell had he let himself get like this?

When I realized none of it mattered anymore.

Brass swiped a hand over his mouth and down his chin, as if he could rub clean the evidence of the physical toll his curse was taking on him.

When he met his eyes again, he flinched at the golden specks that had begun to consume his usual amber irises. Already, his curse was melding with his angel fire, providing yet another hint of what awaited him come the solstice. Would it control his celestial power through subjugation, calling it forth to answer to a new master? Or would his rage snuff out his fire entirely, as the spark of the Eternal Flame that his power was born from was also part and parcel to his humanity?

He swallowed back his revulsion, then turned to look down the hall where Molly's bedroom was located.

Less than three weeks.

The deadline stormed after him like a sea gale, pushing against his back until he could feel the icy snaps of wind kissing his neck no matter the height of his collar. The closer he loomed toward that storm, the more of himself he lost to the same chasm of time he'd been trying to outrun these past two thousand years.

Until Molly, until whatever magic she unknowingly cast about her somehow beat back the storms and allowed him to breathe in a freedom he'd long since forgotten about.

"I can't trust it, the magic," he whispered to his audience of dishes in the drying rack. "But hell if I can deny it either." Nor did he want to, he realized starkly. The force of the admission struck him dumb, so much so that he had to brace himself against the counter.

What the ever-loving hell had he been doing all this time? Had Molly, even in just the short time he'd been around her, not been *his* own form of self-preservation? The very concept he'd forced her to defend, while he stormed all over her life expecting her to answer for things she had no choice in?

Mages, the strength she'd needed to confess her suspicions about a connection between the two of them, suspicions she had no cause to understand but was brave enough to voice regardless...

And he'd shut her down immediately, shitting all over that bravery and dismissing her vulnerable curiosity.

"God-*fucking*-dammit," he seethed into his hands. Then the idea came to him moments before he was tempted to rip off his face from the shame of it all.

They'd landed in this mess because they'd both needed each

other in some way, and if Molly was going to trust him again, he'd have to give just as much as she did, in a currency she could take to the bank.

He didn't spare his reflection another glance before he stalked down the hall.

THE GENTLE KNOCK on Molly's door came sooner than she expected, and her heart ticked up a reciprocal rhythm in time with the stupid sound. Could a girl not even be allowed the time to work herself up to a good sulk before having to face whatever kind of music was coming for her?

Apparently not.

"I don't want to do this right now," she called out.

"You don't have to," Brass's deep voice mumbled against the door. "You just need to listen."

She rolled her eyes. "I get it. You're sorry. Message received." Her flattened palm slashed the air above her forehead in a would-be salute. An answering thud hit her door, and she couldn't be certain whether it was a fist or a forehead. If he made one dent or, God forbid, a smudge on her satin-finished paint job, she'd—

"I'm not sorry."

"You're . . . *not* sorry?" Was he kidding? Had he just let her embarrass herself, stew in her fury, then come and knock on her door just so he could what? *Watch it all?*

Molly scooched off the bed and stalked toward the soon-to-be dead man on the other side of the wall using up all her small apartment's available oxygen. "If you think for one second you can humiliate me in my own home, you've got another thing—"

She wrenched open the door and was stunned into silence. There was no casual fisted forearm resting against her doorframe showing off a toned bicep, accompanied by a charming and disarming smile. No hands in pockets or sunken shoulders demonstrating remorse. All the usual tactics she'd grown accustomed to dismissing from men were stowed neatly away into Brass's leanly muscled frame. Instead, he stood several feet back with his arms braced at his sides and a dejected expression pulling down a mouth that she imagined had always looked more comfortable smiling. The brightness in his eyes had dulled from fiery to flaxen, and dammit all if it didn't kick her anguish in the teeth to boot.

His nostrils flared as he spoke. "I'm not sorry, because *sorry* is what people say to sidestep the consequences. It's a cowardly word meant to reflect remorse, but all it ever successfully accomplishes is sweeping the speaker's discomfort under the rug so they could carry on with their day pretending they didn't ruin someone else's." He took a step forward, crowding out the space between them. "I deserve every bit of your ire. So, no, Molly, I'm not sorry, but I'm . . ." Frustrated fingers found his scalp and dug into the longer locks at the front as he raked his hand through his head.

"You're what?"

"A coward," he forced out, then let his shoulders settle before throwing his arms up in the air. "I am a stray cat, Molly. You were right, and I shouldn't have kept silent just because I wasn't prepared for how keenly and accurately you view things."

Molly stumbled back slightly under the sincerity of his words because, without a doubt in her mind, she could feel he meant them. In her years working in kitchens, Molly had become something of a savant when it came to reading people. It had been a necessary skill, almost as vital as knife work, because when line cooks were throwing around "Yes, chef!" in response to every question or comment, sooner or later it became important to decipher those two words into its own language.

"Yes, chef!" *I'm four orders behind, but I can't be the weakest link.*

"Yes, chef!" *I oversalted the sauce, but my shift ends in ten minutes, so what does it matter?*

"Yes, chef!" *I know I hit the cook temp on that medium-rare sirloin out of the park, but I'm terrified of it overcooking before it actually gets to the table.*

But for Brass to call himself a coward, and not only that but to also admit that she was right? Her well-honed bullshit meter didn't budge one iota, and that freaking terrified her for a slew of whole new reasons.

"Can I come in?" he asked.

Molly simply nodded, folded her arms across her chest, and stepped back into her room, resisting the small tremble that warned her against occupying such a small space with him.

Against occupying *this* space with him.

Brass looked around at her shelves, which were just extensions of what *would have* lived in her kitchen had all the minuscule available wall space not been taken up by 1970s appliances and cabinets. Across from her queen-sized bed, particleboard bookshelves sagged under the weight of estate-sale cooking tomes and vessels and appliances too large or awkwardly shaped to fit neatly anywhere else. But if Brass felt the need to give her shit for her admittedly ingenious wall-mounted immersion blender, he didn't let it show.

Yay for small kindnesses.

He prowled farther into her room, and for the first time, she wished she'd relocated into the room across the hall, which had been Drea's before her best friend had moved out. The space wasn't that much larger, necessarily, but it had two windows facing west and always got the best crisp evening breezes before winter would get its act together and make opening the windows at night unbearable. Molly's lone window remained closed, boxing her and Brass into the stuffy-aired space along with her dusty cookbooks, and boy, did she regret it. With each step Brass took, he seemed to displace more of the air around him, as if moving through water. The result was eerie and yet somehow compelling, urging her to drift closer.

Fully aware of her folded arms and best-get-to-talkin' stance, she only acquiesced by moving one step nearer. Well, two, because her OCD wouldn't consciously allow her to have an uneven stride.

"You were, uh, saying how you were a cat," she reminded him.

His deep chest rose and fell on a tremulous breath. "Molly, there's something I need you to know."

She stilled, then hugged herself tighter, because no good ever came from a statement like that.

"I have a . . . condition."

Now, *that* she wasn't expecting.

"What sort of condition?" she asked, taking a seat on the bed.

Please don't be something oozy. Please don't be something oozy.

"It's not contagious or anything, but it is limiting. My ailment is"—he looked to the window and searched the night sky for words—"mentally debilitating. When it flares up, it affects my personality and sometimes my physical capabilities."

"Is it a brain condition or something?"

The corner of one lip twitched. "That's probably the most accurate assessment. What I have is, well, it's very rare and not well studied." A dark pall fell over their quiet conversation, and Brass joined her on the bed. She turned to face him and instinctively reached for his hand but thought better of it when he kept his gaze trained on the carpet and notably not on her.

Brass was sick? Like, *really* sick?

The idea punched a hole through her chest and robbed her of the remaining air in her lungs. How could he be sick? He was so vital, so stunning and captivating, so . . .

Kind.

With him, it was the sort of silent kindness whose ripples

were felt far more deeply than the initial impact. It was quiet and needed and just . . . *there.*

"Is it fatal?" she breathed out, hating the desperation with which she demanded to know the answer.

Another slow exhale. "Everything is fatal eventually."

"That's a bullshit thing to say and you know it."

Then he lifted solemn eyes to her. "It's the truth. And, yes, sometimes the truth can be bullshit."

That statement sank into her throat, walling off any emotion that threatened to erupt from her.

Why? How? What can I do? How much time?

She'd been around the man for a total of thirty-six hours, but he'd lurked in her mind for months, wriggling in like an earworm, both adding to her discomfort and easing it. This left her with no shortage of strange emotions to sort through when emotional analysis was the last thing afforded to her by her shitty circumstances.

Molly's mind whirled with so many damn questions. Instead of interrogating him with the ones burning on the tip of her tongue, however, she merely asked, "What happens to you, exactly, when you get a flare-up?"

"I am not . . . myself," he clarified cautiously, looking away. "When the attacks come, the logical brain activity is suppressed, so to speak. My fight or flight response is often triggered, except it's usually stuck on the *fight* setting. I turn almost feral, you could say, not so different from a beast that should be put down."

"You're not a beast," she rushed out. Oh, screw it. She grabbed up his hand anyway, knowing full well the contact was probably more for her benefit than his. To her surprise, he didn't recoil. Her heart did a tremulous flip for every second their skin remained connected, and then another when his rough fingers squeezed hers with a firmness that belied the grim subject she suspected taxed him more than he wanted her to know.

She was, however, expecting him to pull away, so much so that she was already counting down the seconds until his touch left hers and took his warmth with it.

Instead, he surprised the ever-loving crap out of her and lifted her knuckles to his mouth. The kiss that brushed the back of her hand was nothing more than a soft press of lips. Combine that with the reverent close of his eyes that lasted a hair too long to be considered an involuntary blink and Molly's mind was whirling like a field of dandelion fluff kicked up by a thousand prancing fawns, along with other long-neglected parts of her.

Holy buttered biscuits.

Before she could think to do or say anything, Brass blessedly saved her from having to form words and lowered her hand back to the bed. Lowered but never released. "That's not the first time I've been told that, but it's perhaps the first time I've ever dared to believe it."

"Why?" She didn't even try keeping the shock out of her voice. He may have deserved many things, but something told her that her artifice wasn't one of them.

Then he lifted pained eyes to hers, and a heated tremor slunk down her spine. "Because you were the one to say it."

CHAPTER 14

What the hell was it about this woman that had Brass scooping out all his secrets and serving them up for her brutal inspection? And to his increasingly infuriating astonishment, he had no desire to call the words back. He *wanted* her to see the hollowness, the scored and scratched shell that he'd wrapped around himself with bitter efficiency for two millennia. One look into the chocolate depths of Molly's eyes and he'd been speared through with something he hadn't ever gotten from his brothers.

Understanding.

Brass tried to blink through what he was seeing, so uncertain as he was to not see the usual suspects casting their shadows upon him: pity, fear, foolhardy determination. Those were the typical *troika* that made up the other sentinels' concerns as time stretched on without the benefit of progress. Despite being in the whole avenging angel business, hope was *not* the currency of the higher realms like the mortals liked to imagine it was.

Oh, no. In Brass's intimate experience, hope was—and he meant this in every sense of the word—a bitch.

Yet damn it all to hell if he didn't allow himself to hang on to Molly's slender hand and pretend, just for a moment, that his most hated four-letter word held out enough of its purported grace to shine some of that shit down on him.

He squeezed her hand tighter and resisted the urge to cradle it against his beating heart. The warmth of her skin still tingled against his lips, and it was all he could do not to hoard other parts of her into his senses like some greedy dragon protecting its treasure. Mages, her touch was exquisite and utterly devastating. Just the single singe of contact was enough to calm any loosening threads that had unraveled around his rage. The simple press of her slight fingers against his beat back the creature and freed his fire to rise just below the surface where it was most comfortable.

Comfort. Fuck, it had been so damn long . . .

"Is your family supportive?" Molly's question broke through the haze of his euphoria, grounding him to the anchor of her words.

"Yes," he offered, unsure how to proceed with what he could reveal. When Drea soul bonded with Chrome, they'd all agreed that the supernatural elements of their lives should be kept from mortals for the humans' safety. Drea, after all, had already learned that terrible truth herself, being born a messenger mage in the Empyrean, only to have been trapped outside of heaven's gates when Brass and the other sentinels enacted the Sealing, a last-ditch effort to prevent Cyro's advancing demon armies from storming and destroying the Empyrean. Drea's fall to the mortal realm had resulted in memory loss, reincarnation, and a murderous human ex-boyfriend who'd been manipulated by the demon leader to try and create a fallen angel army of his own.

Drea's friendship with Molly had been the only thing that was real and worth saving, but to do so meant keeping Molly in the dark about their true nature.

Not wanting to lie to her any more than he wanted to let go

of her hand, Brass settled on a truth that sat somewhere in the middle. "Chrome and the rest of my family are beyond supportive, in their own way. We are all"—he tested the words a bit in his mind before pulling them down—"very action-oriented. Stillness does not become us, if you could imagine."

"Oh, I can imagine." She smiled, and the sweetness in it urged him to keep going. The damn woman was humoring him, he knew, like some psychiatrist intent upon squeezing all the juicy bits out of a patient before the session ran out.

And because he couldn't bear the thought of being the one to chase away that smile—or her hand, which she still, shockingly, hadn't removed—he relented.

"All of us have physically demanding professions and interests, and we don't respond well when we're not able to produce our desired results."

Molly nodded slowly, but her pinched brows told him she struggled to grasp his full meaning, so he tried a different tactic.

He turned to her, grabbed up her other hand, and shifted more of his weight on the bed in her direction. "When you look at me, what do you see?"

Her eyes danced around the room for a moment, touching on each of her familiar creature comforts lining the walls, before landing on their joined hands, all while one thousand percent *not* looking at him. "I see a heck of a lot of charisma," she said through a half-smile, as though the confession both warmed and embarrassed her. "But I also see loyalty, focus, bravery."

She finally lifted her head, and a long-held breath sawed out of his chest. There could have been a meteor shower raining down outside her window, and he'd simply walk over to make sure everything was locked up tight, before returning to her bedside, leaving the world to burn so she might finish her thoughts uninterrupted.

"I also see perseverance, strength," she continued, "and an annoyingly unfair amount of sex appeal."

He snorted at that, more to hide the rush of heat that crept over his couldn't-keep-anything-from-anyone complexion. One couldn't move through life the way he did without gaining some awareness of one's pleasing physical qualities, and Brass was no different. What *was* different, however, was to hear her say it, and damn if he didn't puff up his chest slightly from her words. The instant her fingers pumped against his, he knew she felt his radiating heat there as well.

He cleared the gathering of unease in his throat. "When my brothers look at me, I see pity on their faces. It's constant and damn relentless, and even when they try to put on a show of encouragement or . . . hope," he ground out the word, "the sentiments are always wrapped up in a vile dose of the stuff. We know each other too well to lie effectively to one another. They know it, I know it, and there's no escape from it for any of us."

A silence stretched on between them, thickening the room with the weight of the words he couldn't say. When Molly's knee pressed closer to his in support, barely brushing the denim of his jeans, his angel fire pulsed around the tightening shard of what remained of his celestial soul. Brass wasn't verbose or sentimental enough to think of it as a hug. Chrome would pound the precious right out of him for even thinking such a thing.

But when her leg settled against his and *stayed* there, Brass found that he profoundly didn't care one whit what Chrome thought.

And, yeah, okay, it turned out that . . . Brass loved hugs. Sue him. Especially one from her.

"The only thing keeping me from losing my mind altogether is staying busy, throwing myself into a task or a purpose where I'm useful. When I keep moving and stay absorbed in something else, I'm not thinking about where my path has left me." A foreign emotion teased a smile out of him. "Then I saw your sign in the window. You needed help, and I was available to give it. Isn't that what people call kismet?" He tried for *charming*, but the look on her face told him he'd nailed *corny* instead.

Molly shook her head in disbelief. "You make it all sound so simple. Like you just *happened* to be walking down the street right when you *happened* to be going through whatever you're going through and my little meltdown *happened* to be the remedy to your particular ailment."

He winced. She wasn't wrong. Coincidences were rarely such, especially in his world, but when the last two millennia had been consumed by hourglass sands with an occasional churro thrown in for variety, it hardly mattered whether or not one believed in coincidences.

"You're not wrong," he said, his voice dropping into depths that mirrored his discomfort.

"Well, you *did* sort of waltz in off the street—"

"What you said before, about your stray cat theory, it wasn't wrong. There *is* something here, swirling between us."

Molly's lower lip fell open on a nearly imperceptible gasp, and the sweet tension that had coiled around their joined hands slackened a bit. She slid her hand out of his hold and, mother of all mages above, nestled her palm between her thighs. It was a rote move, something that was an involuntary protective measure, much like a cough or a shiver.

To him, it was a goddamn invitation and—it was important to note—the exact thing she did *not* ask for.

He bit back a curse, both for flaring up Molly's need to protect herself and for the strength it took to hold back his hand so it didn't join hers. Everything about her, from her strength to her sincerity, was just so . . .

"Captivating," he breathed out.

"What?"

"I've always been captivated by you," he elaborated, deciding to follow the course, wherever it may lead. "Ever since I pulled patrol duty at your apartment after Drea was run off the road, my head's been on an incessant swivel drawn in your direction."

Had he meant to say that? Damn.

Figuring there was no turning back, he summoned whatever bravery she claimed to find so admirable in him and plowed ahead, mindful of the muck he'd no doubt kick up along the way.

Desperation was truly a humbling thing.

"During that time, I told my brothers I'd do final checks of the property so I could stay outside your apartment longer. I'd wait by that hideous orange Dodge Dart parked on your bedroom's side of the building." He shook his head at the memory and allowed a single laugh to slip free. "I never was able to tell whether its color came from paint or rust."

A lovely chuckle rose to meet his. "Drea and I took bets on it."

"Oh? And who won?"

"We both did," she said smugly, "because neither of us actually had to drive the thing, and we figured that was a winning situation all on its own. Sometimes we'd joke how, if we ever got broke enough, we could just camp out in the car because it got impounded so often. Aurora's impound lot was right next to an awesome farmer's market that would give away some of their baked goods, produce, and meats right before closing if the items were on their way out and couldn't be sold the next day. Drea had the knack for ingenuity, I had the cooking skills, and we both had an empty freezer most of the time." She lifted a shoulder. "It would have worked out."

"I have no doubt about it. You two are very industrious."

"That we are."

"Had I known all that, I would have brought you sandwiches or something when I was there. It would have been a far better use of my time than waiting by a decrepit vehicle, hoping I'd get to see you glaring at me through the window one last time before my shift ended."

The shy smile she blessed him with robbed him of breath. There was so much humbling kindness in her expression that he'd done nothing to deserve, and he had to tear his gaze away. He jerked his head under the guise of shaking off an oncoming sneeze and looked up. Mounted on the wall behind her was an oil-painted canvas that took up the entire width of her bed. A teal-blue backdrop set the stage for a riotous golden sun. Each flame that spawned out from its middle seemed to snake out toward him like the inviting arm of a sensuous dancer. Yellows and oranges swirled in harmony over each peak, blending in much the same way he imagined the real sun to burn.

Memories churned up and rubbed his vocal cords raw. When was the last time he'd ever thought of the sun? Since he and the sentinels enacted the Sealing, locking them all out of the Empyrean and stranding them in the mortal realm, he'd not really recalled the highest realm of heaven's simulated sun cycles, which were created by the mages to allow for a more comfortable resting place for the souls housed there.

It was a light they'd spent eons trying to get back to and had been, at times, a literal beacon in the dark that all they'd fought for would somehow still be waiting for them when they returned.

When *they* returned, he mentally reminded himself around a pang of emotion. Not him.

"You should be furious at me, you know," he said, forcing himself to change the subject.

Molly lifted her chin. "Who says I'm not?"

"Judging by my brothers' . . . partners," he said carefully, "when a woman's angry, it usually comes with a lot more screaming and an occasional projectile thrown in for emphasis."

"Well, I'm not going to throw anything in here." She scoffed, then swept an arm around the room, indicating her precious shelved items. "A lot of these cookbooks are first editions, and why would I throw my cast-iron enamel-painted apple spiralizer and peeler at you? Then I'd just have to wash all the parts again after I pick your brain matter out of the corkscrew."

Brass threw his head back in the first genuine laugh he'd had in ages. The emotion loosened taut muscles, churning up a foreign joviality that had him playing along with her jibes. Indulging in the moment, he dipped his head and folded his arm over his chest in a sketched half-bow. "Your kindness knows no bounds, truly."

"Yeah, well, don't go getting used to it or anything."

"Wouldn't dream of it," he said with a wink that brought the most delightful color to her cheeks.

"I run a tight ship. I mean it!"

"Of that, I have no doubt." He shifted again, opening more of himself up to her so that he could indulge the selfish bastard within and bask in one more moment of her regarding smile.

"Besides, I can't say for sure that I'm capable of launching something across the— Oh my God, your shirt!"

Brass followed Molly's shocked gaze to his lower abdomen, where the cause of her horror finally solidified. Substances and stains in every color of the rainbow had been ground into his shirt from the waist up, with a stark line of demarcation signaling where his half-apron had ended and the disaster that was his top half began. Some smears were more identifiable in nature, and others were regrettably less so. All were covered with a fine dusting of ash and mages knew what else.

And damn that woman and her infernal distracting presence, he'd not been made to notice. That was, until he'd foolishly slid closer to her on the bed.

Like a cat, he thought ironically.

Molly leaped off the comforter and flapped her hands in front of him. "I am so so *so* sorry! It didn't occur to me that you needed a change of clothes, though why the hell wouldn't it after you put out a literal dumpster fire? My nose is still so filled with all the smoke odors, I thought it was me."

"It's fine. It's probably a good time for me to head home anyway." Brass rose to his feet but froze the second dainty fingers brushed against his lower abdominals.

Every single muscle on his body went rigid, and he quickly closed his mouth to conceal the hiss she tore out of him.

"Like hell you're going home in this," Molly said as she forced him to tug off his shirt with all the gentleness of a sanding belt. Before he knew what had happened, he was following the back of her head down the hall as she pointed him toward the bathroom while calling over her shoulder, "Do what you need to in there. Anything in a squeeze bottle is fair game. Towels are in the bin below the sink. Sorry they're pink. I'm just going downstairs to pop this into the washing machine." Then she walked into the kitchen, grabbed a coffee can from above the stove, and scooped out a handful of quarters while muttering something to herself about, "Eight frickin' cloves of sliced garlic I could smell, but not *that*?"

The front door closed before Brass had any time to figure out just how the hell that woman had managed to strip him raw so thoroughly.

And how he was going to hide an erection hard enough to bang out every single dent in the Dodge Dart.

CHAPTER 15

Normally, hoofing it up the basement stairs, then around the outside of the building, up several concrete slabs of questionable integrity, and another fourteen-step staircase to her apartment was a moderate feat of strength for Molly. She'd been used to schlepping far more up and down to the basement, which had *zero* access points from inside the building itself, especially when all her aprons were dirty and she'd determinedly cram three loads worth of starchy whites into one machine barely up to doing a quarter of the task.

What she was *not* used to, however, was the unfounded need to hustle a barely spun wet shirt inside as fast as possible because the lone drier was, once again, out of order. Sure, she could have hand-washed it in the kitchen sink, as her microscopic bathroom pedestal sink tended to clog on a good day, but then she'd risk Brass smelling of garlic and olive oil. While that was a fragrance *she'd* go feral for, she doubted he'd want to smell like an Italian breadstick on his way home.

So, the fifteen-minute quick wash cycle it was.

This left her houseguest, who was decidedly male and very

much shirtless, lingering in her apartment with plenty of opportunities to analyze all the ten levels of crazy she'd just demonstrated.

Fuckity fuck *fuck!*

Molly leaped over cracked concrete, cradling the sodden shirt in her arms like an abandoned orphan baby, and hurled herself through the shared door to her garden apartment stairwell.

"Please, to whoever happens to be up, down, and all around, let me find one of Drea's hair dryers in the bathroom." Her friend had been blessed with the ass-length hair of a Roman goddess and, as such, often required the magical stylings of not one but several commercial-grade strand scorchers to get her hair even remotely dry. One of those puppies could certainly blast the water out of Brass's shirt sooner than it would take Molly to find the dignity she'd left on the side of her building somewhere…

Again, her mind wandered to where it shouldn't.

Brass.

It did Molly no sort of good to tumble over all the things she'd just shared, both spoken and unspoken, with that man, in her *bedroom* of all places. Though her legs burned with the strain of climbing too many steps in too chilly air, it was her knees that threatened to give out, especially the spot that still scorched from the small contact she'd had with him. And then there had been the hotter-than-hell hand-holding, which her skin still tingled from the memory of.

Stop it, stop it, stop it, she scolded herself. *He is an employee who is clearly going through some stuff in his personal life. You need about as much involvement in that as a plumber needs extra helpings of shit-clogged overtime on a holiday.*

The temptation was there, however, loud, proud, and smack-dab in front of her terrified face, but she hadn't made it up the mountain of male egos and misogyny by giving into every sad story that tugged at her heartstrings. It certainly didn't matter how he'd made her laugh, or confessed to looking for her through the window from the parking lot, or why his brothers didn't understand him but she did . . .

None of it would make any lick of difference if she sent the dude home in nothing but shivering skin and a smile.

And why the hell did that thought pluck up urges that hadn't been stirred in more than a hot minute?

Molly all but fell through the door before she kicked it closed, still cushioning Brass's shirt to her chest and grimacing at the wet spot on her clothing it left behind. "Dryer was out of order, but I think I've got one of Drea's hair dryers that ought to do the trick—"

The bathroom door exploded open, bouncing off the wall with a jarring thud. Wood creaked as it hung off a broken hinge, and Molly had to throw herself backward against the dining table to keep from colliding with a veritable safety deposit's worth of apartment damage.

Brass, in all his half-naked splendor, stumbled from the bathroom in a gale of disorientation, fumbling around for any sort of strong surface that could take his weight. When the wall directly opposite the door met his criteria, he braced tense forearms against it and settled a slick forehead to the surface. Muscles that had only been hinted at beneath form-hugging clothes rippled and jerked in haunted spasms.

"Brass?" Molly abandoned the shirt on the table and inched closer with the care one used to approach a wild animal.

Because there wasn't an ever-loving doubt in her mind that was exactly what he'd become in that moment.

As she stepped closer, doing her best to swallow down the pulse pounding within her throat, more details about him sharpened. Pregnant drops of water slid off the tips of his hair and cascaded through the misted sheen that had gathered on the surface of his forehead. The hair at the nape of his neck held darker shadows of saturation, while other sections of hair had been buffed dry, revealing tufts of the vibrant auburn she was so used to.

The surface of his skin was similarly mottled, with water dripping down the runnels of ridged muscle between his shoulder blades but noticeably absent from the heaving indentations of his ribs.

Molly took one more steady step, close enough to peer into the bathroom and spy a puddle of pink terry cloth hanging off the lip of the still-running-and-now-overflowing sink.

One with the stopper yanked all the way into *thou shall not pass* territory.

"Shit!"

She scrambled around the heaving behemoth in her hallway and flew at the faucet. Only once she saw the water level recede did she drop the towel to the sodden bathmat and turn to the man who would owe her new bathroom linens as well as first and last month's rent.

"What the hell has gotten into you?" The words pelted his broad back like mist on a windshield, and he responded with a startlingly indifferent level of concern. That was to say none whatsoever.

Well, that was just fine. She had more than enough indignation for the both of them. Squaring her shoulders and adopting her best kick-ass kitchen voice, she whirled on him.

"Hey, I'm talking to you." Molly placed a firm hand on his shoulder, stopping just short of grabbing him by his ear and trotting him back to the bathroom. The instant skin met skin, however, the walls spun away and all that wet, silent bulk that had been braced against a much harder surface was now braced against her.

"You left me." Shards of ice punctuated every word that left Brass's lips as he leaned them closer against the column of her throat. "You left and took it with you."

Confused and, yeah, maybe a tad exhilarated, Molly put her hands against his bare chest to steady herself. "I told you I needed to wash—"

"Need. Yes," he breathed against her skin, pulling goose bumps up to taut attention. "You're exactly what I need, Molly Resnick. You always have been. With you, I can fight it. With you . . ." Brass bracketed her hips with his hands and dragged her impossibly closer against him.

Whatever good sense that usually took up residence in Molly's head had wisely chosen to question the hell out of her current circumstances. This was most definitely *not* the Brass she'd left fifteen minutes ago, despite the tantalizingly sexy resemblance. She focused on the mounds of lean muscle in front of her and, for a moment, allowed herself to entertain the idea that, just maybe, could she be whoever he thought she was?

Heat. Everywhere. Scorching, searing heat. Every part of his body on hers emitted the kind of temperatures responsible for volcanic eruptions and liquefying rare metals. And her body responded. Oh, did it respond. It was kind of hard not to after her sexual ice age, and if there had ever been a man to respond *to*, well, Brass checked all the boxes front and back, including the extra credit sheet. Like a damn marionette having her strings pulled, she arched farther against him and sighed as his tongue found the hollow behind her ear. Her nipples tightened when her damp clothing was quickly warmed by his skin.

This wasn't happening. Where did all this come from? A smarter woman would be railing against his shoulders, giving him a good swift kick in the *huevos*, and bolting for the nearest device with 911-calling capabilities.

Instead, a dizzying desire too long leashed flooded her faculties, shooing off any remaining residents of the Logical Thoughts Club, and leaving her with one pervasive question.

Would it really be so bad?

Brass snaked searching fingers beneath her shirt, and they

both sucked in a sharp breath at the contact. "Oh, little witch," he growled against her neck in a voice and tone she further melted for, "I love how responsive you are. I can see your pulse leaping against your throat every time I touch you. Where shall I touch you next, hmm? What will make your magic sing?"

"No-nowhere. There's no magic," Molly rasped out. "Is this one of your flare-ups?" It had to be. He had mentioned how he wasn't himself when they came on. What was the term he used? Feral? That definitely fit the damn bill. "I don't think you want this, Brass, and I'm not sure you're fully—"

"Oh, you're sure, all right." He pulled back slightly, giving Molly an opportunity to catch her first full breath since she'd entered the apartment, and she immediately wished she hadn't. Instead of the toasted citrine she expected to see in his eyes, which always reminded her of a crème brûlée's crust, whirlpools of roiling ochre overtook the simmering heat. They appeared almost like flames trapped within blown glass, writhing and kicking in golden spasms against delicate shells.

The effect startled her, and she gasped, inching back as far against the wall as she could go. "Your eyes!"

Coiled muscles twitched beneath her hands at her sharp intake of breath. That finely stubbled jaw stood locked in rigid repose an inch from her lips, both crowding her and giving her the air she desperately needed. He waited, almost frozen in a spell of indecision, with eyes foggy and far away.

"Brass," she whispered, this time trusting her voice a little more. "Are you all right? Please, answer me. I know this isn't you."

He didn't say anything, nor did he drop his hands from where they rested against her quivering belly. They just settled there, as if coasting to a stop on fumes. A mask of confusion began to smooth over his heated features. Molly watched in worried fascination as the fire fled from his eyes, and the realization of what he'd almost just done crashed over his consciousness in abject horror.

Brass wrenched free from her body and dropped his head down. "I-I'm so, so very . . . Molly, I—"

Never had she known him to be at a loss for words. In their brief time together, he'd never had very many words to begin with, but they'd always been the right ones. The perfect ones, actually. To see him now, stricken and ashamed, shoulders shaking and fingers balled into fists, it broke something within her.

"No, you didn't do anything wrong. No." She hurried to reassure him, but he shook his head and retreated another step.

"I can't be near you. I'm not safe to be around, Molly, do you understand me? You need to be safe, protected, cherished, and I almost *fucking*—"

Molly flew the two steps to him and grabbed his face between her palms. Without giving herself time to question the whys and why-nots, she brought her mouth to his and silenced any further objections.

CHAPTER 16

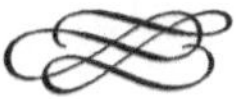

A punch of pain reverberated in Brass's gut, until even his teeth chattered against the force of it. Terror seized his muscles as he looked upon the aftermath of his worst nightmare. Molly, plastered against the wall before him, her dark hair mussed and falling out of her low knot. Her delicate brows, which always gave away more than they concealed, were pinched in confused fear, and shadowed eyes were so wide, the whites nearly eclipsed the irises, except for the pinpoint pupil narrowed directly at him.

Him.

His recollection returned, floating to the surface in sluggish pulls, and *that* was when his fire responded.

Heat.

The perfect curvature of smooth, scorching skin molded to his hands. With each fingertip he dragged along the delicate expanse, mapping every dip and divot, his fire roiled in symbiotic stimulation. A tumult of energy coursed through him, and he had no clue who was driving the bus. His curse? His celestial fire? All of it could duke it out over dominion as far as he was concerned, as long as this intoxication never left him. It was a drug, an elixir of pure magic that lived in Molly's tantalizing essence and commanded him so thoroughly, he'd stay there until all the realms imploded while he tried to consume all he could of her.

Molly.

Molly . . . who was currently trapped beneath him, scared and struggling.

Shit!

With celestial reflexes, Brass flung himself off her. Breaths sawed out of him as he leashed his curse back down. He couldn't look at her, couldn't risk seeing any more of the pain and horror in her eyes after all the broken promises he'd made. Sorry wasn't enough. Her sweet and insistent words of protest weren't enough. And that was just it, wasn't it? She was so damn sweet all the time, even to pricks who didn't deserve to breathe her recycled air, let alone the food she fed them or the smiles she offered.

Molly was innocent, pure, a beacon of perpetual goodness that his fucking fire recognized with more intensity than was safe for either of them.

Brass fisted his hands at his sides and still refused to look at anything but the tips of his boots, knowing full well the steel-toed shitkickers wouldn't offer him any other explanations than what his brain matter was coming up with. A whole lot of *nada*.

When neither of them managed to break through the strained volley of pathetic apologies and *so*-not-needed protestations, he retreated a step farther from her and scrambled for a different tactic.

Until whatever magic that woman held him in cradled the sides of his face and stole his breath with her mouth.

Fire of a different sort flared through him, strengthening his muscles with renewed purpose. Even surrounded by the most decadent softness his long existence could only have imagined in fever dreams, Brass remained a rigid plank of disbelief.

Her mouth was on his.

Holy fucking mages.

How many times had he wondered what her lips would feel like, taste like? The ideas would come at him in tormenting tidbits he rarely allowed himself to consider. What was the point? His destiny had been cemented long ago, and every borrowed breath skated him closer to that cliff's edge.

Death would have been kinder than the reality of her mouth against his. If he wasn't alive, he couldn't linger on the memory of her, knowing it would always remain one.

He was just about to wrench himself away when uncertain pecks of her teasing lips stalled his retreat. Curious insistent presses interrupted thoughts of his morose future, slamming him back into a present he still couldn't believe was his. And then his body responded, deciding on its own to seize the magic of both her mouth and the moment before more logical parts could prevail. Brass tested her eagerness, needing to be absolutely certain this wasn't some delusion.

She was kissing him. Molly was really kissing him.

Fucking. Hell.

He groaned against her mouth in helpless frustration.

I'm already there.

Or he would be in a handful of sun cycles. The realization grabbed hold of his senses and speared him through with a blooming frenzy.

Her soft whimpers dragged him further into her heat, and then he was lost to the burning resignation that gripped him. If kisses were what she wanted, he would redefine the word for her.

Brass opened wider to her distracting caresses, unfurling her to him with greedy pulls. A bold swipe of his tongue had her gasping. A moan vibrated down his spine the moment her exquisite taste flooded his senses. *More. Mine.* The declarations became vows as he sampled more of the siren in his arms.

Was that what she was? A siren of some sort? Some witchy water woman who called males to their doom with unseen lures and sinful promises? Oh, there was definitely magic here. He could feel it pulsing between their skin, transferring in the air they exchanged and melting on their tangled tongues.

It tasted divine, and if Molly's flavor was to be his last meal, he'd give his soul to gorge himself on it before fate claimed him.

The woman had powers all right, powers she had no idea of. They seized him so completely they were like a banshee's keen, drawing his balls up tight and thickening his cock against his thigh. A primal urge to escape tapped out a soft reminder in the back of his mind. A warning, both innate and learned.

Magic swirled unspoken between them, beckoning, beguiling, betraying . . .

His kisses slowed for an instant as the idea began to seep in.

He should be running.

So he did.

Brass pushed forward, breaking free of her mouth and sighing against her kiss-swollen lips until her shoulders brushed the wall where the whole mess had started. Once his forehead touched hers and he'd closed his eyes so as not to bear whatever regret may have lurked there, he trusted his voice to carry him the rest of the way. "You can't be kissing me like that, Molly. You can't be offering me that mouth when I know you're more likely to use it to curse me than keep me here."

"I know." The reply was weak and ineffectual but, surprisingly, held a note of unmet need. "I know."

Despite the mutual protests, neither of them moved. Both their hands rested and remained obediently still on one another, his on her hips and hers on his chest. The only acquiescence to the crackling energy demanding a spark was the desperate press of their foreheads together.

"Tell me to leave," he panted against her mouth. "Push me away right now and lock the damn door."

"I—"

"Do it!" He roared the words and regretted them instantly when her bottom lip quivered and his celestial senses homed in on her elevated pulse thumping against his chest where her hands still lingered.

"I won't," she replied, this time with the returned assurance he knew she could switch on when she needed to.

But he didn't want her to *need* to.

He just wanted her to need *him* the same way that he needed—

Brass's head slid from hers and dropped into the crook of her shoulder. His upper body curled into her with resigned despair. "I will not do this, Molly. As much as I fucking want to, am *dying* to, I won't. It's not worth the cost, and it's a price I'd never ask you to pay." Then he lifted his head slowly and—greedy, pathetic bastard that he was—claimed her mouth in one more drunken, dangerous kiss. A small one, just a token to take with him into whatever version of hell had called his number and would soon invite him in. The pillows of her lips softened beneath his and welcomed his pleas and passion with a hesitancy that made his fire cry out in fresh, new suffering.

It would have to be enough, he assured himself as his fingers curled and retreated inward against the rough waistband of her black work pants. It was a damn torture, one he deserved, to resist raking his knuckles across skin he knew would be just as sweet as it was smooth.

Her hands fell away from his chest, and he felt the loss instantly, mourned it, despite her taking her magic with them.

"Thank you," he murmured against her mouth, and he steeled himself to go.

Molly's sly fingers found his and began to unfurl each of his tense digits until they lay flat against her curved hips once more. "What I was *trying* to say, before you kept interrupting, was . . ."

Brass looked down at their joined hands, then back up at her in wild confusion. Those espresso pools glimmered with concrete certainty.

"I want you to stay."

"No, you don't," he warned her, heat curling his words into a lethal promise.

"Don't tell me what I want," Molly insisted, firing back with a strength that surprised even her. At some point between the soul-searing kiss and the warm, slick muscles sandwiching her against the wall, her defenses hadn't just begun to crumble but retreat.

Ever since Braden, she'd spent untold hours crying into her Cheerios over her poor decisions. She'd gone through the high-light reel of their relationship with a fine-toothed comb and dissected everything, from cheerful words exchanged to teasing body language to the literal counter-testing intimacies they'd shared. Only on the replays had she finally been able to see the penalties that had skirted by under the referee's notice. The lack of eye contact during sex, the gifts given right before he'd ask her for something, even the uber interest in her recipes, which, at the time, she'd been so grateful for and humbled by that it had been easy to ignore the red flags.

Brass's fingers tested their grip against the curve of her waist, seeking, exploring, perhaps begging for access elsewhere, but stayed put beneath her hold.

Waiting for instruction. Or permission. It was an anomaly that kicked her heart into high gear and made her wonder . . .

What else could she ask him to do? Would he listen? Did he still view her as his boss, though no paperwork had been signed, as it was an under-the-table arrangement? Either way, the kisses they'd shared were *definitely* ten kinds of wrong.

Right?

Then why the hell were her stomach muscles already quivering in anticipation of what his hands would feel like if she lifted them higher?

Brass pinned her with a *take-no-shit* glare. "Now is *not* the time to play the boss card."

So, he was aware of that little dynamic between them, too?

Yup. And it's obviously top of mind.

Great.

A thrilling idea came to her just then, and like the Boss Lady she was, she let her bottom lip suffer under her worrying teeth for only a second before she dropped a pebble in the pool to measure the ripples.

If she could be in charge . . .

"What if I want to be the boss?" She barely had time to register the golden sparks in his eyes before she gripped his hands and slid them beneath her shirt high enough for his knuckles to bump against the undersides of her breasts.

They hissed at the same time.

"Don't do that." He moaned between tight lips. "Molly, do *not* do that."

"I already told you, *don't* tell me what to do."

There, she'd done it. She'd made the first calculated move toward her surging desire. Would he run from her, like he kept promising? She, of all people, couldn't blame him if he did.

Please don't run from this.

The thought threatened to rob every ounce of bravery she'd mustered up for a man who set her body to piping-hot levels of combustion with little more than a plate of pasta, some other well-timed acts of service, and, yeah, clothing-incinerating kisses.

But in her experience and with *very* few exceptions, men

were unapologetically men. They had the power to take and trample for no one's sake but their own. A glimmer of that old worry threatened to flare to life within her, tamping down the bravado she'd only just found in Brass's reassuring arms. Would he—

"You have no idea what you've just done."

Buttons pinged against the walls around her, landing like soft projectiles on the carpet. Molly's flannel shirt was ripped away and soon joined its fallen comrades. Her mouth barely had time to fall open before Brass captured her lips again, stealing her shocked cries and mingling them with moans of his own.

There were no words for the heat singeing her skin. Brass unleashed was a force only ever written about in odysseys and epics. Entire cities could have been laid to waste from the potency he wielded, and those left behind would have thanked him for the opportunity of a fresh start.

He was fire, ice, rage, and sin all balled together in a mortal man who refused to let the span of a breath go by without some part of him caressing some part of her.

"Tell me what to do." He said this as his hands crept higher up her abdomen, pausing every inch or so to sweetly brush his knuckles over some of her softer, more rounded places, as if lingering over something lovely.

"Higher," she commanded, half out of her mind with the thrill of his touch and her sex-fueled power trip.

Brass responded with the efficiency of a soldier, coasting over the delicate bumps of her ribs until her breasts became wanton prisoners of his expert hands. She hissed and arched into his grip. Before she could say the words, he'd peeled down the thin cotton cups of her bra separating her aching nipples from the firm touch they craved.

"May I?" Golden eyes peered up at her from a head dipped lower than she recalled it being a moment ago. When the hell had he moved? Not caring to contemplate anything too closely at the moment lest she scare away the most erotic experience of her life, she simply nodded.

His stubble abraded a delicious track along the underside of her breasts, carving out a path that every fiery sense tried and failed to follow. Her brain was awash of sensations both foreign and completely unimaginable. It had never been like this with anyone else, where she came alive from little more than the caress of a fingertip or the simple press of lips.

Nothing was simple with Brass, and the prospect both thrilled and frightened her.

Molly's head fell back at the same time her jaw nearly hit the floor. Brass's tongue slid over and around her right nipple while his left hand toyed and pinched the other. When the sharp sting of teeth was added to the mix, she could hardly get her legs on board with the whole support thing. She buckled and dipped slightly, before her hand flew to the wall behind her.

She really needn't have bothered. Brass's arms were under her thighs before she even had a chance to rally the troops. And most miraculously of all, that mouth of his never left her breasts. In fact, the sudden change of position only seemed to spur him on more, giving him a better angle, offering up more of her flesh to a man who devoured her like she was the lone slice of triple chocolate cheesecake in a sea of imitation vanilla pudding.

"Brass, I need something," she panted, not caring how desperate her Boss Lady voice sounded.

"Tell me, Molly."

"I need . . . *more.*"

"More what?"

The bastard was teasing her. In between the most erotic nipple action of her life, the man causing it wanted to play word games.

"You know what," she gritted out.

He lavished attention on her other breast, this time drawing out his torture with one long slow lick. "Do you want me to choose?"

"Yes. Yes, that one. Option A. Just do it."

"Only because you said so."

It all came together faster than a mother sauce in a blender. One moment, Molly had been mostly naked from the waist up with her back against the wall; the next, her pants and underwear had been stripped away and her thighs of questionable strength had been hoisted on Brass's impossibly wide shoulders.

"Oh my God!" The cry that left her from her near-upended equilibrium was premature but still very much appropriate as Brass's mouth kissed a pathway toward that growing ache. A soft peck on the inside of her thigh was all the warning she got before his tongue swiped a long, slow lick up the very center of her. A pulsing tension bordering on pain trembled under the onslaught of his clever ministrations. His tongue—that infuriating *tongue*—swirled a seductive track just above and to the left of the one place holding every bit of her together. Like a man savoring the final licks of his dessert, he lavished his attention on everything *but* the one final taste that would end it all for both of them.

The experience rocked, not only her core but every muscle her body had previously laid claim to, before Brass had stolen command and coaxed ripples of exquisite pleasure from parts long dormant.

It was a stark breach of contract, and she was totally okay with it.

Molly flung her arms wide, searching for anything strong enough to suffer under her nails as she suffered under his skillful mouth. What she found were Brass's shoulders, tight and torqued with tension as he supported every ounce of her above while increasing his onslaught below.

He deepened his ruthless explorations until, finally, even

he'd had enough teasing and captured her clit in one swift strike.

Waves crashed over her with penetrating pulses. Every muscle quivered in soul-shattering tandem, from her stomach to her thighs to intimate spaces that exploded free from locked cages only a master could pick.

Brass was that master. Holy shit, was he that master.

Molly relinquished her hold on his shoulders and silenced her screams as best she could, trapping her mouth beneath trembling fingers. She cried and cursed and begged for mercy from foreign gods she'd never known. Surely, there must have been something out there worth blaspheming over. Orgasmic death by Brass's mouth seemed as good a reason as any to test the theory.

As she descended from heights never before seen, Brass's muffled purr of satisfaction squeezed out one final tremor in her thighs. Those precious kisses she would keep for eternity. Small, sacred pecks of affection that no one but her would ever know they'd shared.

When the light of all they'd done ascended over her little quadrant of the world, would he think of those kisses still?

She needed to think so.

Especially as he dropped to his knees, gently lifted her from around his shoulders, and settled her comfortably against the wall, careful not to let her skin touch the cold paint lest she get chilled. When they raised their heads, his with no shortage of disheveled hair and unspent desire, twin orbs of riotous ochre flames pinned her to the wall.

She gasped and pegged him with a question her soul demanded answers to long before her head thought to ask it. "What are you?"

Fear, cold and lethal, chased away the heat of their exchange. A stunned expression fell over his face, followed by the stony silent treatment visage that he'd throw on from time to time like a well-worn sweater.

It was armor, she realized. Armor against her.

With his drawbridge fortified and without answering her question, he surged to his feet, grabbed up his trench coat and sodden shirt, and shut the door on the best thing that had ever happened to her.

Of all the beings in the mortal realm who'd possessed the singular ability to see into Brass's soul and play connect the dots with the shreds of his humanity, of course it'd be Molly. His goddamn lips were still warm from her flavor, and his fire thought it was the perfect time to show its belly and beg for a rubdown. The more time he spent in her presence, the harder it was to remember just how deep his desperation was. But to feast on her pleasure and then have her mocha gaze tunnel into his scorched insides and rip out whatever soft bits were left? To touch him and not only spy his despair but truly *see* it?

To borrow a favorite idiom from his brother Chrome . . .

Brass was well and truly fucked.

Over the past few weeks, the swearing had become an odd comfort, and he'd begun to understand his brother's preference for the flare much more. Sometimes, there was simply nothing better than a well-timed fuck.

Mages knew his head had been more than run through the wringer on that one.

His bare feet rasped out soft slaps among the granite-carved stairs descending to their den's sparring ring. He brushed his twitchy fingers against the great mountain's stony walls, structures that had been carved by the angels back when mortals were little more than amoebas. With each bounce of his thighs, his heart pumped harder, forcing blood to places that still remained impossibly full. And sticking with the theme of too much steam and not enough pressure release valves, the mountain wasn't helping. Each night, the sediments and minerals would feed his fire, strengthening his celestial senses and refueling his power over the metals and alloys he commanded.

Well, he was right full up at the damn moment, wasn't he? Any more energy would only serve to push out what his snake of a soul craved to keep close to him.

That would be Molly. The strength of her thighs settled on his shoulders as he licked her to oblivion was the perfect weight his body demanded to reach its full physical potential. Her ripples of pleasure became his sustenance, drawing more vigor out of him like a marathoner chasing a runner's high.

Except there was no high, only height. A singular summit that, once she'd crested it and he'd felt her nails scoring his shoulders with every sure step he ascended, her sighs of pleasure went right to his cock. The breaths she released were affirmations, endorsements he'd readily brand across his back with a blade of her choosing.

Because, somehow, she'd already inscribed her name on his soul.

And that *somehow* was the thing that curled his gut and chased him into the pit of the great mountain hoping to beat the shit out of something.

Every boiling kettle eventually found release, and Brass was a millisecond away from erupting. The only way to do so without leveling Aurora and taking half the White Mountains down with him was through practiced form, patience, and a shit ton of padding. Though he was loath to admit it, polyethylene foam was one of the better inventions mortals had figured out. Sure as hell beat three-quarters of their processed foods or anything sold at those dollar stores. Personal protection equipment, however? Now there was something he could get behind.

It was a start, at least, though the jury was still out on exactly how many mountain peaks he needed to keep intact and still have the mortals call them a mountain range.

As he rounded the corner of the stairwell that dumped into the open sparring ring, soft clacks rose up to greet him, engulfing the steps of his approach. Swirling in the center of a veritable ocean's worth of blue floor pads were Iron and Rhode, who, like him, were bare except for matching white *karate gi* pants. The angels tracked each other in slow, measured circles, two predators sizing up their opponents. Rhode's umber gaze marked Iron's larger strides through the spaces made vacant by the former's *bō*. His frame, once so wiry and emaciated from eons in captivity, had begun to pack on lean muscle and regain some core balance. Blue, blown veins no longer protruded from too-pale skin, and clothing, while still several sizes smaller than Brass remembered, clung to hips and thighs that had begun to fill out with long-forgotten strength. And though it had only been a few months, ripples of abdominals had started to form below increasingly powerful pectorals. It would still be some time before Rhode's hair grew back, and the Seraphim commander's war braids again hung from his temples, but he was up and moving and, judging by the blossoming bruises on Iron's ribs and shoulders, regaining a bit of his former ruthlessness.

Brass slid into the room, tucked his arms across his chest, and waited for the drop he knew was coming. Where Iron mirrored their great mountain in size and strength, with boulders for biceps and impenetrable stamina, Rhode had always been a viper. A supreme master of patience and ambush foraging. When Chrome served as intelligence master of the

Empyrean, Rhode had been hand-selected by him to command the sentinel's spy legions. Despite Chrome's profuse protests, Rhode had insisted on infiltrating Cyro's surveillance network the night before the Sealing in hopes of discovering anything that could have helped the sentinels prevent the impending attack by Cyro's forces on the Empyrean.

Rhode had never returned from the mission and had only been discovered by Chrome and Drea a few months ago when they raided the demon grotto under the pretense of Drea's false employment there. He'd been held as Cyro's captive all that time, and though he claimed he had very little memory of his time there, Brass had his doubts.

When it came to staying immobile for the sake of the hunt, there was no one more adept at the skill.

Even through eons, apparently.

Iron slowly crossed one bare foot in front of the other, his dual-colored eyes trained on Rhode's hands gripping the *bō*. Before he stepped out of his stance entirely, he spun his right shoulder around and kicked out his powerful leg toward Rhode's head. The crack that echoed along the craggy cavern walls was the only measure of impact that preceded Iron's back crashing against the foam mat.

In a blur of white and wood, Rhode had swung up his *bō*, deflecting Iron's foot a moment before it connected against the side of Rhode's head. With a reverse sweep of his staff, Rhode ducked low and swung his weapon behind Iron's ankle, felling the giant like a two-hundred-year-old oak.

Never remarking on or even smiling at his win, Rhode angled his staff down to Iron and, with a heavy dose of sportsmanlike conduct long missing from the sentinels' brutish habits, pulled the angel to his feet.

Iron grunted his appreciation, then rubbed at the back of his head just beneath where his russet hair was bound in a knot. "Good. A little too good."

Rhode nodded his thanks but leaned heavily against the staff. The angles of his chest expanded with an effort that belied the stealth he'd demonstrated a moment ago.

"You've still got a ways to go, my friend," Brass remarked, stepping onto the mat.

Iron straightened and pinned him with a menacing glare. "He's doing fine." Then those eyes, one hazel and one brown, swept down the length of Brass. Iron stilled his solid frame, then lifted a brow and flared his nostrils with a great inhale. A creeping recognition awoke the spark of his fire. His eyes erupted with molten topaz, trapezius muscles swelling like raised hackles on a wolf. "You fucking touched her," he snarled.

Brass dropped his hands into fists at his sides. "Mind your own— *Oof!*"

Brass's heels scraped across the mats as Iron's transformed metallic bulk pummeled him into the granite wall behind him. Charcoal-gray wings burst from Iron's back and held the angel's body above the ground, giving him the perfect amount of leverage to rain down blow after blow upon Brass's face. The second time his neck jerked to the side, however, Brass's rage responded in kind, armoring every inch of his body with his own metal. Fire erupted from his core, shooting down his limbs and consuming Iron's wings.

Then the familiar cackle in his mind returned. A voice as cold and calculating as the taunting sands of his diminishing time left coiled around his self-control, fueling his flames with a power he'd never reached for.

Hotter. Burn hotter.

A blue inferno engulfed Iron's wings as Brass dodged the next blow. Iron's fist met the granite beside Brass's ear. The angel snarled and reared back his fist again and recocked. "I told you to let us know how bad it was getting. I told you we would find a way. And now you put your fucking hands on a mortal! A *woman!*"

Woman . . . My woman. Mine.

The declaration was a vow growled by his soul long before his mind or body could catch up. There was no time to analyze or question, only feel and react. Intellection fled the field, until all he was left with was a consuming need to destroy.

Iron's hands descended, poised for Brass's throat, but before he could tighten his grip, the great mountain seemed to vibrate from the force of Brass's wail. The voice was his, but the pure gleeful devastation projected through the bellow shook his body with an alien sensation.

Hotter. Make him feel what you feel.

Brass roared into the face of his brother, pushing, pressing, screaming a power he didn't comprehend against a male he'd otherwise die for. "She is *mine*! Nothing will take her from me." Then he leaned into his brother's face and flashed his teeth on a growl. "And with one word from her, I will happily melt you into ore, brother, just so she could command me to remake you into a likeness of her choosing."

Iron froze above him, as if jerked to a halt. Thinned lips relaxed over bared teeth and wild eyes blinked through a sudden shocked confusion. Then he whipped his head toward his wings. "What's happening?"

Brass's angel fire surrounding Iron's wings had burned beyond its celestial electric blue, pulsing and pounding into writhing swirls of white-hot fire.

Hotter. More.

Brass roared against the inferno, spread his wings and, gripping Iron by his neck, hoisted him above the floor. A hissing drip permeated the screams, followed by the unmistakable fumes of metallic oxides.

Through the haze, Brass peered down from his screaming brother's face toward the mats below and the rising smoke that drifted above two small puddles of molten iron.

Puddles that still bore the outlines of Iron's flight feathers.

Before he could comprehend what he was seeing, a blaze of dark wood swiped down on top of Brass's wrists, jerking Iron free of his hold. Startled, they both fell to the floor, but before Brass could rise, Rhode's *bō* cracked him across his temple. His head swiveled around violently, breaking the curse's claim on his concentration and extinguishing his fire along with it. Then he was pushed forward until he was facedown on the mat with Rhode's foot compressing his neck and the butt of the staff levered under his chin.

"Enough of this." Rhode's stern words carried a weight that had been born of eons commanding legions of the Empyrean's finest spy networks under Chrome's instruction.

And the dude had subdued Brass with no more than some meager body weight and an overgrown toothpick.

"Sorry," Brass breathed out, blinking away the fog of the moment and feeling the repercussions of his loss of control press him farther into the mat. Had he really just done that? Had he just—

"Iron! Let me see him!" Brass roared, struggling against the weapon at his neck.

Rhode didn't move despite his body straining against Brass's flailing. "Are you calm?" Rhode gritted out. "You must be calm."

"I'm in control." It was as good of an answer as he could give, and judging by the decrease in pressure against his neck, Rhode knew it as well. As soon as the weight was off him, Brass scrambled forward to where Iron lay on his hands and knees, panting and spitting on the foam mats. His wings and metal had receded, revealing red and mottled flesh that stretched along the column of his spine where his wings had sprouted. Some patches of skin puckered with minor burns, while others were blackened and flaked by advanced degrees.

"Shit. Fucking shit!" Brass cried even as Iron waved him away.

"I'll be fine," Iron breathed out as he fell back on his ass and leaned his weight on his forearm. "Chrome will fix me up. They'll regrow."

Regrow. Like his flight feathers had received no more than a bad goddamn haircut.

"But I—"

"*You* did nothing, brother." The topaz had fled from Iron's steely gaze, but the meaning was there all the same. It always was. Pity. "But next time, it might not be me your curse decides to take it out on." Iron spat onto the mat beside him and gave no concern to the blood that he'd coughed up as well.

"He's right." Rhode sat next to them, legs straight out in front, elbows resting against the staff he held horizontally across his lap. "How do you know your little mortal won't be next?"

His little mortal. Why did the simple ownership in those three words make him want to carve Rhode's tongue out just for mentioning her? A possessive spark flared within his chest where his fire had just raged, as though his pathetic heart only bothered to beat when she dominated the subject matter.

"Her name is Molly," Brass whispered, staring daggers at a hole in the mat by his foot where metal had melted through it. "She . . . I . . ." He sighed, uncertain how to vocalize his concern. Fucking mages, he'd nearly killed his brother, and he was over here playing footsie with some scorched foam instead of saying what those males damn well deserved to hear.

Brass dug his fingers into his hair and lowered his head. "I think she's a magic user of some kind." The confession stole his breath and that of his brothers. He regarded it for the terrible sign he knew it to be. For all three of them. "When we were at the restaurant, I was rummaging through the dumpster in the alley, investigating a small fire that had erupted beneath some copper wiring. The next thing I knew, orange flames turned blue, and my fire was pulled out of me, lighting up the entire dumpster's contents. I didn't do it, but she was the only one around, and—"

Fuck, he couldn't say this. Every aching part of him swelled and roared against sharing what felt like a precious confidence. What if it put her in harm's way? What if whatever had slated him for slaughter learned of her magical counterbalance and went after her?

What if she knew and the fire was intentional?

It was that question that turned the crank on his mindfuck, even while his fingers scratched against his palms, itching to feel her soft skin instead of the roughness of his own.

But these were his brothers, brothers he had just tried to kill for even speaking of Molly, even if the intent of their words was to protect her.

From him. Again.

"I'm better around her," he rushed out before he could see the distrust on their faces and had to answer for it. "I don't know why, but I can just *breathe* when she's near. There's no choking tether I have to keep lashed down all the time. My rage is free, yes, but it's almost like it has a different motivation, if that makes any sense."

Rhode and Iron exchanged puzzled looks. "Your curse is sentient?" Iron asked.

"No. Yes. I mean, fuck . . . I don't know what I mean." Any explanation his brain offered up fled the station as soon as it boarded, because anything that couldn't be explained away was a result of one thing.

One very significant and vile thing: magic.

"She doesn't know." Brass lifted his head and met the solemn eyes of two angels who had their own reasons to recoil at the word. Bless the mages, they didn't judge him for it.

They didn't judge him, but oh, the pity was there loud and proud like always.

"She doesn't know," he went on, "and she never will. At least, I won't be the one to tell her."

Rhode leaned forward. "Are you sure that's wise?"

Brass shook his head. "I'm not sure about anything, and I can't afford to go in blind. Molly's . . . I don't believe she's aware of her power, but that doesn't mean she's not dangerous. So, until I can figure out what she's playing at, her ignorance of her condition is the best thing for all parties involved."

Iron grunted and wiped his forearm across his mouth. "You still touched her today."

If there was a point to be made, the bastard would always highlight the direct path and still somehow find a damn shortcut.

"Yes," Brass gritted out.

"You touched her today," Iron indicated, "and lost your shit soon after."

"Please don't mince words on my part."

"I don't believe in coincidences, and you can't afford to either."

Brass bared his teeth. "Just what are you fucking saying?"

Iron leveled his even-keeled stare at Brass. The effect was made more ominous due to the rapid bruising already beginning to show around the thick column of his neck. "I'm saying you can spend time you don't have cracking her magical nut, or you can stay the fuck away and deal with your shit. Mages know you have enough of it."

There. Right there. Iron not only gave a voice to the elephant in the room but named it, adopted it, and set it up with a visitation schedule.

You can stay the fuck away.

As much as he hated it, the idea pinged around his cranium more than it should have. What if he stayed away, perhaps for a day or so? Just long enough to get to the bottom of what the hell was going on. His fire immediately revolted against the concept, though, as was recently evident, his powers couldn't be trusted to act in his best interests, not anymore. That was far more terrifying than all the other alternatives laid out before him.

What if he hurt her? Or worse, what if he did more than just taste her?

Brass shot to his feet and gave his back to his brothers. He wouldn't offer them his hand, knowing they'd see the assist as more insult than aid. So, instead, he threw his shoulders back and padded out of the sparring ring on limbs that had never truly regained their strength since the moment he'd untangled Molly from them and likely never would.

CHAPTER 18

While most people would have been dragging ass at five in the morning on a Wednesday, Molly was infuriatingly awake as she turned the key and let herself into Suerte and Honeysuckles. She didn't bother to punch on the lights in the dining room or set up anything for Benny, who always trampled in a hair shy of fifteen minutes before the place officially opened. The dine-in breakfast rush didn't usually get going until after school drop-off, so until then, their customers were mostly just commuters of the coffee-and-muffin-grabbing variety anyway.

Fine with her. There was only so much peopleing she had in her after a night that devolved from mind-blowing to second-guessing to tossing and turning amid twisted sheets wondering just what the hell she was going to say to Brass the next day.

A lot of things tended to flare up in the light of a new morning, not the least of which were regret, bad decisions, awkward silences, and the realization of a shared moment that her pea soup brain could only describe as . . . significant. Oh, and because she was one of the few people on the planet who was *more* neurotic when not caffeinated, she'd spent otherwise good sleeping hours agonizing over all of it.

Would Brass regret their time together? Had he landed on the same no-employee-relationships conclusion and then fiddled his game piece around the board like she had, secretly hoping the spinner had landed in the middle of two impossible choices, therefore warranting another turn?

Molly ambled into the office and dumped her exhausted body into her chair while she emptied out every last ounce of her frantic thoughts all over her desk like a field of mismatched puzzle pieces. Blue velvet cushioned her neck, and she allowed herself a few quiet moments to breathe through the events of the prior evening.

One event, in particular, kept surfacing, and in the quiet of her private office, she finally gave herself permission to revisit it.

What if I want to be the boss?

The whispered command had shocked her almost as much as Brass's hands on her skin. It wasn't just out of character for her, but out of the question. She had more than enough bossing to do in her waking hours, so why the hell did the thought thrill her when alone with Brass? And more to the point, his responding words had stunned her as much as they had seduced her.

Tell me what to do.

It had all unraveled from there in the headiest combination of power and pleasure. Everything she wanted, she didn't just ask for but took without apology or explanation. And he gave with equal zeal, so much so that even when his actions were leashed while he waited for her instruction, he still doted on her with a devotion to rival that which ancient civilizations showed to immortal gods.

And holy shit, it had been amazing.

With Brass, the sexual acts they'd shared had gone so far

beyond pleasure. Somewhere around the three a.m. mark, when she was staring at her bedroom's pre-1970s popcorn ceiling and counting the pockmarks to try and fall asleep, a strange image arranged itself among the mélange.

Two golden eyes staring down at her. Not amber or hazel but a blazing gem-colored ochre that swirled with an inexplicable fire. They were the same eyes Brass had trained on her before he blinked the moment away and fled her apartment faster than a building inspector who hated paperwork. All she'd been left with was the parting shot of fear twisting his features into something she didn't recognize and a boatload of confusion on her part.

Instead of dwelling on the misshapen pieces, however, all she could focus on was the one insistent word that wouldn't let her sleep, strategize, or even scream.

Significant.

Whatever she'd shared with him wasn't just sexual but significant, like a change had occurred, one where she'd chase down lifetimes to experience it again.

Even if it was unnerving or—she hesitated to say her growing suspicion out loud—unnatural.

"I know what I saw," she whispered to no one before opening her eyes. "I'm not crazy, and I'm not entirely convinced Brass is either."

"Yoo-hoo! Anybody home?" A man's voice filled with far too much humor than the hour called for preceded Brass's brother Bronze into the open doorway of Molly's office. A graphic tee stretched across his lean chest, which was covered by a barely acceptable winter layer of what she'd seen some of the touristy boutiques in town refer to as a fleece-lined flannel *shacket*. His charming demeanor seemed to hold up more of the doorframe and conversation than Molly had the energy for, so much so that she couldn't even muster the appropriate response for what amounted to an unannounced guest in her closed restaurant at the ass-crack of dawn. Though, given that said guest jangled a familiar set of keys next to his ear—a set she'd supplied a certain new employee with—she figured it was in her best interest to call on her remaining active brain cells to stand at attention.

Without coffee, however, that was a lost cause. Instead, she let fly the first thought her cranial team could muster.

"Why are you all so tall?" she grumbled, debating whether closing her eyes again would make more or less of Brass's family appear in her restaurant.

Wait . . .

Remembering what time it was, Molly shot out of her chair. "Where's Brass? Is he all right?"

Bronze, who Molly had only met once before, shrugged and lifted one corner of his goateed mouth in amusement before attempting to tuck his unruly shag of red hair behind his ear. "A healthy mix of fiber-filled carbohydrates, lean proteins, and a whole lot of avocados. Makes us shoot up like weeds in the rain. And gummy bears. Can't speak for the rest of my family, but something about that red dye 40 just really agrees with my constitution." Bronze gave his abdomen a soft pat of appreciation.

Molly blinked, then let her head drift to the side as if processing what he'd just said would make more sense from a different angle.

"And to answer your other questions," he cut in, "Brass is taking a bit of a *siesta* today. He sent me to help instead." Bronze waved his arms to the side in a *ta-da* moment and threw her a smile so wide not even the most aloof of preschool drop-off moms stood a chance at resisting his charms.

"You're here to help?"

"Sure am." Bronze threw a thumb behind him in the direction of the kitchen. "You got any spare aprons?"

"I . . . um . . ."

"No need. I'll find 'em. May as well start up the coffee."

That got her attention. "I find it hard to believe you haven't had any coffee yet or that Brass would have skipped out after only one day of dish duty."

After only one day of being with me, and after we—

"Your boy just needs a day or two."

"Oh, he's not my—"

"And as for the coffee, why bother filling up on boring old French press at home when you've got the single-origin pour-over set up here? Besides, how can I chat up the customers about the coffee if I don't make every attempt to become a first-rate connoisseur of the good stuff?" Bronze yanked a half-apron from a hook in the hallway outside her office, replaced it with his shacket, and ventured off into the kitchen. "I'll get the grind going. It's a ten-minute pour on the coffee, right?" he asked over his shoulder.

A surge of emotions battled for dominance. Hurt, embarrassment, foolishness, they all had it out in a battle royale-style brawl that did more of a number on her sanity than anything that had kept her up last night.

He's not coming back.

Before she let the realization take root and grow into something not even an industrial soil tiller could yank out, she gritted her teeth against the sting forming behind her eyelids and set to rights the one thing she could control.

"No more than six to eight minutes on the pour-over," she called out.

There was already more than enough bitterness to start the morning. No need to make it worse with shitty coffee.

As THE SUN set up shop over the restaurant's sleepy street, two things became abundantly clear. First, a proper pour-over went a long way to enhance Bronze's charisma even further, turning him into every restaurant owner's wet dream. The second, despite the draw and appreciation of such a stellar staff member, tables were emptier than they'd ever been. Molly suspected that news of the fire hadn't quite settled yet, and her regulars were waiting to hear any potential outcomes before trusting her again with their butts in seats and credit cards on counters.

Molly turned over her phone on the desk and reached for another sip of coffee, her third cup of the morning, though at some point, Bronze had been astute enough to switch her out to decaf. Normally, at ten thirty on a Wednesday, she'd be knee-deep in neglected table tickets while Benny would bark out egg inventory numbers and complain that the bakery they ordered their bread from was late on their delivery again. Instead, she took a rare opportunity to steal a few precious moments for herself and work out her dishes for the Winter Whimsy Festival, which was only about two weeks away.

"Hey, boss!" Bronze peeked around her doorframe. "Got a customer who wants to talk to you."

"Sure thing. Tell them I'll be right there."

Molly tucked her notebook in her drawer and followed Bronze out into the dining room. An older blonde woman stood just inside the front door with her arms folded across a form-over-function wool coat that had exactly zero chances of batting away a snowflake, let alone a sea gale. Judging by the hairspray-stiff bob and her eerie lack of age-appropriate facial lines, the woman likely had *I'd like a word* tattooed on her dimpled ass.

"May I help you? I'm Molly, the owner." She smiled and extended her hand in greeting, but the woman retreated a step instead.

Oookay . . . so it's going to be like that.

"I guess you're the one I should speak with," the woman remarked after waiting one more protracted second to no doubt see whether anyone else would step forward to address her.

Molly sighed. It was an act she knew all too well.

"If you're looking to speak with the owner of this restaurant, then, yes, that'd be me." Molly threw all the cheer the woman didn't deserve into the words.

"I was here Saturday afternoon with two girlfriends of mine to discuss the plans for our bunco league's holiday party. We are Aurora's top-performing players of the dice game, and the town's recreational committee will be honoring us with an award for our achievements at our annual gathering in a few weeks."

"Congratulations." It was the third thing Molly had thought to say, right behind, *What the hell is bunco?* and *Was the award along the lines of the complimentary holiday chocolates given to all the businesses, committees, and clubs by the mayor's office each year?*

"Well, I'll have you know that the date for our party has now been postponed." With that, the woman pulled a folded piece of paper from her pocket and shoved it at Molly.

"What's this?" She unfolded the paper. *Aurora Laboratories and Diagnostics Patient Report* was displayed in bold letters across the top. As Molly tried to make sense of what she was reading, the woman—Roberta McCall, according to the document— gladly offered clarification.

"That is my toxicology report for blood work I had taken the day after I ate here." She leaned forward, and Molly caught a glimpse of red lipstick on the woman's eyetooth. "Shortly after I ingested the mahi-mahi tacos for lunch at your restaurant, I became severely ill and was hospitalized for the next twenty-four hours." She tapped a lacquered nail at a row of numbers categorically higher than any other.

"Your histamine levels were high? I don't understand."

"Scombroid fish poisoning," the woman enunciated like one would a three-syllable word to a first grader. "Also known as histamine fish poisoning, where the victim suffers severe allergic reaction symptoms following the ingestion of contaminated fish."

And then the cogs clicked into place. "Wait, are you suggesting you ate contaminated food at my restaurant?"

"My dear, I'm not suggesting anything. I'm merely informing you of what I've already told the health department. The poisoning spawns from bacteria as a result of improperly refrigerated fish. When fish is not chilled appropriately, it allows for histamines to form in the fish's flesh and get infected with bacteria. *Heat-resistant* bacteria, I'll have you know." She lifted her chin higher with the authority earned through extensive Internet searches and scanned the few restaurant customers who looked up from their tables at her with worried interest. "No amount of cooking can cover up the spoilage, which I'm sure you're well aware of. Many of these establishments often resort to using subpar ingredients to improve their bottom lines."

"Hold the heck up." Molly raised her hand. "Please do not tell me you're coming in here to accuse me of poisoning my customers. I can assure you, I recently had all my equipment inspected. I've got the satisfactory sanitation inspection certificate hanging right over there " Molly gestured toward the framed piece of paper that sat on the wall next to the register.

A piece of paper she'd already hung up—in its sparkly document holder frame she'd had custom made, no less—before the inspector's heels had fully cleared her doorway.

The woman snatched back her lab report and pocketed the thing. "However you choose to come by your documents is no concern of mine. I figured with it being the holidays and all and with many local businesses often seeking vendor booths at the Aurora Winter Whimsy Festival, it would serve you to know what kind of response you'll receive should you go forward."

"Mrs. McCall, I think there's been a mistake. I've taken every proper precaution to ensure—"

"Save your pleas for the health inspector. They should be paying you a visit shortly." With one more meaningful glance tossed to the remaining customers, the woman swept out of the restaurant. Moments later, wooden chair legs scraped against the floor as diners quickly wrapped up their meals, paid their bills, and left on her coattails.

"What the actual *fuck!*" Molly screamed as she slammed the front door. Before Bronze or Benny could say anything, she ran toward the kitchen and examined her walk-in chillers. One by one, she opened each fridge and stuck her hand inside, ensuring the temperature reading on the outside of the equipment was accurate.

Benny turned off the stove's burners and came to her side. "No way those were malfunctioning. I would have known it."

"I know," she whispered as she leaned her head against one of the fridge doors.

"She could be lying," Bronze offered. "Trying to get press for her club, scare tactics, what have you. There are any number of things that could have caused what she's claiming, the least of which wouldn't even start or end with this place. Did you see her face? The woman had more foreign matter floating around in there than space junk in an asteroid belt. It's nothing. She's nothing, Molly. Don't worry about it."

"I *have* to worry about it," she said, then spun to face them. "You saw how those customers left after hearing what she said." Then Molly recalled an earlier conversation with a diner a few days ago. "She's not the first one to tell me they've gotten sick after eating here, either. I can't prove it, but even if I could, it wouldn't matter. Image is everything."

The line had been something her old catering boss touted with more flair than a firecracker. The words had been ingrained into her and every chef under his employ since day one. It was why she'd spent so many nights perfecting the presentation of her cold apps, while commiserating with Braden and falling into a hole it would take her years to crawl out of. And now she was in another hole, this one born of her financial foolishness and stubborn pride over not wanting to go down with a ship that, in so many ways, she'd help set sail.

The back of Molly's head went numb against the fridge's soft incessant vibration. Above Benny's and Bronze's heads, painted into the wall with swirling lavender strokes, the words *Suerte and Honeysuckles* flowed like a river offering to sweep her away.

No matter that she couldn't see the bottom or where she was headed. She never could and never relied on promises of luck and fortune to guide her anyway.

This was yet another reminder of the one constant in her life, and she wasn't about to let some lab report sideline the opportunities the Winter Whimsy Festival could bring.

"We're closing tomorrow," she said on a swallow. "I need to get to the bottom of this, and it's not like we'll have customers beating down the door for eggs and coffee anyway, not if Mrs. McCall's motormouth has anything to say about it. If a health inspector's going to show up here, I want to be ready."

Molly pushed off the fridge and stormed into her office, never once meeting the eyes of the two people who had the lovely distinction of seeing her at her worst.

She didn't know why Brass's golden gaze also flared in her mind or why it remained with her as she shut the door to puzzle out her next steps.

CHAPTER 19

The only thing worse than rage cooking a smorgasbord of potential choices to showcase at a make-or-break winter festival was doing so in a temporarily shut-down restaurant full of doubt, debt, and despair. There were a lot of things Molly could face. Deceitful ex-boyfriends, criminal bosses, and trumped-up male egos were some of her greatest hits. What she couldn't stomach, however, was standing in a kitchen, with counters laden with goods she wasn't sure would ever see the light of day, and *not* having a piping-hot churro waffle, made decidedly by someone who wasn't her, sliding between her lips.

After all, if cinnamon sugar dough, spiced chocolate sauce, and humiliation couldn't pull her out of her spiral, she wouldn't like to meet the thing that could.

Probably had too many calories anyway.

Molly locked up the restaurant, wincing at the *Closed* sign that had been getting its share of sunny-side-up action for the past five days. After Mrs. McCall stormed into the place touting all sorts of vitriol Molly couldn't defend against, the woman had made good on her threat. Sure enough, like a fly to shit, Aurora's health inspector came knocking on the restaurant's door the following morning.

The findings had been interesting to precisely no one. All of Molly's equipment, food practices, and sanitation procedures were as aboveboard as could be. There were no signs of any malfunctions, poor food storage, and—thanks to Molly's industrious late-night scrubbing session and the small fortune she'd invested in cleaning supplies—even her grease traps were spotless. The inspector was clearly hoping for an *I've got you now!* bust of some kind, as if the man earned a healthy commission for every dream he shut down. Instead, he'd begrudgingly supplied Molly with an updated permit of satisfactory inspection, mumbling the word *unremarkable* against the too-long fringes of his mustache.

Despite the clean bill of health her restaurant received, Molly had kept the place closed through the weekend. It was a hit she couldn't afford, but like it really mattered? Debt was debt no matter how long it went unattended, and unless she figured out how to spin bullshit into bullion, a few days wasn't going to make a difference. Besides, she knew better than to think her regular customers would be so forgiving so soon. The odds of her tables being filled after her weeklong disasters were, if she had to take an optimistic approach, slim to freaking none.

And then there was also the little wrinkle of not hearing from Brass since what her dramatic mind now referred to as The Incident.

Five days. Five days of not seeing him and her mind had devolved into nothing but lingering worries, dissolving sensations, and a shitload of self-important regret.

It was true Molly had never been musically inclined, but as the saying went, she could still name that tune in three notes . . . and apparently live off the royalties for the rest of her life.

Stupid. Stupid. Stupid.

So, she decided some cheer in the form of sugary carbohydrates was in order. It was the only sensible route at that point and had never steered her wrong before.

Molly shoved her icy fingers into her coat pockets and tramped toward Spruce Path, journeying to the local mecca that was Chunky's Churros. She'd always hoped the food truck's name was more of a cute moniker for the owner, rather than a commentary on his customers, but her confidence had long since fled the scene on that one.

Just like everyone else.

She ambled toward the eyesore that was the safety-orange and Barney-purple monstrosity that made up the churro capital of Aurora—well, for as long as he parked the truck there, anyway. A soft whine interrupted the decent brood she'd worked up, halting her from going up to the window. Four russet paws poked out from around one of the town's boxwoods that had been pruned to within an inch of its life. Short, black fur took over where the red coat ended, revealing familiar curious brown eyes.

"Hey, sweetheart. I was wondering whether I'd ever see you again." Molly squatted down and gave the hound dog that had been in the alley next to her restaurant the rubdown of her life. The pup wasted no time rolling onto her back and lolling an approving floppy pink tongue in Molly's direction. "You want some treats?"

At that, the dog's ears performed a miracle of gravity, perking up despite their droopy weight. Determination, it seemed, was a cross-species trait.

"What do you want? They have churro waffles, which are my personal favorite. Think waffle fries, but with sweet dough instead of salty potatoes, though I think we'd skip the chocolate sauce for you. They've also got more traditional churros, which are stuffed with pretty much anything. I highly recommend the caramel, unless you're more of a vanilla cream gal. No judgment."

At the mention of caramel, the dog rolled over and licked the tips of Molly's fingers. "Message received, my dear."

After a harried exchange of coin for confections and a renewed determination to fit a gluttonous amount of good stuff in too few hands, Molly dangled a churro in front of her new four-legged friend before taking a bite herself. "Not sure caramel's good for dogs, but who the hell am I to judge, right?" she said around a mouthful of sweetened nirvana.

"It's not." The bass timbre of a voice she hadn't heard in several sun cycles almost caught her as off guard as the startled slender tail that had whipped around and nearly nipped her nose.

Damn if her body hadn't remembered exactly how that resonance had scraped across her skin. Once Molly recovered, both females, two- and four-legged, stood to address the intrusion. She opened her mouth, preparing to blast him with a tidal wave of indignation that had been brewing the past few days, but what came out was anything but. "You look like shit."

Brass's pallor had become even more evident, slashed by the shadows of the boxwoods and petite arborvitae. The high-necked collar of his black trench coat brushed against a chin stubbled and stained with several days' worth of growth. Some of the familiar starch had left his shoulders and seemed to weigh down his forlorn frown. His forelock, which always acted with a will of its own, stood at an odd angle, as if it had been repeatedly pulled in directions both unnatural and unwanted.

But it was those infuriating eyes that worried Molly the most. They weren't just dim but dead.

Brass took a step forward and only spared the dog a glance before returning his attention to Molly. "Can I walk you back to the restaurant?"

"How did you know I was even there today?" She lifted her chin. "It's not like you bothered calling or showing up when I expected you to be there."

Shame crinkled the edges of his eyes. "I was not myself. I needed some time—"

"Away from me. I get it."

"No, you don't." The finality with which he spoke the words had her stopping short. Even the dog issued a growl of warning at Brass's uncharacteristic tone. "Not yet, anyway," he continued with only slightly more composure than a ruffled understudy on opening night. "But you deserve to. I'd like to explain if you'll let me."

Again, Molly mentally amended.

And wasn't that just the kick in the pants Molly should have been used to by then? She could teach a class on groveling and even secure a college tenure track for the subject matter. What she was *not* used to was the stark role reversal. She had been on the receiving end of a good grovel the sum total of zero times in her life, and with Brass's current look bordering on dragged-through-the-mud chic, she couldn't say her curiosity wasn't a bit piqued.

It's not going to change anything.

She played the reminder on repeat even as she stepped forward with one churro waffle extended.

Skepticism and perhaps a dash of hope lifted Brass's brow. "Is that a peace offering?"

"Nope." She popped the unsauced treat into her mouth and chewed with vigor despite its undressed state. "It's a count-down. You have until the time it takes for Churro and I to finish our dessert before I decide whether I want to stop listening to you and forget your face entirely." Molly began walking, and the dog, right on cue, took up her stride alongside her.

Faced with a choice to either follow or fall behind, Brass joined them. "You named the dog Churro?"

"I like to think the name chose her, but yes. And time's a-wastin.' You better walk and talk. I'm only even entertaining you because you've already ruined enough. I won't let you ruin my snack as well." She bit down on another churro, this one filled with caramel, and tossed the rest to the dog, who snuffled it up in solidarity before a single sugary drip marred the sidewalk.

"Duly noted."

———

THEY WALKED in silence the few blocks back to the restaurant. The only sound permeating Brass's thoughts was the rhythmic clacking of claws on concrete. The damn noise had become a metronome against which his troubled thoughts paced. It seemed Molly was content to give him enough rope to hang himself, allowing him to indulge in his mental strategies while she indulged in her sweets. The dog was an entirely different ball of wax, however. The hound's chocolate eyes cast their northward suspicion his way every few feet. While he could appreciate the little thing's protective qualities, especially where Molly was concerned, there was something about the canine's energy that irked him.

Perhaps it was the paranoia courtesy of five days with nothing but his worsening curse for company.

Perhaps it was a different kind of paranoia, one that thoroughly disliked the idea of a forty-five-pound hound running protection duty for a woman Brass would merrily step in front of a Gatling gun for.

The idea was only one of several that had kept him quiet while Molly, saint that she was, took her time savoring food he knew full well she would have devoured in four bites tops.

She was *still* holding her fucking hand out for him and all he could do was stare at it, hoping like hell whatever magic he sensed in her skin didn't also come with a hefty dose of pity.

He'd had enough of that to last lifetimes.

Instead of dwelling on the present and future, Brass had spent the past several days away from Molly delving into the past—her past, specifically. With Chrome's help, the two of them had pored through all they could find about Molly's family history, which, as Molly had confirmed with her adoption story, was a whole lot of bupkis. He'd never been able to discover more about her birth parents before they died or, more troublingly, why her official birth had never been recorded in Latvia. Because of her scarce family history, Brass had no leads, be they magical or mortal, to chase down regarding her true background.

Without a clear map to follow, Brass had quickly begun to spiral. The longer he stayed away from Molly, the louder that pervasive cackling in his head grew. The tether leashing his curse had worn down to strings no thicker than shoelaces. Somewhere around the second day, he'd stopped eating entirely. Every crumb that touched his lips reminded him of the perfection he'd last tasted between Molly's thighs and the magic she somehow held over him.

A magic that both soothed his curse and riled his soul.

After he'd incinerated three trays of food and burned through every round of ammo in the armory before melting the firearms soon after, Brass had gone to Iron and Chrome begging to be lashed down in the pit of the mountain where he could wreak his curse's fiery destruction in peace.

It was Rhode's suggestion they'd followed instead.

They kicked him out with a warning that if he didn't return to Molly to ease his beast while they searched for a cure, they'd find a way to bring her to him, whether or not she went willingly.

It was as final a resort as any of them were prepared to make, which only served to highlight just how little time he had left until the solstice.

Fuck.

Molly's footsteps slowed as they approached the restaurant. Brass hung back a good distance, not assuming for one moment he was welcomed into the place, not after how he'd left her.

And he was right. She'd unlocked the front door and went inside without so much as a backward glance.

The rope she'd offered him had officially been reeled back in.

Brass scrubbed a hand over his chin, wincing at the days-long growth that abraded his palm and just how much he had let everything tumble out of control. His hygiene, his curse, his family, his fate . . .

His woman.

Blinking away the thought, he turned to go, not missing for one second the smug look on the hound's face and how Brass had incorrectly assumed that animals were immune to pettiness.

Yet another thing he was wrong about.

"Here you go. Eat up! There's plenty more where that came from, though we should probably keep this in the alley and not near the main entrance. Lord knows I've got enough people watching this place, and I don't need any more unwanted drama." Molly bustled out of the front door. In two hands, she held stainless steel mixing bowls, one filled with water and the other filled with—Brass sniffed—was that bratwurst?

Intrigued, though still not invited, he followed Molly and the dog around to the alley, well aware of just how much he resembled the stray cat she always seemed to think of him as. Even though she was angry at him and despite the silence between them, just being near her again made his soul . . . happy. Sated. And damn if that wasn't the precise drug he needed after five days of hell.

Molly tucked the bowls behind the dumpster, and the happy hound got to work eating her little heart out, shaking her slim tail in a rhythm that matched her obvious joy.

When Molly went back inside, Brass braced for the harsh

metal clang the back door always made when it sealed shut. Instead, a dull thud echoed through the alley. Not metal. Wood.

A door stopper had been shoved between the door and the doorjamb.

He paused, staring at the intentionally placed block of wood. It was as much of an invitation as he'd be lucky to get, and they both knew it.

Urged by his fire and no small amount of desperation, he surged toward the door. With a quiet kick, he'd cleared the wood and shut himself inside.

CHAPTER 20

Birchwood and brown sugar were the first scents to assault him. Maple and molasses quickly followed suit, drawing him farther down the hall into the kitchen, where he was promptly and thoroughly overcome with a new type of ambrosia.

Massive stainless steel pots stood sentinel on the commercial range and were lit to life by sure flames that never faltered in their purpose. He'd take his job seriously too if he was in charge of whatever heaven was in there that could make his mouth water from fifty paces and keep pulling him in.

Just what kind of siren soup was this woman cooking?

Wafts of cider-scented steam curled above one pot, while the other bubbled away, enticing Brass closer to discover its secrets. He leaned over the lip of the brazier closest to him, inhaled with his celestial senses, and nearly dove in headfirst. Plump bratwurst simmered in a pool of malted cider broth, while its sibling vessel cradled tight little jewels of molasses baked beans studded through with glistening hunks of applewood smoked bacon.

He would have said he'd died and gone to heaven if he hadn't already seen the place.

Molly, not Benny, had made these, and mages above, she'd somehow managed to wrap up her entire essence into tiny morsels of ecstasy. Even without tasting, he knew what he'd find built in: joy, pleasure, skill, succulence.

This was her. *This* was what she'd fought so hard for every day of her life.

And he'd abandoned this? Her?

He was just about to reach for a spoon when another intriguing aroma had him turning around. On the counter in the middle of the kitchen sat a tray of amber crystals cozied around the tips of popsicle sticks. He lifted one to his nose and smiled.

Maple.

"It's hard maple taffy, but it's not perfect yet." Molly walked into the kitchen with the same steel in her spine that had lashed his tongue down the entire walk back.

"It sure looks perfect to me."

"Yeah, well, looks can be deceiving. The only thing perfect in this kitchen is the bourbon bread pudding that's still in the oven." She glared at him with the quiet feminine rage of an ancient goddess. "The jury's still out on everything else. Here." She thrust a white envelope at him.

"What's this?" he asked, taking it from her.

"Your wages for the time you worked here."

Brass's fingers halted at the envelope's flap, never even reaching the cash inside. Then he tossed the whole of it on the counter as understanding dawned on him. "You think I came back for the money? I don't need your money, Molly."

"I don't really care what you need. I'm paying you for the hours you worked, as we agreed upon. It's a simple transaction."

Simple transaction? The words tumbled through his mind like a paraglider meeting the sharp, craggy edge of a cliff.

Had that been all this was? Did she think he'd just been there for *money*?

A shrill cackle, feminine and fiery, sizzled his senses, riling his rage into a burgeoning tempest of torment. His lip curled on a snarl, and the array of silver kitchen equipment before him began to blur into a blanket of hazy metal. A low growl formed within his throat like some baser animal whose only known language was that of a mindless captive.

No. Not now . . .

Brass swallowed, doing his best to blink away the reactions. When he risked opening his eyes once more, soft elfin features leveled him with wide-eyed concern.

Concern but not fear.

In a moment of inexplicable clarity, Brass saw his reflection in the espresso depths of Molly's eyes.

And holy hell, was it just as pathetic as he felt. A true dressing-down of epic proportions.

Abandonment. Betrayal. Every unspoken hurt written in the tight lines of her face whipped him across his own, firmly cementing her shit stain opinion of him. With a single disappointed frown, she'd essentially piled him high on the heap of every other man who'd ever taken advantage of her and treated her like the thing she feared most: a transaction.

"Molly." The plea thundered past his lips on a pulse of power. Just breathing her name when she was near was enough for his internal fire to beat back the beast and lift his lungs with a hope he didn't deserve.

But he'd already been in this position before, hadn't he? Asking for her forgiveness as though it was some pantry staple commodity for him to seek out whenever he had wounds to lick and peanut butter to indulge in.

Damn.

"Yes? Do you finally have something to say?" She placed her hands on her hips.

He risked a glance at her eyes once more and welcomed the chastisement he saw there. Welcomed it and selfishly indulged in any length of time she chose to look at him. "You're not a transaction, Molly."

She started at his words, and he leaped at the opportunity to finally say what he needed to.

"Do you know how much courage it takes to even breathe the same air as you? How my favorite sound in the world is the first sigh on your lips after you've tasted coffee I've brewed for you? I can't feed you, not in the way you should be fed, because anything I can make wouldn't come close to what you can manage with a tenth of your skill. I can't support you with anything more than my strength and stamina, which fail me more each day."

He risked a step toward her, his breaths easing and lifting in time with hers. "I can't take your eyes with me where I go, because even that feels like a damn betrayal of your trust, like just another thing stolen from you. I can't be the one to indulge in your sweet scent, even though it's the only thing on the planet that has arrested my senses so completely, it's prevented me from agonizing over what's to come."

Molly didn't retreat from him, but neither did her subtle veneer of protection crack against his onslaught. The only hint that he was getting through at all was the small quiver in her bottom lip. That mouth drew all his attention, and he called on the strength of his memory of her lips on his to see him through.

"But I can't do it anymore, Molly." The admission was the first one he'd said out loud, and it stung not only his ears but his soul. "There are so many things that are not in the cards for me," he whispered, extending his hands, palms up, out to his sides. "Forgiveness is one. I won't risk you tarnishing your integrity by even asking it of you."

"Brass, you don't have to say—"

"You're damn right I don't have to say anything," he seethed. "Words are wasted breaths, and I've never been a fan of speaking for the sake of doing so. But in my foolishness, I've learned that *not* speaking has failed me just as much as running off at the mouth."

A confused wrinkle marred her smooth complexion, and it was all he could do not to reach for her and polish it away with a kiss.

Instead, he braved a different action. "Let me show you. Please."

Never, in all the eons he'd been alive, had he begged for anything. *He* was the one charmers begged for their lives when the muzzle of his gun was at their temples and his fire was licking a deadly path up their skin.

But with her, he would beg. He would roar and slay and sacrifice the skies and seas if she'd asked him to.

Brass didn't wait for a nod of approval. He wasn't likely to get it anyway. So he shucked off his trench coat, grabbed a bunch of hotel pans of varying sizes, and started arranging them into overlapping structures.

"The bread pudding can be served here, high on the top shelf. I'll build a plexiglass cage around the sides, but leave the top open. Customers won't be able to touch it, but it'll be easily accessible for you. Plus, that smell is money. I don't need to tell you how leading with carbs and sugar is a surefire way to get 'em in the door and hungry for more." Brass upturned one of the medium-sized pans, which was longer than it was wide, and sidled it up to the larger display. "Simmer extra sauce here, and don't even deal with those garbage canned heat gel fuel things. I've got something better and more easily adjustable so the sugar in the bourbon sauce doesn't burn. I'll build out a frame for ramekin holsters as well, all heated off one source. I don't want you fiddling with fire. Leave that to me." He quickly paused for a moment, then looked at her. "Unless you want to," he amended.

Molly stepped forward, eyeing the mess of steel pans that had begun to take shape into a building project any LEGO fanatic would be proud of. "What are you talking about? What is all this?"

"For your vendor booth at the Winter Whimsy Festival. Caterers live and die by product delivery. No point in making the best brats this side of Lake Champlain if your setup's not optimized for heat retention, aboveboard searing capabilities, and distribution efficiency. Leave the subpar stations for funnel cake and twelve-dollar caramel apples. You think restaurant groups and food industry professionals are going to want to invest in a chef asking top dollar for dried-out bread pudding and scorched beans, all because she couldn't get her heat right?"

Once he'd settled the pans in place, adjusting things here and there, he stepped back and swung his arms wide, offering his chest and every shriveled, damaged thing caged within it to her. "I'm all in. For you, for your dream, for whatever the next week and a half brings, I'm here." Then he walked around the counter with steps far surer than he felt, until only a few feet separated his breaths from hers. His soul immediately relaxed under her aura in a cloud of exuberant relief. He didn't want to examine that too closely, or why a different heat had begun to lift the hairs at the back of his neck.

"Please say something," he pleaded.

Molly stared at him for a time, her eyes giving nothing away. It was a habit he'd noticed when customers would come to her with initial complaints. She'd entertain them, hear their gripe, and then, as was so often required in the service industry, give them what they wanted regardless of everything, always with a smile on her face.

How he wished she would smile now. Even just one corner, a quirk, a tilt, fucking anything to hint at her true thoughts.

Instead, she volleyed that icy gaze back and forth between him and the countertop display he'd built. When she finally settled on his features once more, the expression she wore had changed from unreadable to unmistakable.

It was heat, not anger, that simmered between them, touching and licking at the small spaces on their bodies only greedy grasps remembered. He noticed it the instant it fell upon them both. Her perfect nipples tightened beneath her thin sweater, forming delectable beads his mouth watered with the memory of. That bottom lip of hers fell open, releasing a soft gasp that wrapped around his thickening cock.

Brass gritted his teeth against the pleasurable pain that held him immobile. He wouldn't touch her like this, not as the raging, rutting animal within surged to the—

A different flare of power lashed through his senses, one both foreign and familiar. He frantically searched his mind for any memories of what it could mean, what he was feeling.

Then he stilled as the answer punched through his core, emboldening his limbs with a celestial power he'd not known since he fell from the Empyrean.

My full angel fire. The thought was a hymn to his heart and something he'd never truly thought he'd feel again. His complete celestial fire coursed through him, unlimited and unrestricted by what he could charge into it from the earth each night.

I am as I was before—

As soon as the hesitant joy settled into his bones, a dark pall swept in on its heels.

I'm not commanding this. I have no control. It's Mol—

Molly silenced his racing mind with a mouth so sweet, not even his memories could do its flavor justice, and damn it all to hell, he fucking let her. Slim arms snaked around his neck moments before her intoxicating scent invaded his senses. With limbs far greedier than his worried mind could control, he moved with her, gathering her close to his chest and infusing his kisses with every word he never said. He could bathe in her brown sugar and bourbon flavor, score it into his skin and bake it onto his body, and it'd never be enough to last him the handful of days he had left with her.

"Molly," he groaned in supplication against her seeking lips. "I need to taste you."

She didn't reply, apparently taking a page out of his playbook. Instead, she simply dug her nails into the meat of his shoulders, widened her mouth against his, and breached his lips with a sweep of her seductive tongue.

Booming rattles sputtered through the wall moments before a sharp metallic clang pierced the kitchen. The baseboard heating pipes exploded at their feet, releasing a torrent of boiling water right at them.

CHAPTER 21

Molly could honestly say she'd never given thought to just how hot the water in her baseboards got until it started pummeling her ankles with unrelenting pressure. Despite the thick denim cuffing her legs, the water still managed to soak through with surprising speed, searing her skin with pain rivaling the hottest grease fire.

"Aah!" Molly made to jump back, but before she could get her legs out of the spray's range, both her feet were off the ground.

With inhuman swiftness, Brass maneuvered his body between her and the water and lifted her onto the counter. Trays of maple hard taffy cluttered to the ground, their golden gem-like passengers abandoning ship into the puddling water and melting on contact.

"Do you know where the heat shutoff is?" Brass roared as steam rose around them and water continued to pulse from sheared pipes.

"Uh, yeah. There's a utility room near the back door."

"Go! Turn the heat off now!"

"But your legs!" she cried, watching with panic as the steaming water crept higher against his khakis.

Her next words of protest were swallowed up by a growl so inhuman, she was sure it would reverberate in her dreams for nights on end. Brass had her off the counter and clutched her high against his chest, sloshing through steaming water that was now ankle-deep. He must have been in excruciating pain, but even as she clung to him, he showed no signs of discomfort or agony.

How the hell is that possible?

Instead, a different mask consumed his features. One of cold, calculating anger that vied for airtime with ferocious worry and concern.

Over her.

Once he reached the edge of the kitchen, he set her on her feet where the water had not yet spread to the hallway and pressed firmly against her shoulders. "Go!"

Molly ran to the one room in the building she only ever entered when she needed to show the service technicians where to go for scheduled maintenance. She shouldered through the gray door and scrambled on slippery soles for the HVAC cheat sheet she'd typed out when ownership of the building officially passed to her.

"Baseboards . . . Baseboards . . ." she breathed as she scanned her color-coded instructions with a shaky finger. "Ah, there!" Once she located the appropriate lever and the ancient pipes churned to a foundation-rattling halt, she flew down the hall back to the kitchen.

What she found stole the next breath from her lungs.

Wings. Two floor-to-ceiling wings burnished with dusty gold feathers curled inward into a metallic column thick enough to rival Grecian architecture, facing the wall gap in between the ranges where the pipe had burst. Though the water still hadn't been contained, its sprays were less forceful and pattered, rather than pelted, against the lower feathers that formed a watertight seal against the ceramic floor.

Impossible.

As if the damn things heard her, the wings shifted slightly outward, scraping the water away like a giant squeegee, revealing Brass on his knees with his hands around a baseboard pipe . . .

And his entire body was covered in the same gleaming metal as the wings cocooning him.

Holy. Freaking. Shit.

Brass hunched over a length of pipe that he'd yanked out from beneath the baseboard. With the heat off and no longer pumping hot water through the old building, the steady stream had slowed to a trickle, which allowed Brass to grasp each jagged edge more securely. Molly took a step closer and watched in terrified awe as blue flames engulfed both his arms before skating down his hands with an eerie controlled efficiency. He didn't scream or run or do any of that stop, drop, and roll stuff she'd been taught as a kid.

Instead, the fire raged on, consuming his arms and hands and, by extension, the pipes, as if the flames were merely following orders instead of incinerating everything in their path.

And Brass was most definitely *not* being incinerated. The copper pipes in his hands, however, glowed molten orange as the blue flames around them burned brighter. Even from where she stood by the door, she could feel the heat being given off by the fire. Was that even normal? What kind of small soldering fire could be felt from ten feet away?

The kind that arced painlessly in electric blue waves over a winged man made entirely of metal.

The stuff was so hot, it warmed her cheeks and she had to blink several times to keep her sweaty tears at bay. No freaking way was she risking one blind second of whatever she was witnessing.

As quickly as any metal worker, Brass brought the softened pipes together, and with a final roaring blaze upon where the metals had been joined, the fire extinguished as fast as it had ignited. Molly waited for the black smoke to waft up from the welding job and trigger the fire alarms, but none ever did. It was as if the flames existed in heat only, with no carbon footprint.

How the hell was any of that possible?

It wasn't. None of this was real. It was all some cosmic joke the universe got its jollies from. She racked her brain to think of the last thing she ate. Had she eaten any fish from the walk-in? Was this a symptom of that histamine poisoning thing Mrs. McCall nearly had her shut down over?

No, no, no . . . This isn't happening.

She felt around for the nearest chunk of wall that wasn't taken up by sheet pan racks and promptly slid down it until her butt hit the damp floor.

Those massive wings curled back behind Brass's shoulders, and he stood to a height that not only looked menacing but miraculous. Every single bit of skin and sinew glowed with a pristine metallic opulence that only bronze sculptors could hope to capture. But the features were there all the same, and she panically sought out every familiar frown line and furrow until her mind was absolutely fucking sure it was the same man in front of her she'd left there a moment ago.

Except with wings . . .

And the same glowing ochre eyes she hadn't been able to get out of her head for the past five days.

HOURS LATER, Molly sat at one of the tables in the restaurant's dining room and accepted her second can of nitro cold brew from Drea courtesy of Chrome's private stash.

As it turned out, Chrome wasn't just Drea's boyfriend but her *mate*. Oh, and he and his brothers were angels, as in wing-wielding flyover feather boys, except with metallic powers and fire and stuff.

Angels. Brass was a freaking *angel*?

"I know it's a lot to process," Drea lamented, pulling out the chair next to Molly and sliding over a napkin-turned-coaster.

"No, itemized deductions on your tax return are a lot to process. Municipal permit applications are a lot to process. This"—Molly swung an arm around the room, encompassing the four angels gathered there— "is fiction. None of this is real. My brain just hasn't figured out a way to explain it all yet. But trust me, there'll be a way. There's *always* an explanation."

Drea smiled softly and didn't bother to keep the pity out of her amethyst eyes. "Is there? Or are you just still angry at me?"

Oh, Molly was angry all right, if anyone would call it anger when her best friend, who was also not entirely mortal, didn't fess up to dating—sorry, *mating*—a fallen angel, then, yeah, she was still angry.

In the corner of the dining room, Bronze and Chrome were huddled together with another man, one with golden hair just past his chin, who'd been introduced to her as Tungsten. Though just as deep-chested and imposing as Chrome, he had an air about him that suggested his strength came from sources other than physical demands. The lines crinkling the corners of his eyes told her he laughed easily and often, but his attentive expressions were ones she'd only seen on men who valued insight and advice over barking orders.

True to form, Brass wasn't among them. Instead, he stayed hunkered down in the kitchen, giving some excuse about inspecting the rest of the plumbing.

Guess the best way to avoid the elephant in the room is for the elephant to avoid the room altogether.

Tungsten, whom everyone called Tung, finished his quiet conversation with the others and grabbed the vacant seat opposite Molly. His smile was a kind condolence, obviously meant to smooth over the hard parts of a very jarring realization. It stung more than soothed, however, because all she wanted was to see that same smile on someone else's face.

Someone who, once a-fucking-gain, was avoiding her like he hadn't just saved her from partial-thickness burns and prevented her restaurant from a months-long HVAC-and-water-related shutdown.

"I'm sure you must have many questions about what you've learned," Tung offered by way of an icebreaker.

She was silent for a moment, fiddling with her coffee can and scanning the nutrition information for the fifth time. When her thoughts became too oppressive to bear, she mumbled, "It really is all true, isn't it?"

Two sets of sad eyes confirmed the answer to her first question, and all she could do was shake her head in disbelief.

Angels were real. Brass and his brothers were honest-to-God fallen angels, had all hailed from somewhere called the Empyrean, and were trapped in the mortal realm, fighting legit demons—no, charmers, they were called—and searching for sparks of an Eternal Flame that could get them all back home.

Drea, her best friend on the planet, was mated. Soul bound to a fallen angel. She wasn't even human.

Just like Brass wasn't even human. Not only was he not human but he was immortal.

It was more than a lot to wrap her head around, especially after the day she'd had.

Tung was right. Molly had a litany of questions piling up, but after a kitchen full of water droplets she had no hope of finding before they inevitably turned into doors-closing mold and her second can of Chrome's consumable rocket fuel, there was only so much of her energy left for interrogations. So, she offered up the one question she could still bring herself to ask, the one that had never stopped plaguing her.

"Why?"

Tung sat back. "Why, what?"

"Why did this happen?"

Drea leaned forward and gripped Molly's hand. "Oh, honey, Brass and the others are trying to figure that out right now. Though, there is a working theory that it might not have been—"

"No, I mean, why did this happen to *me?*"

Drea looked to Tung briefly, but Molly didn't have the energy to try and read what passed between them, so she let every pent-up worry tumble out of her and land where they may. The floors were already a mess anyway. No harm adding to it at that point.

"Every time I try to seize an opportunity, or a little bit of good decides to come my way, some monster-truck-sized slice of shit comes to steamroll me as if the luck granted to me was a mistake to begin with. My best friend is some sort of celestial messenger, I've had fallen freaking angels cleaning up spilled juice and schlepping garbage out to the dumpster, my customers are being poisoned, some dice-throwing retirees are gunning for me to close up shop because they don't like my tacos, and now my building's pipes decide to—"

"Your customers are being poisoned?" Chrome barked.

Bronze lifted the unopened can of coffee out of Chrome's hand, did the honors, and gulped back a swig before Drea's mate could close his fist around the can's vacated space. "Sorry, you're too slow, bro," he said before returning it to his brother.

Chrome swiped the can close to him and muttered, "Asshole." Then he knocked back the rest of the thing with three long swallows.

Molly nodded. "I've had two customers complain of food poisoning within the past week. One even came in with a patient lab report showing high levels of something or other. Some chemical found only in spoiled fish. She insists it was from something she ate here, as if I had any way to prove it," she said with resigned frustration.

"That's common though, isn't it? Food poisoning? It could come from anywhere, really," Drea provided with hope in her voice.

"Not really, no, at least it's not common among small operations like mine. I source the hell out of my food, and Benny runs that kitchen tighter than a military operation. He's always the first to notice when equipment needs servicing long before there's ever a problem. Also, thanks to my little taco terror, the health inspector came to pay me a visit. He didn't find anything and reissued my sanitation certificate, but that doesn't mean something else hasn't happened already. All it takes is one more public complaint, and I don't think it's something my reputation can easily come back from. People talk. The Internet can be a brutal place." Molly spilled her proverbial big-fear beans all over the floor and waited for the problem-solving suggestions to attempt to vacuum them up.

As she suspected, none came. Apparently, three strikes and you're out was a universal phenomenon among humans and angels alike. She may not have figured out how to wear *lucky* very well, but *despair* she had down pat, especially when it was all wrapped up in a feather boa of *pathetic*.

Molly ached to turn around, to see whether Brass was still deep in his Mr. Fix It due diligence or whether he'd quietly entered the dining room to see her. It was killing her, not being able to sort through this mess with the one person who she'd literally gone through it with.

As much as she still loved her best friend, and as kind and wonderful as these people were, she didn't want to hear any of this from them. She didn't want to hear how the man who'd begged her for everything except forgiveness, because he knew it was the one thing he needed to win back rather than plead for, hadn't even looked at her since the explosion. Yes, he'd arranged for his family and Drea to come and be there for her immediately. Yes, he'd left her so he could work tirelessly shoring up the one thing that mattered to her, the restaurant.

But it didn't change the fact that she didn't want to hear that he was an angel from anyone else but him. A part of her felt that, even though his true nature wasn't a secret any longer, it was still his story to tell, if he truly wanted to tell it to her.

Obviously, he didn't.

Why won't you tell me? Why won't you just talk to me?

"Molly." The floorboards creaked behind her, and she turned to find Brass, soaked and solemn, drying his hands on a dish rag. The look on his face was so heated it could have burst the remaining pipes in a five-mile radius.

Molly shot to her feet. "What is it?"

"Has anyone else been in the kitchen?"

She shook her head. "No, just you and Benny."

Then he nodded and turned to his brothers. "Thank you for coming out. I'll update you guys later."

Reading the message behind Brass's words, everyone emptied out of the restaurant, leaving behind soft sentiments of encouragement and reassuring condolences. When the two of them were alone again, Molly's heart resumed the same unsteady rhythm from when she'd last spoken with Brass.

When she'd last kissed him.

He stepped forward then, with her coat in his hands. He opened it wide and held it out to her to put on. "I'd like to show you something."

"What is it?" she asked, already sliding her arms into the sleeves. Somewhere, she was sure there was a set of rules she was breaking about being too eager or showing your hand, but when Brass clutched her to his side and escorted her out the front door before locking up behind them, she didn't care.

She'd waited all night for any sort of contact or connection. Like hell she was about to ruin it based on someone else's ceremony.

His hand never left her hip as he tucked her close and led them toward her car. "Answers."

CHAPTER 22

Molly held Brass's hand as he led her down a set of carved granite steps polished to a shine so high they rivaled the glinting flecks of mica studded throughout the stone walls. Normally, her underground experiences were limited to basements, the occasional cellar, and that one school field trip in fourth grade where they visited a cavern carved out by a prehistoric river.

The hallways she passed through now had none of the stalactites or weeping walls she expected to see. Oh, who the hell was she kidding? Like she had any real expectation of what an underground angel den buried deep beneath the White Mountains could possibly encompass, especially after the revelations that had been dropped on her thus far that day.

Fat fucking chance.

Even as Brass led her through his home, casually remarking on the rooms they passed with the alacrity of a distracted museum docent, she didn't have the bandwidth to process what he actually showed her.

There'd be time for that. There were only so many wonders the human mind was capable of absorbing in such a short period. Especially when the biggest wonder of all had reverted to his customary silence while he led her down a flight of stone stairs and into—

"Oh my goodness."

The lights flicked on around a room that she could only describe as, not a library, but a book sanctuary. Where Molly expected to run her fingers across worn wooden bookshelves that perhaps sagged under the weight of hefty leather-bound tomes, she was met with more granite instead. All along the walls, slabs of stone had been hollowed out at deliberate intervals, creating formidable ledges far sturdier than any bookshelf a master furniture maker could hope to construct. Every wall-to-wall indentation in rock was home to rows upon rows of carefully cradled books. Glass windows with handles shielded the stacks from any elements and allowed for easy perusal and selection.

The space wasn't particularly large, and it didn't have that cavernous flair of old-world libraries, but what it lacked in size, it made up for with a presence of permanence. Every shelf was lined with a luxurious fabric Molly suspected was free of acid and safeguarded against mold. Whatever books they stored here hadn't earned their spots due to being on any bestseller list.

These were the Nelson Mandelas of books, ones that had given so much in their heyday that they were rewarded with an eternal spot in biblio-heaven.

Molly stepped in farther and ran her fingers along the nearest glass shield, marveling at how some spines were constructed in a familiar modern-day fashion, while others seemed pieced together by one who needed like pages to be with their friends. Others, still, featured names of authors, where some books only had symbols or carvings on the spine.

All of it stole her breath.

"This is truly unbelievable," she whispered but jumped back quickly when she'd gotten too close and her exhale produced a foggy patch on the glass in front of a tome that seemed older than the mountains surrounding them. "Shit! Sorry."

"No need to be sorry. You can't hurt 'em." Brass closed the door behind them and adjusted some dials in a side panel before explaining, "This room is regulated to within an inch of its life. Everything here is controlled meticulously, from humidity levels to temperature to light and even dust." He gestured toward the stone shelf in front of her. "We carved these way before mortals began using wood for bookshelves. Wood contains natural oils, acids, and lignin, which can erode texts quickly. Stone does a much better job of keeping the crud out. The lining is an acid-free polyester, and all the lighting down here is free of UV rays."

"I know you're stalling, but I'm not mad about it," she breathed out, scanning the rows of books.

His lighthearted chuckle brushed against her skin, even from across the room. "Having a Beauty and the Beast moment?"

"Yes, and you're ruining it, so stop." The gentle humor petered off as quickly as it had come on, and then Molly remembered why he'd brought her there in the first place. "You promised me answers."

Brass's face fell, and for a moment, she regretted bringing up his original intention.

"I like the taste of teasing you," he lamented, though his voice was tinged with a dark note of wistfulness that troubled her for reasons she couldn't say. "I'm going to miss it."

"Why are you going to mi—"

"Have a seat." He nodded toward the array of couches that formed a tight rectangle around the sunken floor occupying the center of the room. In the middle was an oval glass coffee table just close enough to each couch to be handy rather than a hindrance. If the rest of Brass's brothers were anything to go by, banged knees was likely a real concern.

Molly relaxed into the nearest couch, instantly appreciating its mocha buttery soft leather and, despite the obvious age of the room, the angels' clear preference for furniture that was both masculine and comfortable. There was something to be said for those who cared not a whit for room aesthetics.

Brass took the couch end opposite her and rested his elbows on his knees, hands fisted in front of him. His attention seemed to hover just above where the coffee table sat, and he stayed silent for some time. If uncertainty was a language, it'd be scripted in the coiled strain of his scapulas and the tension mounding his trapezius muscles higher against his ears.

Should she say something? Remind him that he'd brought *her* here? Was he having second thoughts about sharing whatever occupied his mind to the point of so much distraction?

What in the hell is he not telling me?

Just as she mustered up the courage to squeak out a few words of *Hey, remember me?*, his resonant voice filled the silence.

"The pipe didn't burst by accident."

Molly sobered. "What? How is that possible? No one else was there. Was it sawed or weakened somehow?"

"No, not sawed, but it *was* weakened. From what I can tell, the building's plumbing system probably dates back to the fifties, when everyone and their mother used copper to outfit the piping in their heating systems. I found evidence of stress fractures in the copper pipes running through your baseboards. The fracture patterns on the metal were consistent with what would happen if water froze inside a pipe, then melted as it was heated up again. That type of repeated behavior puts undue strain on the metal and can cause it to rupture, which is what happened."

"That doesn't make any sense, though. I mean, I know our town hasn't invested in natural gas lines yet for the business district and all the shops are still on oil heat, but I just had an oil delivery two weeks ago. I shouldn't have run out already, and I never keep the restaurant colder than sixty degrees when I'm not there. Pipes don't freeze at that temperature."

"They do when the temperature of the water in them is below freezing."

Molly shook her head. "I'm not following."

Brass leaned his forehead against his fists and took several deep breaths that rattled his strong frame. When he looked at her, a light sheen of sweat dappled his temples, and an air of vulnerability she hadn't seen from him before morphed his stern gaze into one of wariness.

She sat up slowly and leaned closer to him. "Tell me."

"You saw me in my metallic form. My brass form."

Well, I guess we're just going to get right down to business, then.

"I did," she answered.

"When the pipe burst, the water was a few degrees shy of boiling temperature, five at the most."

"Okay . . ."

"Industry standards dictate that baseboard heating water usually runs around one hundred and eighty degrees."

"And water boils at two hundred and twelve degrees Fahrenheit," she supplied most unhelpfully.

He nodded, encouraged that she'd caught one of his unraveled threads, and continued. "I switched to my brass armor to protect myself from being burned, and also because my metallic power can manipulate and sense when my metal's components are present . . . and when they've been tampered with."

That got her attention. "Tampered? You can tell that just by changing your body into—"

"Brass. Yes. It was a power that came to me once I landed in the mortal realm, and thank the mages it did because I'd happily endure a geyser full of boiling water if it meant its attentions were trained away from you."

Her heart stammered at the simmering aggression and the implications of his words. Their eyes locked, and ochre flames overtook the gentle amber that was so bright and eager in her memory from when they last held her as he helped shape her future with a mountain of hotel pans and hard maple taffy.

A strange calmness soothed her senses, and she could finally see the accompanying signs of what his fire, as she understood it, cost him. Strained muscles, tense jaw, eyes dipped down at the corners. Even his lips curled back slightly, as if he was fighting off something.

Molly put her hand on his thigh. "Brass—"

"Baah!" He heaved himself off the couch and stalked toward a row of books not far from where Molly had begun her earlier perusal. She felt the loss keenly but said nothing. Regardless of what her emotions were lighting up with, she wouldn't do him the dishonor of calling him out on his emotional dysregulation, not when he was clearly troubled by something she couldn't yet understand.

Once Brass had found his selection, he lifted the glass case— the seal around its perimeter releasing with a soft sigh— removed the book, and offered it to her by way of the strangest explanation she'd ever received to dismiss one's angered outburst.

He kept his back turned to her. "Forty pages from the last. Read it."

"Um, all right." The book in Molly's hands wouldn't have been a book by today's standards. Loose leaf sheets of similar-sized parchment were bound between two wooden covers. Symbols she didn't recognize were scrawled on the front. When she opened it, to precisely no one's surprise, there were no page numbers, so she did as instructed and counted forty pages backward from the last one. What she found were letters in a language that wasn't the least bit rooted in Latin and, therefore, one she had no hope of reading.

What she *could* read, however, was the translated notes on a loose white piece of modern-day notepaper that had been stuffed between the ancient pages. Molly barely had time to comprehend what she was reading before Brass turned back around, a new mix of composure and compromise armoring his stance.

"That book dates back to first-century Latvia and holds the recorded accounts of a tribe of Baltic pagan elders," Brass explained.

Molly carefully set the book down on the coffee table. "Yeah, I'm pretty sure I shouldn't be touching this."

"Of all the gods and goddesses those ancient people prayed to," he continued, ignoring her attempt at levity, "Ragana was the most mercurial."

"Ragana . . ." Molly leaned forward to consult the translated notes. "Goddess of witches and death. She sounds peachy."

Brass nodded and, having seemingly recovered himself, resumed his seat next to Molly on the couch. "She's a shapeshifting goddess who is queen to all of her kind, lesser goddesses and such. When it comes to mortals, she's the great equalizer and balancer of excess among the seasons and during the harvest months. In her realm, life cannot exist without death. The Baltic people would pray to her, leaving her sacrifices and the shearing of their first crops of the season to ensure healthy harvests and prosperity for their tribes."

Molly didn't know where Brass was going with the story or what it had to do with a blown pipe in her restaurant, so she remained silent while he continued.

"She is named for the moon, and like the moon, her moods and powers come in phases." His words took on a darker tone. "A tribe can only experience prosperity for so long. According to Ragana's principles, in order to appreciate how fortunate a group of people truly are, they need to endure periods of drought and pain. That was her edict, and the reason for all the sacrifices. They weren't just any sacrifices, however, but the best and, in many cases, rarest. The first eggs of spring, the cow's first milk after its calf was born." Then his voice softened abruptly, and Molly had to strain to hear him. "Blood from a girl's first cycle into womanhood. A virgin's evidence when she no longer was one. The sick and twisted list goes on and on."

"Oh my God," Molly rasped.

"It was a power move, like any god or goddess of legend. For Ragana, she required the people to give her their best so they always knew she could take it all away at any moment. That the balance of their lives existed only because she allowed it to."

"That's . . . intense and, as a modern woman, if I'm allowed to be a little judgy on the subject, really awful." They were pitiful words for a pitiful ancient belief system, but she couldn't think of anything more forceful to say that would change anything. Most of humanity's less-than-stellar moments were recorded by the era's winners who never knew better and never cared to learn.

"Yes," he agreed solemnly. "And it seems she is not quite finished with her balancing act."

Molly's thoughts ground to a halt. Her head snapped up from the open book in front of her. "What?"

The stiffness in Brass's jaw had returned. Golden flames danced in the depths of his gaze and melted any amber that had been there a moment ago. "The water in your baseboard pipes was frozen repeatedly but not at a time when you would have noticed, and it was done so in a way that was otherwise unde-tectable. With speed, efficiency, and perfect fucking timing."

"You're not suggesting that—"

"In the evenings, while you were away from the building, the water in the pipes froze quickly and remained frozen during the night. Then, what I suspect would be an hour or two before you opened up the place in the morning, the ice thawed just as quickly, and the heating system returned to normal before you noticed. Two nights of this would have been all she needed to cause the explosion."

"When you say *she*, you mean . . ."

"Ragana. She's the one spoiling your fish and poisoning your customers. She's the one who can freeze water with a thought and destroy the earth's and ocean's bounty with a breath."

Any other evening, Molly would have tipped her hat to the crazy man spinning tall tales and run screaming in the other direction. Any other evening, she would have thought angels were nothing more than Christmas tree toppers and her restaurant had been experiencing a sky-high amount of totally unrelated tummy-troubled customers.

Except she and Benny had inspected her walk-in fridges half a dozen times in the past few days and found nothing. The health inspector had found nothing.

And Brass . . . he was definitely *not* nothing. As frazzled as her mind was, there was no explaining away his wings or his armor. For as long as she lived, she didn't think she could ever erase the image of him kneeling in her restaurant's kitchen, a golden-yellow god armored head to toe, with metal wings both fabled and ferocious. He had been terrifying on the inhale and glorious on the exhale, and with his silent stoicism and flaming gaze that touched every part of her, he'd heartily stolen all her breaths since.

He was real, all right. Her heart knew it, and most convincingly of all, her damn body knew it, too. Was it so hard to believe, then, that an ancient goddess could exist as well?

"Why?" Molly asked. "Why is she targeting me?"

An animalistic answering noise rent from deep in Brass's chest. "Because you are important to me, and she fucking knows it. Because she wants me to know she can take you away from me at any time."

Then the fire in his eyes snuffed out, revealing those whiskey amber pools again that screamed out a wild and raging sadness.

"Because I'm not ill, Molly. I'm cursed—cursed by *her*. And come the winter solstice, I'll cease to be who I am, *what* I am."

He hissed in a deep breath and grabbed both her hands in his. "You're the key to breaking my curse. I've known it since I felt you through your apartment window that first time we were patrolling the grounds and I had the good sense to look up. I've known it since I relieved you from carrying a Dutch oven when we helped Drea move and you rewarded me by running away." His words came faster now, more frantic. "I've known it since I ripped that *Help Wanted* sign from your window and kissed you not nearly fucking enough." He squeezed her hands tighter, pressing a foreboding sense of urgency into them.

"And now, she knows it, too."

CHAPTER 23

It had been so long since Brass had spoken that bitch's name, he was surprised his mouth could still form the word without spitting. He'd thought it would have brought him some small measure of relief to at least share that truth with Molly. Instead, he wished he could take it all back, that Molly's alluring and attentive gaze hadn't dimmed to the degree it had when he'd dumped the first of many sinful confessions at her feet.

Of course she would have questions. Her brilliant mind was a treasure the mortal world had no hope of learning how to appreciate. With all that inquisitiveness trained on him, however, a familiar sickening emotion returned to the pit of his stomach.

Fear.

And this time, none of his usual coping mechanisms were available. His brothers usually frowned upon weapons training or hand-to-hand fighting anywhere other than the armory or the sparring ring. Tung would kill him ten times over if any of the books saw a speck of dust, let alone damage.

Which meant he had no choice but to face Molly's inevitable

line of questioning . . . and endure her wrath when he couldn't answer her.

"You're cursed?" she asked. "How?"

And so it begins.

"Do you recall when I told you about my ailment?"

Her eyes flitted through her memories before alighting on the one in question. "You called it a brain condition. A limiting ailment that, when it flares up, affects you physically and also your personality. You said it makes you . . . feral. When I asked whether it was fatal, you fed me some arrogant bullshit about everything being fatal eventually."

"That's all true." He lifted his gaze, then, and his lips curled into a small smile. "Including the bit about my arrogance."

That line of cheekiness earned him a snort and an eye roll.

"As for whether it will kill me . . ." Brass shrugged and rubbed a thumb across her knuckles, loving the way her skin was always just as warm as his. Another thing he'd miss.

"I won't know who I am any longer," he continued. "There is a fury inside of all of us, a necessary rage for any sentinel to dispatch who we must. It's tempered by our celestial power. Rage and right have always been in balance. It was how the prime mages created us. But my rage has been trapped within my soul for almost two thousand years. When the winter solstice arrives, my full fury will finally be unleashed, over-coming my celestial power and trapping it within the vacated cage that once held its oppressor. Without that balance, I'll go mad. It's . . . it's a blind madness. I won't recognize myself, my brothers, you, anyone. There would no longer be any humanity left in me. I'd become a mindless animal hell-bent on little more than destroying any living thing that crosses my path."

Molly shook her head in disbelief. "That's not possible. How is any of that possible?" Then her shoulders stiffened, as if settling on a solution. "No, that's not happening. I've had to come to terms with a lot of strange stuff over the last several hours, but *that* I refuse to allow."

The indignation in her voice on his behalf would have been heartwarming if it wasn't so heartbreaking. She spoke her declaration with enough assurance to chase away any lingering doubt, as if she were some wayward traveler who knew all she had to do to correct her course was ask for directions and that would solve everything. It was the tone of a woman dominating a male-dominated profession who regularly dealt with entirely too much bullshit before breakfast and was no longer interested in hearing any of the lunchtime specials.

Brass shifted his weight and smiled sadly. Her gumption was one of the most captivating—and arousing—things about her. Damn, he was going to miss that, too.

"How did this happen?" she asked again with a quieter desperation.

Brass sank back into the couch and let the weight of the cushions support more than their fair share of his burden. "Around the turn of the last century, I was in the Baltics hunting an apex charmer who had just raided a nearby village for souls."

"Apex?"

The little furrow that had formed between her brows melded with the shadows cast by the dim lighting, creating golden accents across her cheeks and nose. Lucky bastard that he was, he wanted to grin for all the beauty locked away in this room with him. For every sparkling smile she gifted him, a thousand had lived in his memories. He'd called upon every one of them over the past few days, when he'd slashed his fury at the stones and screamed his release into a sky he'd soon no longer recognize.

"Charmers are demons born of the shadow realm. They can make themselves appear like mortals and act accordingly. They're animals like any other beast, really. They can eat, sleep, have sex, and otherwise assimilate seamlessly into the human race once the sun goes down. There are three classes: mystic, elite, and apex."

"Let me guess," she cut in. "Apex are the really bad guys?"

He cast her a sidelong look. "The really, *really* bad guys. It's what you get when you pool all the dark magic practices of a mystic with all the brutal combat training of an elite. They excel at everything, are incredibly hard to kill, and are particularly adept at snuffing out mortal souls. Cyro, the demon ruler, truly broke the mold when he made those assholes."

The shiver that reverberated through Molly's hand made him wonder just how much truth he should share regarding the origins of his curse. When she sidled closer to him on the couch and the warmth of her thigh began seeping into his, he made his decision.

Like it was ever yours to make?

He'd share it all.

Around him, the shelves of books faded to the barren, snowy birch forests of his memory. "An unusual number of people from a local tribe had been dying unexpectedly. Children, women, elders, you name it. It didn't take long to figure out the deaths weren't natural and who was causing them." Brass leaned into the warmth of Molly's presence, using it as an anchor against a storm he was loath to relive.

"I found the apex responsible and tracked him to a farmer's cottage at the edge of the forest, not far from where the cliffs abraded the sea coast. At first, I thought the poor structure was abandoned. It was the first day of winter, and the small hovel hadn't had much to speak of in terms of fortifications. No smoke from a heat source, no livestock, no barrels of grain, nothing to suggest it was inhabited by a mortal. So, I attacked."

"Was he there? The apex?"

Brass's fire simmered beneath his skin. "Yes. When I ambushed him, I swarmed in on a tide of fury and rage, intending to end it quickly. I scorched everything in that cottage with my angel fire, including the demon. Unfortunately, he had not been alone. Ragana was there and, as she is a being of the elements, was quite immune to my flames."

Haunted images rose from the depths of his mind, choking off his resolve. Then he forced his power into his words, willing them to recount what his entire being balked against. "In my haze of power, my flames swept through the cottage and left nothing behind. I hadn't truly comprehended all I was destroying at the time. As a result, I had . . . taken something of hers. Stolen something precious and impossible to return." He shook his head against dark memories. "Once she'd realized what I'd done, her wail was terrifying and anguished beyond imagination. Even as a sentinel, it froze me where I stood, and that was when I knew . . ."

A soft breath hitched in Molly's throat as she saw the road down which his tale would soon take them.

"Her judgment was handled swiftly after that. She cursed me, trapping the very wrath that allowed me to burn down the cottage inside me for two thousand winters as retribution. If she had to endure the agony of what she'd lost, then so would I."

"The winter solstice," Molly confirmed. "So, that's when it all . . ."

"Yes."

"And those flare-ups? All those times I've seen your eyes change?"

He swallowed hard. "I'm losing control. Every day closer to my final one brings with it a thinner tether with which to secure my sanity, along with my rage. It's like trying to lash down a bucking bull with a piece of dental floss. There *is* no stopping it, no slowing the freight train I'm tied to the tracks in front of. Except, then you come along, and every time you spear me with those chocolate eyes of yours, that rage is strapped right back down and held tighter than before. I can fucking breathe again and have a few hours where every thought isn't weighted down with who I need to protect from myself in that moment."

"Not me," she whispered as she took his face in his hands. "You don't have to protect me from you. All you need to do is be honest and tell me what you need. If I can help, I will."

He stalled and stilled his touch against her.

"If you can help . . ." he enunciated slowly, turning the words over on his tongue.

Had she really just said that? And more to the point, was he that much of a bastard that he'd allow himself to even entertain the idea? Because he was more than happy to provide her with a list that started and ended with her. There was such little time left, and she was just so . . . so . . .

And then her hands were on his chest, pushing him back against the cushions. Caught off guard, he went down faster than a felled tree and burned where the imprint of her palms remained above his heart.

"Molly," he warned. "You don't know what you're asking—"

"I'm not asking. I'm done asking. I want this, and if I can ease your suffering, even for one night, I want to."

"I don't need your fucking pity," he ground out. "I won't have it, not from my brothers, and mages dammit, *never* from you, do you hear me?"

"Good," she challenged him. "Because I'm not giving it to you." She lifted a sleek eyebrow in response. "Besides, did you ever stop to think about what this day has been like for me? You're not the only one with a temper, and you're sure as hell not the only one who's been holding it together with nothing more than a force of will that's been running on empty for the past few months." Then she shifted her legs around so they straddled his calves. A safe distance away but still way too intentional with their suggestion. "I want this, for both of us. Do you?"

Danger lurked in her offer. She'd asked for honesty, and he thought he'd given as much as he could in that regard.

How fucking wrong he was.

There was so much magic in her touch, her taste, her tempting smiles, and her sonorous laughs. All she had to do was bark an order at him and his fury, his nightmares, would become distant memories.

She was worth so much more than the dregs of his humanity that had managed to leak through the sieve of his torment. Knowing all that, could he accept what she was offering?

Would it make a difference to his damned soul?

Brass reached for her legs and swiftly drew her up his body until she was situated on top of his growing arousal. Primal possession had his fingers curling around her thighs, and the answering light in her eyes instantly read his response.

"I've been fighting for myself for so long. Do you have any idea what it feels like to have someone else, someone like you, to fight for?" he asked.

A velvet warmth blossomed beneath her flushed skin. "Show me," she whispered.

The insistent command on her lips had the weight of a general's order. Molly wasn't searching for a way to win the war, only the battle ahead. And the next. And the next. Her single-minded grit was a tactic he'd not considered, and yet everything else in his world no longer bore any consideration.

Except her words. Her mouth. Her fucking scent and magic and magnanimous spirit. He'd claim it all, live as an avenging servant to her muse, and take her spirit into the next world with him.

But for now, he'd claim her, and damn it all, it would have to be enough.

With a speed to rival the stormiest wind, he scooped her beneath him and answered her order with a soul-searing kiss.

CHAPTER 24

Though it wasn't always easy to tell based on recent events, Molly loved many things about being a boss, and being her own boss in particular. Using that Boss Lady confidence, the only kind she had nowadays, to assure Brass that she wanted this, wanted *him*, had been her most powerful move yet.

Until he'd pulled her under him so quickly, her lungs had missed a breath or two. And that was a major problem because her brain desperately needed the oxygen to comprehend everything he'd just revealed. An angel, a demon, a goddess scorned.

A curse. A deadline.

And then there she was, some sort of savior. Well, she wasn't sure whether that had any truth to it, but his lips on hers definitely went a long way to silence her doubts.

Hell, she needed this. Not only the weight of Brass on her, both cradling her body and crumbling away any final defenses, but to indulge in a delicious distraction where no harm could come to either of them.

Here, they were safe, protected. She within his arms and him within her pounding heart, which threatened to punch through her chest and fling itself at the one person it never managed to effectively ignore.

Based on the limited sample size of men Molly had been with, she was confident enough to assert that none of them held a candle to the strength that surrounded her.

Brass kissed like she suspected he killed. Efficiently, swiftly, thoroughly, brutally. His punishing lips gave her no time to retreat or seek salvation elsewhere. And why the hell would she want to? The skill of his mouth and the appreciative growl that rumbled in his throat made it damn clear he found everything he needed in what she had to offer. The mountain around them could crumble, and she'd have a hard time tearing her mouth away from the passion he commanded.

Their kissing had become a private language between them. Each swipe of his tongue spoke of desperation, while her nibbles along his bottom lip sang a pleasure she couldn't comprehend.

Molly brought her knee up higher, wrapping it around his powerful hip. Brass leaned impossibly closer, grunting against her mouth and crowding out any remaining doubts with his all-encompassing hardness. The man—*angel*—had strength for days, and instead of using it to fight whatever was coming for him, he was at her mercy and used that delicious strength for *her*.

"You keep making moves like that and this will be over before it starts," he murmured against the curve of her jaw.

"No it won't," she assured him in some sex-kitten voice that had never in the history of ever left her mouth before.

What the hell was this man doing to her?

His answering chuckle vibrated against her skin, causing her nipples to pucker beneath her shirt. "Always so bossy."

"You like it."

"Mmm."

Brass extended his arms, holding his massive torso above

her, and locked his appreciative gaze onto her hardened nipples. A spark in his eyes hinted at a memory that sent a pool of warm arousal flooding between her thighs.

She knew that look and knew the exact memory he was recalling. Molly tensed beneath him, and with a boldness that surely must have been on borrowed time, she arched her back and offered her breasts to him. A dangerous smile curled his full lips into something sinful.

"Do they hurt?"

"Yes," she begged.

"Are they tight, wanting?"

Brass curled his hips forward, rocking against her and pressing the full length of his cock against her aching core. Her breath hitched as he did it again, slower, making damn sure she felt every single inch of him through their layers of clothing.

"They're all those things. Please, I want your mouth on me."

Then he pinned her with that fiery stare, seducing her body with his intense regard. Though there was something different in it this time. There was heat, yes, always that, but a different kind of alarm also drifted through the silvery fire of his irises.

When he spoke, she curled closer to him, somehow knowing that his next words would carry a weight to them that neither of them could bear on their own. "I will always give you what you want, Molly mine, for as long as there is breath left in my chest to give it."

She didn't have time to analyze the depth of his promise before he tore away every stitch of clothing she wore. An unwelcome urgency charged into the room on the heels of Brass's conviction.

Time. They didn't have any *time*.

The realization punched a crater of despair into her soul as it dawned on her what he was doing. What both of them were doing.

Were they saying goodbye? Was that what this was?

Molly gripped his shoulders and struggled to keep the emotion out of her voice. "Brass."

Then he cradled the side of her head in his strong hand and swiped away at that tension tightening her jaw. "Not here. Not now," he demanded.

And just like that, the man of few words silenced her with even fewer explanations. Passion pushed out any further worries. Instead, Molly let the urgency fuel her into taking what she wanted, what she *needed*.

While she still could.

Brass's clothes fell away under Molly's insistent touch. With no barriers and no more words left, Brass brought his mouth to her quivering stomach and licked a trail of scorching kisses up her body. Thought didn't just leave her but leaped off the fire escape of her mind in a gleeful exodus. There was danger in being devoured so thoroughly and consummately, she was sure of it, but hell if she could bring herself to care when those wicked lips of his captured her nipple. Each small hurt he bestowed with teeth and tongue was instantly smoothed away with a supple mouth that shot arousing thrills to every awakened nerve ending.

Molly squeezed her thighs tighter against his arms, half urging, half pleading him to deliver on whatever anticipation the angel had masterfully worked up.

Brass paused only long enough to worship her other nipple, but his free hand didn't remain idle for long. Her next sigh mingled with a masculine groan, causing the muscles in her lower belly to tremble with anticipation. It was a predator's warning and the only one she got before his hand settled between her legs and he parted her intimate flesh with two fingers. Then the man settled into an expedition, exploring her heated arousal with studious swipes.

Sensations assaulted her from every angle. The warm, soft leather beneath her. The tepid air filling her greedy lungs. The intense focus on the combination of his hard fingers and feathered tongue ripping out vibrations only her soul had ever known.

Molly had passed *too much* miles ago and was currently rounding *glutton for punishment*. Then Brass sank a thickly knuckled finger into her most intimate channel while working her clit with expert tormenting pressure. Her breaths sawed out of her, each inhale bringing her shuddering breasts further under his scrutiny.

Before she knew what her body was doing, the bastard picked up on the rhythm and circled her swollen nub just so, coaxing her to squirm exactly where his waiting mouth wanted her.

His expert ministrations made her reckless, like a trapped wild thing made rabid by its surroundings.

And then he added a second finger.

"Brass, please. It's too much. I need to feel you."

Her words were robbed from her throat as his insistent fingers burrowed deeper, eliciting a rising tumult that she had to clap a hand over her mouth to trap inside and keep from rattling the books against their glass houses. As soon as her hand solidified its cage over her lips, Brass's hand was there, peeling hers away and kissing her palm with a soft reassurance.

"What's too much is for me to have you beneath me and *not* hear your cries of pleasure. I'll be dead and dust before I'll be asked to bear such a thing."

Moisture slickened his hastening movements as she fought for purchase, for *anything* that would prevent her from soaring away from herself lest she never return to him again. Then a pulsing power overtook her, cresting over her heated skin and crashing upon her with relentless ecstasy that consumed more than it gave.

Brass was there before her trembling subsided, kissing her fluttering eyelids, her pulsing temples, even the hollow of her neck where what little breath she had still struggled for purchase. It was as if he needed to be there, guiding her down from the pleasure he wrought, ensuring she came back to him.

Her thighs relaxed away from Brass's hips at the same moment his forehead fell against hers. Her dewy skin, coupled with his cock nestled against her swollen sex, made the contact far more intimate than it otherwise would have been. Brass leaned his hips further into the V of her legs and slicked his length with what he'd coaxed from her. His patrician nose nuzzled against hers as they savored the tenderness of a moment they both knew would be gone far too soon.

"I've wanted this for an eternity," he whispered against her lips. "For lifetimes, for eons. Before languages existed with words to describe how good you feel against me, around me. Even now, with all the known vocabularies, words still fail me when I'm around you. They always have."

Now, it was Molly's turn to be utterly speechless. Her heart hammered out a frantic rhythm in time with his. She did her best to savor the echo of it as it reverberated from his chest to hers. How she wished she could memorize the whispers of his need for her and how stiflingly cherished it was to exist under Brass's regard.

This can't be the last time.

That final thought pounded through her skull with a relentless insistence, even as he slicked himself farther against her heat but never moved to claim what they were both breathless for.

If she was ever to take charge of anything in her life, let it be this, with this man, at this moment. If she didn't, the regret would not only wear her down but eat her alive for as long as he lived in her memory.

So, like any expert Boss Lady, she took charge and surged her hips forward, welcoming the entire length of him into her body.

Brass threw his head back and roared to the ceiling. Every glorious tendon was on display as his body strung tight through the adjustment of their joining. The fullness was as exquisite as it was tormenting. She fought against shutting her eyes, against lashing her head back and forth or burying her head in the crook of his heavily muscled shoulder. She needed to see this, to see all of him.

She needed to witness him falling apart just as much as she was about to.

"Fucking mages, Molly. You're so damn tight." The growled pleas traveled across the sensitive skin of her breasts where he breathed the words against her, bathing her in his exultation.

Look at me. Please look at me.

He hadn't yet opened his eyes. Did he not want to acknowledge this in some way? Was it better to live it through his mind than acknowledge the woman beneath him who he'd eventually no longer recognize?

"Don't preserve this, Brass. Just let go. I need you to let go and live."

The veins at his temples fluttered under her command, and then he reared up and opened his eyes.

Molly smiled widely at her reflection in the dancing ochre flames of his gaze.

There you are. I missed you.

And then he pulled his hips back and slammed into her core. Again. And again. The sweet seduction from earlier had been replaced with good, old-fashioned fucking. It was the kind of lovemaking that scored marks on not only skin but souls.

And Molly was *so* there for it.

Her heels dug into his ass as she urged him on and bucked her hips in time to his penetrating rhythm. He poured everything into the act, every unspoken word, every missed opportunity, every mistake, every regret.

They all filled her to an impossible fullness, reaching parts of her that had always bore a hollowness.

Until him.

Her orgasm curled up her spine before she was ready for it. The mounting pleasure arched her hips, causing her to buck more tightly against him. His hands were under the curve of her back instantly, supporting her through a climax so brilliant, so scorching, it could white out the sky and extinguish entire galaxies. Through it all, Brass never let up. His hips pistoned faster, deeper, harder, until his final release racked his powerful muscles with a shudder that caused the glass coffee table beside them to tremble.

When Molly slowly opened her eyes, content to luxuriate in the newfound heat of what they'd created and perhaps lean into a good cuddle session or two, what she saw froze her blood where it flowed.

Brass, his face twisted in agony, was completely engulfed in flames.

CHAPTER 25

It came to him in bolts of brittle awareness. One second, Brass had been sheathed by the most exquisite heat he'd ever had the good fortune to burn under, and the next, every cell of his body was lit to literal flame.

A deafening roar tunneled through his throat and erupted out of him with a bludgeoning force. His body jerked against a rush of power that punched through his core and radiated along every nerve ending with a fire no mortal heat could match.

Brass gritted his teeth against the onslaught and braced against waves of a familiar energy that, with each crest, crashed into him with a commanding strength that teased at ripples of memories long lost. Muscles flexed anew, blood ran hotter, and an intimate fire flared to life within him.

He'd known this fire. His soul bore the imprints of its former glory and freedom. They were celestial flames he hadn't been able to fully command since before he fell from the Empyrean.

Freedom.

My full angel fire!

Brass wrenched his eyes open quickly enough to catch the sight of an electric blue inferno writhing in the reflection of Molly's terrified gaze.

And then he saw it: the flames. They had engulfed his entire body and gotten to work singeing the leather couch under which Molly was pinned. Not pinned . . . Trapped, while he burned above her. Already, her face had reddened, and her bangs had coiled closer to her forehead.

Shit!

He wrenched himself off her and threw himself against the nearest slab of stone that wasn't already protecting shelves of flammables. Once his inflamed skin hissed against cool granite, Brass extinguished his fire and scrambled back over to Molly, who was shaking slightly but mobile enough to still reach for her clothes.

"Molly! Are you hurt? Did I burn you? Show me where. *Show me, dammit!*"

Subtle trembles skittered along her skin. He was surprised, in his fevered rush to get to her, just how attuned he was to such a thing as the minute workings of her nerves. Muscles and senses he'd long commanded now heightened to peaks he'd not known how to climb before. The thrumming awareness pulled every perception he had toward Molly, who looked at him like he'd grown a few more appendages.

"Are you hurt?" he screamed again and ripped at the shirt she'd hastily draped over her nakedness. He had to see for himself. Until he could inspect every inch of her skin for burns or so much as a fucking heat rash, he'd not let her even attempt to stand.

Then she stood.

Insufferable woman.

"Will you get off me? And stand over there, will you? *All* the way over there, by the books that were probably bound in petrified wood from prehistoric volcanoes or whatever. Go!" An insistent finger pointed to the farthest corner of the room while her other hand clutched a large shirt—his shirt—to her chest. The fabric barely covered the tops of her thighs, which was a far better arrangement than he'd found himself in at the moment.

Molly's outstretched directional wasn't the only appendage barking orders, and his was still fully trained on the woman who was ordering him around the room.

Grateful for the tepid air, Brass retreated his naked ass the sum total of two steps, then froze.

When Molly waved her arm at him again in the classic *shooing* fashion, a golden crescent on the underside of her wrist caught the lamplight.

"Do that again," he rushed out.

"Do what? Order you around?"

"If it'll make you move your wrist in that way, then yes. Tell me how you're not getting involved in any of this and swipe your hand at me."

"I am *not* taking orders from a naked angel who just erupted into flames after one orgasm! Do you have any idea what kind of mindfuck that is for a woman? That you'd rather *catch on fire* than cuddle after sex?"

As predicted, Molly slashed her hand horizontally through the air between them. When her fingers started their return trip, Brass grabbed hold of her wrist and carefully, with his hand on the small of her bare back, ushered her toward one of the library's wall sconces.

"What are you doing? You're kind of freaking me out a bit."

Brass rotated her wrist back and forth beneath the dim orange glow. Nothing appeared at first, but when he maneuvered her at a different angle, a shimmering golden crescent no larger than a quarter winked up at them.

Molly's breath hitched. "What the hell is that?"

Her question traveled through the quicksand of his mind as his newly suped-up brain matter tried to process what he was seeing.

"It's a symbol," he managed to say.

"Why is it on me? What does this mean?" Molly rubbed her fingers across the gold looping swirls that decorated the delicate blue veins of her wrist.

"Molly."

The tremble he couldn't keep from his voice pulled her attention northward until she finally looked at him. He tried to will some sense of understanding into what he was about to share.

She's going to hate you for this.

Brass gathered her wrist into his hands, cupping it like the precious offering it was, and brought it to his lips. The kiss he placed there surprised even himself, underscoring the dire seriousness of what it all meant.

"This is significant, isn't it?" she asked, cradling his face against her trapped hand despite her confusion.

Embrace this moment, for she may not touch you again once she knows.

"It's a name," he clarified.

"Who's name?"

"Mine." The fire within his soul flared brightly at the confession, as if sighing in relief after endless captivity. "It's my real name, written in the celestial language of the Empyrean." A heavy breath lifted shoulders that had never felt so light, yet still bore such a burden. *"Restor."*

Molly fingered the tattoo again while the shirt she held to her dipped lower, revealing one last peek of a supple breast. He'd never been more grateful and tormented by the distraction. "It's a beautiful name," she offered.

Brass blanched and was surprised she hadn't run screaming

from him. Then, because life-changing realizations were making him fucking stupid, he surprised himself further by saying, "It's yours now."

She tore her gaze away from her wrist and looked at him. "What? Why?"

He swallowed past a truth he never thought he'd have the providence of testing on his tongue. "Because it is the mark of the soul bond, a connection of the Eternal Flame's light within two individuals. The tattoo is a symbol of our mated joining."

"Mated joining," she clarified slowly.

"Yes. We are mates, you and I. And it was that bond that brought back my full celestial angel fire. I am finally whole again, all because of you." He brought her wrist to the center of his chest first, then tucked the rest of her body into the shelter of his.

As he held her, deafening power thrummed through his veins, along with several earth-shattering realizations.

He was wrong. His fire would never hurt her, couldn't. It was a power he would wield in protection of her, in defense against all that threatened to take her from him. His curse. Ragana. Cyro and his charmers. He'd rain his angel fire down on them all just to lay their ashes at Molly's feet in tribute.

All this and more ran through the tracks of his mind so quickly, he almost didn't notice the tendrils of a foreign power mingling with his own.

As Brass sat next to Molly on one of the sandstone-colored sectional sofas in the den's empty great room, he couldn't ignore the effect a tray of leftover croissants and French press coffee had on brightening her mood. He may have been an immortal angel, but he was still not above taking notes when it came to a woman stating the importance of carbohydrates and caffeine.

What could he say? Like all males, he loved a list.

While the rest of his brothers were out on charmer patrol, Brass took the opportunity to ensure Molly was properly fed and watered before he answered any more of her questions.

Because, of course, she had more questions.

And so do I.

After they'd gotten dressed and Molly requested a few minutes in the bathroom to *make herself human*, whatever that meant, he'd wondered how the soul bond piece fit into his doomsday puzzle. Entire essential parts of him revolted against the idea of leaving her unprotected, and for a brief, blissful moment, hope had flared in his chest that the mages wouldn't be so cruel as to continue him careening toward his current fate. Why gift him with a mate, only to have her memory ripped from him days later once the madness took hold?

What if Ragana's threats had been true? What if he truly wouldn't recognize her once his humanity had been ripped away from him?

What if I hurt her? What if I kill her?

And then there was the one line of questioning that worried him most of all, the one thing he couldn't parse out quite yet and he feared he was running out of time to do so . . . *What of her magic?*

The questions had played out on a morbid greatest hits reel in his mind. Each time the record spun around, it picked up more and more worries, until the panic pile was so high, there was no longer any room for the elation granted him in finally accessing his full celestial power.

In finally having *her.*

Molly peeled back the buttery layers of a croissant and popped each one into her mouth, though her face didn't reflect her usual exuberance for the act. Several times, her eyes wandered about the room, though whether in avoidance or curiosity, he couldn't be certain.

Brass tried to see what she saw and look upon his ancient home with the eyes of someone entirely new to his world. Slabs of carved-out granite stretched high around them, curving into a ceiling that hugged the cavernous space. The rock walls were studded with elaborate wall sconces, which threw off just enough light to cast entrancing shadows over the bachelor-pad-standard overstuffed sofas and nicked-a-plenty walnut coffee tables. Aside from the stone support pillars and general cave-like structure, he supposed it wasn't that different from any other mortal dwelling . . . except for the far corner, which housed a row of practice targets, breakfronts gleaming with every sort of weaponry, and, as was standard, a pool table.

Once Molly had taken several passes of the space, she chewed the inside of her lip, and Brass braced for any number of possible things to come out of her mouth.

"I don't really know what to say," she offered before blowing away the steam curling from her open mug.

"You don't have to say anything."

"Now, we both know that's not true."

He shrugged away the statement, but it didn't escape her notice. Always so damn observant.

"Always with the nonanswers," she griped.

It was on the tip of his tongue to argue, to fire back with something snarky that would get her blood pumping high enough to fight with him so he wouldn't have to explain things that would otherwise send her running again. So, instead, he remained silent and went back to stroking her wrist where it draped across his lap. Mages damn him, her wrist. He hadn't been able to let her hand go since she'd settled on the couch and likely wouldn't be inclined to do so anytime soon.

The woman truly had no idea of just how important she was to him.

"So, your angel fire doesn't need to be recharged anymore?" Her question drew him from his thoughts.

Ah. His fire. *That*, at least, he could address. "No. I have all my full celestial fire available to me once more. It's no longer drained away with each passing hour."

She squeezed the hand that held hers, pumping his heart as well. "That must be wonderful for you."

"It is," he agreed. "More wonderful still that you were unharmed. My fire will never harm you, Molly. It recognizes you now. You have to know that."

An adorable wrinkle formed between her brows. "It's sentient?"

"More like emotionally charged," he clarified. "When I experience heightened bouts of anger or fury, it acts on my behalf. It protects me even when my mind may otherwise be distracted."

"You make it sound like it's some kind of flaming dog or something, like it has unending loyalty even while it's . . ."

When she didn't finish her thought, Brass peered down at her. "Is everything all right?"

"Loyalty," she said distractedly into her coffee cup. "And it acts on your behalf."

Brass sat up slowly, still not letting go of her wrist. "Yes . . ."

What was she getting at? Of all the things he prepared himself to answer for, his fire was way the hell down on the list. She knew it was one of his powers, after all, so at least on the surface, its appearance shouldn't have been *that* unusual, except for the literal flaming orgasm bit. Did she really have no questions about his mark, though, about the soul bond, hell, even the fact that they'd made love to begin with?

A new fear gripped him then.

Mages, did she regret what they'd done?

"Is it possible," she continued, "that your full fire could act on your behalf even through, let's say, the rage of a goddess's ancient curse?"

He shook his head in relief, though still regretting the way he'd robbed some of the brightness from her eyes. "I already told you, Ragana is a goddess of the elements. Fire is as natural to her as the lunar tides or the chlorophyll in a blade of grass. My fire has no effect on her. I already tried, remember?"

"Wait, here me out!" Molly sat up straighter, a curious excitement highlighting her features. "Your fire isn't of the elements. Not anymore, right? You said you don't have to charge your power beneath the ground each night. Before our"—she looked down at her wrist, and a delicious blush crept up her cheeks—"well, *that*, you always had to rely on the elemental energy of the metals and minerals around you at night to feed your fire. But now it's pure celestial power, right?"

That time, it was Brass who let go of Molly's wrist. "Celestial power requires balance." He repeated his earlier explanation for the benefit of no one but himself. And certainly not for the hope that had begun to put the light back in Molly's smile.

Hope for him, for a way to end the curse.

"And so does rage," she reminded him.

Brass quickly lifted the coffee out of Molly's hands and brought it to his lips. It took the span of three scalding swallows for the idea to surface and a plan to form. Silently, he reached inside himself to test the strength of his power. It was there, all right. All of it. Every kernel of celestial fire that had ever roiled within him floated within his core, ready to do his bidding. A spark of elation lifted his chest. He sensed no elemental nuances or signatures in the flames. The only connection to the earth that still lingered was his metallic power and that he knew to never use against an earth goddess.

Molly was right. His fire may just be enough to stop her, perhaps even temper the effects of the curse long enough to prevent it from fully taking hold before he had a chance to destroy the witch.

"Yes," he stated slowly, still processing the possibility of having finally found a way to end his torment once and for all. He searched inward again, double-checking the energetic makeup of his power. In this, he couldn't be wrong. Only absolute certainty would be enough to propel this plan forward. However, upon further inspection, another component lurked in the shadows of his flames, inking tendrils of temptation around the seed of hope that he'd hastily begun to nurture.

Fury. It remained in his soul like a deeply rooted weed, as alive and active as it had ever been.

It raged like a silent predator lying in wait among the shadows, with infinite time and patience. It was the king cobra slithering about his mind and had no qualms about going weeks or months in between feedings. Sooner or later, it would strike. Hard.

Would it end with Ragana? If he destroyed her, would his rage, which had been his constant mercurial companion for centuries, truly be destroyed with her?

A trickle of doubt crept into his mind, turning his head toward the woman who'd planted it there, along with his hope.

"Do you feel any different?" he asked.

She balked. The question had clearly taken her by surprise. "Uh, now that I think about it, maybe a little? It's from the mark though, right?" She offered him her wrist like a summer camper offers up a boo-boo to a counselor for bandage duty.

She still doesn't know about her magic. Or does she?

Brass hated the skepticism invading his thoughts. It shamed him, even as her smile, and the fact that she hadn't run from him this time, brightened his soul. And yet he couldn't help it. Life lessons were harder to learn when one was immortal. One act of fury followed by a single spell from a scorned goddess and his very existence had warped under her evil magic.

Was Molly capable of the same?

Even now, the most she'd alluded to their soul bond was an innocuous raise of her wrist. She hadn't mentioned it by name, hadn't mentioned *him* or even yet questioned the significance of what now lay between them.

Yes . . . she has doubts, secrets of her own. Magic she keeps from you . . .

The cackling feminine voice blazed across his consciousness, stirring the silt floor of his fury's cage until the monster banged against its bars with hastening force. Brass's fire answered instantly, beating back the beast with a quickness he hadn't been able to manage in millennia.

She mustn't know, he decided grimly, not willing to risk the opportunity before him. *Not yet, but soon.*

Soon, if the mages willed it, they'd be able to have a very different conversation. Until then, he'd focus on the here and now, on what he could manage.

Fighting Ragana. Tempering his rage. Welcoming his mate into his world.

"Yes," he lied to her. "From what my brothers' mates have said, there are new sensations that arise from being soul bound."

"I guess that makes sense," she conceded, rubbing her shoulders for warmth or comfort, he couldn't tell which.

It didn't matter. Brass was intent on providing her with both.

He clutched her by the shoulders and welcomed her against the wall of his chest, wrapping her in his arms and warming them both with the banked heat of his core's fire.

Molly sighed against his neck, sending shivers along his spine. "That feels *sooo* good."

"Let me put you to bed," he whispered against her temple, nuzzling some of her bangs aside to take in more of her natural scent.

"I *have* had quite the day," she murmured, already half asleep.

"I'm pretty sure my brain's about to go on strike and make demands I'm not prepared to defend against at the negotiating table."

"Best not have that, then." Brass swept Molly into his arms and carried her to his suite, wondering how much time they had left together and whether his fire would be enough to keep her with him.

CHAPTER 26

It was a strange thing to sleep surrounded by stone. In Molly's thirty-one years on the planet, she'd had some stellar opportunities to spend time in numerous hotels, visit countless old-timey bed-and-breakfasts, and even endure all New Hampshire had to throw at her on a camping trip or two.

Shudder.

None of them, however, compared to sleeping in a king-sized four-poster wrought-iron canopy bed next to a fallen angel whose scent she'd give her good cast-iron pans for to bake into everything she cooked from now to eternity. There was something about the minerals and metals around her, even the dormant ones that lived in Brass, that calmed her to a point of deep tranquility. At home, when her mind couldn't settle, she'd give in to her compulsive urges and trace her fingers along wallpaper seams or rearrange the pleats in her curtains so the billowing gauze all hung at even intervals and widths.

Here, the stone took all that away. Though there was no mistaking the walls for anything other than what they were—craggy rock slabs carved out by means she couldn't imagine—

they were perfect in their imperfections. While her OCD would normally have jumped off a cliff at the incongruity of it all, it was oddly comforting. It was an impossible task to try and smooth out the stone. Within its walls, all secrets were safe, protected. Perhaps it had something to do with the lack of windows, but she had a feeling that, were she so inclined, she could scream her concerns to the top of the arched ceiling and the mountain would instantly know to hold them close, rather than fire her fears back at her in a stream of echoes.

And oh boy, did she have a lot of fears.

The hands on the bronze ormolu clock that gilded Brass's mahogany dresser had just passed midnight. Indiscriminate shivers that had pricked along her body ever since her sweat session with Brass decided to be relentless in their attention, regardless of the hour.

How frickin' courteous.

While Molly had hoped to tumble into an exhaustive state of deep sleep only night workers and sleep apnea sufferers ever fantasized about, her feat ultimately alluded her.

Was it possible for one's mind to shiver? Was that a thing? It certainly felt like a thing and had been the driving catalyst pulling Molly away from Brass's deliciously warm embrace. The soft hem of his borrowed T-shirt brushed against the tops of her thighs as she meandered through his spacious suite of rooms.

If she could say one thing about the man who lived there, it was that he had a taste for the fancy. Four-poster bed aside—because who even had one of those?—the space was decked out in more bright and shiny than a pharaoh's tomb. Rows of golden trinkets anointed stone shelves like a glittering jeweled tiara topped off a royal. Hanging—though she hadn't yet figured out how—on the wall behind the dresser was a massive antique arched mirror that would have looked right at home during the Baroque era.

Knowing how old all of them were, she probably wasn't far off with that assessment.

Molly wandered in front of the thing and admired the sleeping giant reflected in its depths. Behind her, Brass's resplendent body was laid out like a Greek god of carnal sin, if one had ever existed. He'd slept shirtless. Of course he did. After all their earlier exertions, it was kind of silly to stand on a ceremony neither of them particularly cared about. But the fact remained that she was never comfortable sleeping naked, and he was apparently all about her comfort. Hence the sleepwear compromise. Flannel pajama bottoms for him, and a T-shirt and underwear for her.

Amicable sleeping arrangements aside, it didn't stop her wrist from warming just at the mere sight of all that bronzed flesh on display. At some point in the night, he'd rolled onto his back, leaving his beautifully sculpted chest uncovered by the comforter. Taut muscles stretched across pectorals that, even in sleep, seemed to house an inner reservoir of strength always at the ready. Then her greedy gaze slid to his abdominals, which were a corrugated and dangerous terrain all their own, one she'd hoped to map the topography of very shortly.

Not to be left out was The Trail. That tempting thatch of tawny hair that stretched in invitation from his navel to the base of a cock her innermost muscles still hadn't fully recovered from.

And that was what worried her the most.

Ever since their carnal clash on the couch, her body had decided to mutiny the brain barking orders to it. Muscles hummed with an energy comparable to what she'd experienced that one time after Drea had dragged her to that indoor cycling class. Problem was, Molly had just been sleeping and hadn't exerted more than a heavy breath or two.

So, why did she feel like she'd run a marathon that *wasn't* sex related?

Heat quickly crept up her cheeks. She pinched her T-shirt and held it away from her in the manner of all hot flash commiserators. It was another unfortunate symptom that had sprouted up out of nowhere. Throughout the night, her body temperature had vacillated wildly.

One more worry to add to the pile, chief among them having to do with the warming tattoo on her wrist and the slumbering sex god who had somehow put it there.

That had to have been it. She didn't care how supernatural her acquaintances had become. One did not burst into flame upon gifting her the most toe-curling orgasm of her life without marking her as the proverbial summit of where it all took place in hopes of one day returning.

Returning. That thought alone had been enough to pull her out of bed and examine the permanent symbol on her skin that marked her connection to Brass. The soul bond. Had there ever been anything so permanent as what that represented? Marriages failed just as often as they succeeded. Parents could die. Homes could be shattered. Bosses could lie, and men could steal women's trust faster than a french fry off a passing party tray.

But to be soul bound to an immortal angel carried its own air of immortality that went beyond the petty gripes of the human world she'd thus far lived in. And where did love come into play in that everlasting dichotomy, if at all? They hadn't spoken of it, and she wasn't sure how to take that. Was love a distinctly human emotion or only so much in the way that humans had learned how to exploit it?

"I can hear you thinking over there." Sleep rasped Brass's voice into a register that burned her skin even hotter and pulled her nipples into stiff points. How the hell did he always do that?

Through the mirror, she watched him rise from the bed, unfurling his body from the covers with a jaguar's grace. "That's not fair, you know," she whined. "You can't come out of a dead sleep and have perfectly tousled hair. It's against the rules."

His warmth blanketed her back as he lifted her tangled tumbleweeds of hair away from her neck to plant a kiss there. "I like to make my own rules."

"Do you also like to make your own bad boy biker clichés?" She arched a brow at him through the mirror.

"What I'd *like* is to know why you're not in bed keeping me warm."

She sighed, totally unprepared to lead with the heavy stuff. "Why do you always like to cut to the chase? Sometimes—hear me out—*sometimes* build up is good. Necessary, even. Words are not always bad, you know. They can do a girl wonders for ramping up to an argument just long enough so she can figure out the right words."

Her worried tone clearly conveyed all Brass needed to know about her state of mind. He gently spun her around but left his hands on her shoulders. "What's all this about?"

And then she said the *wrong* words. "Is there a choice?"

Brass's hold stiffened against her. "A choice in what?"

"A choice in the soul bond?"

The stoic calm that had carved itself into Brass's features cracked and quickly crumbled around the edges. "Not for me there isn't."

"But how do you know that? How do you know that your prime mages or whoever didn't make a mistake?" She lifted her wrist, presenting it to him like evidence to be entered into the court record. "How do you know that I'm the right one for you?"

His jaw ticked back and forth. "Does it feel like a mistake?"

A painful sob lodged in Molly's throat once. Twice. By the third time it tried pushing through to the surface, all her defenses had flown the nest.

"No!" she cried, her exclamation stunning them both. "And

that's the problem!" Molly stormed over to the bed and plopped down. "Ever since you charged into my restaurant with far too much sass in your ass for me to deal with during a midweek breakfast service, I've felt . . . right. Relieved. Content. You don't hover, but you're always there. You don't say anything most of the time, yet your silence gives me more reassurance than a barrage of bullshit compliments. You're supportive without smothering and . . . and . . ." She was blabbering, having a full-on bleeding-of-the-soul moment all over Brass's Egyptian cotton sheets, but she couldn't patch that dam with all the granite New Hampshire had to offer. "And I *like* the idea of being your mate."

There. She'd said it. The confession that had taken root so deep within her, it could hardly reach the light long enough for her to examine it.

But it was there, in their face for both of them to see and scrutinize. To accept or reject.

Molly summoned the courage to look at him and wished she could read the stern expression carved into his glacial features. Still, he said nothing, so compelled as she always was, she filled the silence with the panic of her heart.

"What does that mean? What does it mean that I want you?"

One moment, Brass was frozen in front of the mirror; the next, he was on his knees in front of her, a blur of red and gold, with his warrior's hands cradling her face. Golden flames danced in eyes so wide and wild, they illuminated every dark corner of her soul's desire.

"It means," he growled, "that you're mine. And this," he breathed against her mouth while holding her wrist to his bare chest, "is yours. All of it. My mark. My soul. My fire. All of it is yours."

The thrum of his heart beat a wild symbiotic frenzy against her pulse, as if his very life's blood was learning her, adjusting to her.

Accepting her.

Shock had no place between them, nor did doubt or any of the people who had come before them. In that sacred space, carved among the secrets of the great mountain, there was only Brass and Molly.

Then her heart punched a final answering beat within her chest.

He is more than enough.

Brass surged forward and claimed her mouth with his, commanding a kiss that never had the time to bloom into second-guesses, for there were none. She groaned against the warm, silky invasion of his tongue as he maneuvered it with more skill than any man had a right to possess. She knew instantly that she'd remember that kiss forever. It wasn't just an exchange of passion but of poetry. A lesson for all future generations to study in what happened when two souls collided into one.

He broke the kiss just long enough to tug her shirt off. The natural chill of the stone walls sought the nearest living thing, leeching heat from her body and kissing her breasts and stomach with goose bumps. The fire in Brass's eyes danced with delight at what the chilly air brought. Already, her nipples had pebbled to aching, beckoning peaks. Behind his flannels, the outline of his thickening arousal left nothing to the imagination. True, she'd seen it all before—lucky woman that she was—but never with the kind of dangerous intent that sizzled in that moment.

Brass didn't plan on having sex with a woman he merely liked.

He planned on fucking his soul bond until she screamed his name and rattled the stars.

Oh, Good Lawd.

Eager to have his mouth on hers again in *all* the ways, Molly curled her fingertips into the waistband of her underwear and began to pull them down.

"No. Don't."

Shocked, she stalled mid-strip. "Don't?"

"That's my job. I plan on baring you to me. All of you. Body and soul."

Oh, shucks. Well, if you say so.

He lifted her off the bed and placed her feet on the ground in front of him. Then he gestured toward the nearest bedpost with that wicked fire in his eyes that still scorched her skin everywhere it touched. "Grab it," he ordered.

On legs barely sturdy enough to hold up an objection, she bent over and gripped the bedpost fist over fist.

Then his voice, heated and silky as dark caramel swirled with cream, floated into her ear from behind. "I'm going to make love to you, Molly. No hiding beneath me this time. I want to see you come apart around my cock. I want to own every ripple of pleasure that lights up the body baring my mark."

Before, Brass passing himself off as a man-of-few-words mortal had been a feast for her senses. But the soul-bonded Brass who worshipped her body like a shrine at an altar *and* offered up benedictions to the cause?

As in, actual full sentences of adulation from his mouth? To her? *For* her?

Somewhere between Brass's slow slide of her underwear and the tender kiss he placed at the small of her back, a very unusual word floated around her mind.

She *loved* this.

For a woman who made a thousand and one decisions every moment, she thought she knew her preferences and what she needed to do to get shit done. She'd commanded kitchens, cooked for celebrities, bought a fucking restaurant on nothing more than borrowed credit and creativity. And it had all been . .
.

Really, *really* exhausting.

"I don't want to be in charge right now," she whispered to the bedpost.

"You don't have to be, baby. Not with me. Not ever with me. It'll always be your choice."

"Yes." She sighed, tilting her head back. "Yes, that's what I want."

It damn sure was what she wanted. To not be on all the time, to let go on occasion knowing someone would be there to catch her and keep the ship running. A partner. A lover.

A soul bond.

Brass.

He gently kissed her neck as he dragged a slow, toying hand down the cleft of her ass. She hitched a breath that quickly turned to a moan when he found her heated core and slid his thick fingers through her pooling arousal. "You are so wet for me," he murmured between her shoulder blades before bestowing another far-too-chaste kiss there. "Perfection. You were made for me, Molly mine."

"You . . . sure do . . . talk a lot . . . when you're . . ."

"Hard?" He pressed his steely length against her ass, and she gasped at the smooth hot flesh that connected with her. Just when in the hell had he removed his pants?

"That's not very angel-like," she informed him.

A searing chuckle left his lips and snaked down her spine. "Hang on tight. I'm going to make you fly."

Brass lifted her hips to his and slid himself home in one smooth stroke. Her body arched back into the prison of his hard embrace as she moaned against the inside of her bicep. Sweaty palms clung to the bedpost as he retreated in an effortless glide, then drove into her again with a force that lifted her heels off the floor.

Each penetrating thrust was an answering cry to every single doubt she'd ever had about him. Every tightened grip on her hips was an imprint on other parts of her. Every hammering pound of his body against hers, inside hers, awakened her soul in a way she never thought possible. It was a striking pressure that spurred her on toward an intensity that had always been denied her.

Until now. Until him.

It was utter ecstasy down to her very core.

With a final punishing grunt, Brass lifted Molly off the floor entirely and rocketed her into pleasure spasms that rent her body into the sum of its parts. Tremors transfixed entire limbs and cast her into a universe where only she and Brass existed.

He truly sent her flying.

Guttural sounds joined her chorus of cries as Brass followed her into the abyss. Once the waves crashed and their exhausted bodies were heaped onto the sands of their post-orgasmic sex frenzy, Brass swiped the bed covers onto the floor. Too sated to move, she just lay against his chest as he wrapped them up in multiple layers of fluffy feather down comforter and dragged them both into a sleep so deep, even their dreams were mated.

CHAPTER 27

Harsh wind slammed against the back of Brass's cloak and hood. Already, the forest floor had hardened and bore a dusting of frost that had settled over the land. The sea to the west churned with shards of ice that had formed in the bay to the frozen north two months earlier and now drifted southward.

Winter was an icy breath of warning along his neck. Something was coming.

Him.

Once the sun went down, he tracked the demon charmer to the forest that blanketed the spruce- and pine-rich lands east of the sea and north of the gulf. There were no footprints to follow, save for the few a frightened hare left behind before its tracks were swallowed up by the larger pawprints of a lynx scouting its supper.

Good. It meant Brass's prey wanted to remain hidden. It also meant that his prey thought it wouldn't be found.

The mortal pagan elders had requested aid from all of the

surrounding villages following the mysterious disappearances of several tribe members. A dozen taken within a fortnight: four men, two women, six children.

Fucking children.

A dozen souls who would never see the Empyrean and never know true rest, for Brass knew what had befallen them.

The most recent mortal stolen, a child, had been taken from his pallet in the predawn hours. All that remained was a threadbare blanket and a child's sock that boasted far more darning than wool. At least, that was all the boy's family had noticed disturbed.

Brass, on the other hand, had more specific tools at his disposal.

Upon his analysis of the small dwelling, his metallic senses were called to the speck of brass that had embedded itself in the wood of a traveling trunk. The metal had the patina of armor and hummed with a signature dark magic born of Cyro's shadow realm demons.

An apex had been there, and Brass would make the bastard pay for every soul he'd stolen.

Brass ducked below birch and black alder branches, tracking the dark magic through the forest, until the small farmer's cottage appeared in a clearing at the edge of the tree line. There was no pasture and no smoke curling from the structure's chimney. What was there called to his metal like an oily caress of the dark sea.

A demon.

His soul's fire thrummed with vengeful power. There would be no mercy, no forgiveness. Just utter annihilation.

It would never bring back the souls lost, the souls he and his sentinel brothers were charged to protect, but by the mages, he'd deal out swift justice in anguish and ashes.

Brass pulled his sword free of its baldric and called upon his angel fire until he was a raging inferno from his toes to the tip of his blade. With a war cry that sent the larks scattering from the trees, he exploded through the small door.

Ivory skin flashed in the firelight. Curves caressed the hourglass of a woman's naked backside as it rose and sank above a man's bare body. Chestnut waves fell to the dip in her waist in tantalizing tendrils, gripped at the ends by large meaty hands. Her face, a mix of fairy features and sensuality, was lax with ecstasy before her dark eyes alighted on her intruder with shock.

The man beneath snarled and bucked her off immediately. Then the light of the flames illuminated the rest of him. Sickly pallid skin swirling with gold and teal tattoos stretched across unnatural strength. A hairless scalp, fuming gold eyes, and three gilded bands corded around his neck and biceps marked the male for what he was: an apex demon.

Brass erupted, shooting flames of angel fire into the prone charmer's chest. The apex, whose body was still sluggish from sex, reacted a breath too slowly. The inferno engulfed him before the first of his cries reached the buckling roof rafters.

"No!" The woman, now covered in a hunter's cloak, screeched a wail of agony while Brass's power ignited the small cottage into tinder. Before the roof collapsed, he'd rushed forward, grabbed her about her trim waist, and shuttled her outside as the apex smoldered into ashes along with the structure's remains.

"You . . ." the woman breathed once Brass unhanded her. "You killed him. He was my sword. My salvation in what was to come. My lover! And you killed him!"

Wind whipped through pine boughs on a furious sea gale and battered Brass's skin with unrelenting pressure. Trees toppled around him, crashing to the earth with the rage of a thunderclap.

Her lover? An apex? Who was this woman?

Brass had never contemplated love for longer than it took to lace up his boots or sharpen his blades. He was a fallen sentinel angel. Immortal and doomed to wander the mortal realm, hunting down charmers while searching for sparks severed from the Eternal Flame that would one day return him to the Empyrean. What use had he for such an emotion? Certainly, not the kind that evoked such torment that wailed forth from the woman before him.

A woman who clearly spoke of madness.

"How is this possible?" he cried. "Who are you?"

A frightening cackle rent the night sky, infusing the crisp air around him with shards of ice that pricked his skin and tore at his lungs. Wrath stretched her features into savage snarls. "May you forever know my name, sentinel, for it will haunt you all your days. I am Ragana, goddess of death and witches."

A . . . goddess?

Brass sent bolts of flames at her from every angle, but they no more scorched her skin than they heated the winter's air around her.

Then she was flying, her pale toes levitating above the earth, while that crippling chill burrowed farther under his skin. She stretched her arms wide as if in offering or bestowing an omen. "Hear me, sentinel! You have taken from me, and so I shall take from you. Burn! For two thousand winters, you will burn with your fond fury, until it claims what is left of your humanity. Hear me! Hear me!"

Brass shuddered awake with Ragana's tormenting cackle still resounding in his mind. Sweat dampened his chest and soaked through the sheets beneath his thighs.

Then came the pain.

Blinding agony contorted his muscles, anointing them with a new master. When he levered out of bed, he didn't recognize the man in the mirror who stared back at him. Teeth bared. Eyes wild. Nostrils flared like a bull eyeing down a matador.

No . . .

The nightmare that plagued him in sleep for two thousand years had gotten its act together and finally decided to fuck him over in the land of the living. Looking for something, *anything*, to fight off the rage curling up his spine, he reached for his nightstand. Not the lamp on top of the nightstand but the solid piece of mahogany furniture itself. With one hand, he lifted the thing and hurled it at the mirror. The glass practically atomized on contact.

The seal had officially broken.

The oak armoire was next, its perfectly crafted doors turned into little more than driftwood. The suite of rooms became a den of destruction as he fired his fist into anything smart enough to splinter into pieces at the sight of him.

"More," he roared, twitching his head from side to side. "More!"

A muffled murmur pressed against his senses with frantic insistence. Something soothing, familiar, a sound that caressed his temples with tenderness and evaporated the red haze painting his surroundings.

"Brass . . ."

The dulcet lullaby of a woman's voice, this one a sweet serenade to the harpy's cackle, pulled him back from the tantalizing flames.

"Brass!"

Molly.

Her warm hands grabbed his face and yanked him toward her. The instant she touched him, rage fled the scene, but oh, it didn't go quietly. This time, his mind's captor snaked a curved talon along the edges of his soul, whispering promises of *mine* and *soon.*

Brass collapsed onto the bed, sweat coating his skin and blood funneling to far too many parts of him all at once. As if on cue, his suite's door slammed open to allow entry to three very bloodthirsty armed motherfuckers.

"Holy fucking shit," Chrome commented, accenting his observation of the destruction with a low whistle that hinted at him being equal parts impressed and terrified.

Bronze stormed in on Chrome's heels, followed by Titan, a dark and bearded badass and second-in-command to the prime sentinel.

Molly deliberately kept his eyes on her while she whispered, "It didn't work, did it?"

"What didn't work?" Titan asked, turning over a gutted armchair.

"The soul bond," Brass confirmed through heavy breaths. "Now that I have my full fire back, I thought I could use it to beat back the rage. To beat the curse."

Three sets of worried eyes met each other before looking decidedly elsewhere. The pity party had returned, with more concern than ever. Wonderful.

Bronze lifted a scrap of fabric that had once been a . . . fuck if he knew. Carpet? Comforter? "Yeah, I'm going to have to go with a no on that one, big guy."

"It's okay," Molly assured him, still bright and cheerful despite the shitstorm he'd ushered into his room and her life. "She can't stop us from living."

"No, she can't." He breathed a vow into the words that was as unbreakable as the sea. "This ends. One way or another, this fucking ends. But until then, we live."

Molly nodded, a worried mist clouding her eyes. "We live."

***

IF ONE COULD BOTTLE up an entire week's worth of euphoria, cork that sucker, and sip its nectar whenever a gray cloud threatened to show its ass, Molly would have invested in home bottling equipment, complete with a label maker and cut crystal decanters for extra-fancy indulgences.

Turned out, when one wasn't so intently focused on preventing her soul bond from going all scorched earth every waking second, she got a lot of shit done. Of course, it didn't hurt business to have a rugby team's worth of fallen angels running regular rotations at the restaurant. Post-preschool drop-off breakfasts had never been so bumpin'.

And speaking of which . . .

At some point between when she'd closed the place and when she'd flipped back over the *Open* sign, balance had been restored to the universe. That or someone had left their golden goose parked under one of her tables and Benny must have scrambled that egg and put it into the quiches because holy hotcakes, business was booming. Things had gotten so crazy that one of Brass's brothers, Steel, bless that angel, even volunteered to work under Benny and bang things out in the kitchen. Brass, as always, had also been there for her, doing everything she needed front-of-house wise before she even had the wherewithal to ask for it.

Fine by her. During their more idle times together, they'd also learned that having intentional tasks for him to complete helped keep the rage at bay. Currently, he was set up in the boiler room, the only place with a floor big enough to spread out and work, nailing together the final pieces of her event displays. The Winter Whimsy Festival was tomorrow, and after spending all of freaking ever boxing up her supplies and prepping what she could in advance, she had nothing left in the tank other than whatever dark roast coffee Brass had handed her an hour ago.

"Be right back!" she called to Benny, who was instructing Steel on the finer arts of the perfect reverse sear. "Going to the dumpster. Final cardboard box run."

When all she got was a two-fingered salute from both parties for her efforts, she rolled her eyes, hefted her cargo beneath her arm, and headed out to the alley. She'd made it ten feet out the door before four russet paws pitter-pattered over to her.

"Churro! Oh my gosh, I didn't think I'd see you again! I've been leaving bowls of food and water out for you. Have you noticed? I hope you noticed. I'd hate to think those dry-aged steak tips were being snuffled up by some random alley cat or, worse, a trash panda who wouldn't appreciate the tenderized funk of all that meat, you know?" Molly crouched down and gave the scratches of all scratches behind the hound dog's gloriously floppy ears. "What, no licks this time? Can't say I blame you. Tongue is a very personal boundary. Oops, hang on. Let me toss these in the recycling bin real quick."

Molly hefted her cargo up and over, then yanked out the two-by-four Benny used to hold the lid open for her. Once the plastic slab slammed shut, she tossed the hunk of wood in between the garbage and recycling dumpsters and started turning back to Churro.

"I was thinking, since you don't have a collar or anything, how would you feel about— Oh, hi. I'm sorry, I didn't see you there. Are you, uh, looking for someone?"

Standing right where Churro had been was a woman, and boy, did she take the ancient Yule celebration vibe *very* seriously. Rich crimson robes draped her shapely figure in fur-lined elegance before expanding to her wrists in wide bell sleeves. Mahogany hair fell in loose waves around alabaster skin that would have rivaled the moon for its reflected glow.

The woman's forest-green eyes pegged Molly with a strange insistence. "I have found who I'm looking for." Then she took a step closer.

Whatever shit luck that had been on Molly's side since she slid out of the womb regretfully decided to show up for work that day. "I think you have me confused with someone else," she offered, retreating a step toward the door.

The woman mimicked Molly's movements, inching closer. "I don't get confused. You are who I came to see."

Warning flared within Molly's chest.

"Who are you? What do you want?" Another step back. Something about the woman had her instincts recoiling, and Molly had always made it a habit of trusting those puppies. She slid her eyes around and quickly examined her surroundings. Would it be better to run for the open end of the alley where there were more people, or should she fumble for the back door knowing she could lock it behind her?

Keep her talking. Keep her talking.

"You have been making things rather difficult for me," the woman crooned.

"Oh?" Another step.

"Yes. You see, I have an arrangement with someone who, tomorrow, shall be joining me for a"—she pursed her garnet lips—"long-term contract. Your involvement with my protege has impacted his training."

"Yup. You must have me confused with someone else. I'm just a cook, lady."

"You are *just* nothing!" The verdant forest of her eyes darkened to onyx pools. A *whoosh* of robes was all the warning Molly got before the woman's bony hand was wrapped around Molly's throat. "*You* are a rejected orphan bastard who doesn't know the power she wields." A long, thin tongue traced a line under Molly's trembling chin. The woman sighed and smiled, tightening her grip even more. "Little orphan girl has been keeping secrets, hasn't she? Does our sentinel know from whence you hail?" Then she leaned closer, bringing with her the smell of decaying forest and death.

"Do you know what I'll do to him when his humanity is but a distant memory? Animals, after all, do make for some *wild* lovers, especially the mindless beasts. All they want to do is fuck and fight and fuck some more. They never truly learn who their master is until every last ounce of understanding has left them. What's left for me, then, is the exquisite fury to fuck out of them until their cocks are bruised and their wills are broken. And *you*, Molly Resnick, have interfered for far too—"

The alley door exploded off its hinges, shattering the brick facade into mortar and stone shards. Brass erupted from the shadows of the dark hallway, two silencer-clad guns primed and pointed at the woman's face. Twin ochre flames raged in eyes that promised death.

"Look away, Molly."

She barely had time to process his words before two electric blue streams of fire arced in front of her, finding their home in the woman's eyes.

The hissing cry that left Molly's captor was enough to deafen the dead. The woman threw her head back and screamed through a mouth that widened to unnatural proportions.

Molly stood there, frozen, half expecting the woman's head to spin around on her spinal column, when Brass's boot met the bitch's face and Molly's neck was finally free.

A split second later, angelic backup joined the party. Steel, Bronze, and Iron all had fire dancing in their eyes and the most unique assortment of weapons trained on one very immortal and pissed-off goddess.

"The dog. It was her. Ragana," Molly confirmed into Brass's heated shoulder blade from behind him.

One moment, the witch was on the ground. The next, she levitated above the dumpsters, blood streaming from misshapen eye sockets, while she pointed a knobby finger at Molly's soul bond. Brass's bullets, which still glowed with the angel fire he'd fused into them, slowly squeezed out of the torn hollows where Ragana's eyes had been until the shells clattered onto the pavement with a taunting tinkle.

"That is not enough to stop me, sentinel. There is nothing you can do to slow the course of time." Then she floated in a clouded mist that blurred the edges of her gown and hair. The lascivious smile that stretched her face wide, and the blood from her eye sockets leaking over her lips, cast a sickening queasiness in Molly's stomach. "Enjoy your final evening. Tomorrow at sundown, before the first day of your two thousandth winter comes to an end, you will be mine." Those crimson lips spread into a grim smile, revealing the suggestion of delicate fangs where blunt incisors had previously been. "There will be time enough yet for you to thank me, sentinel. What is an extra day to say goodbye when I'll have you for eternity?"

Ragana winked out of sight before the rest of Brass's bullets found their mark in her skull.

A permeating feminine cackle drifted through the wind tunnel created by the buildings on either side of the alley. It chilled Molly so thoroughly, she wondered whether she'd ever be warm again.

CHAPTER 28

The first day of the season ushered in a barrage of Aurora's deepest pockets to the town's recreation complex-turned-winter wonderland. Frosted sports fields had been gridded with rows upon rows of happy little pop-up tents. Anchored at the end of each aisle was a carefully curated food vendor, hawking their wares in the form of eats and sweets.

Molly was certain Suerte and Honeysuckles had secured one of those coveted locales only because of someone *else's* borrowed luck. Her little booth sat situated across from the aromatherapy candlemakers Transcendent Times and the guy who print-screened absolutely anything on a sweatshirt and sold it at two and a half times the market value.

Her booth was little due to the ever-rotating sets of broad-ass, though thankfully wingless, shoulders widening her tent flaps like murderous Winkie Guards from *The Wizard of Oz*.

To say Brass and his brothers were *kind of* on high alert for Ragana would be like saying a defensive nose tackle only *kind of* wanted to ram the center offensive lineman into the quarter-back until the dude choked on his own teeth.

At least football players wore face masks.

"That's it. We're officially out of the bread pudding and taffy. I've got about"—Benny peered into the pot of molasses baked beans, his face contorted with focused assessment—"a dozen or so servings of beans and twice as many brats, if that. Could cut those puppies even smaller to stretch 'em out if you'd like."

Could you also cut up the remaining minutes until sundown and stretch those out for, I don't know, forever?

Thankfully, how busy she'd been was the only thing keeping Molly from not handcuffing Brass to her side and smashing the shit out of every mahogany-haired woman with her ladle.

Amazing what having her highest-ever earning day did for taking her mind off losing the one man she'd trade it all away for.

Molly took the last of the bourbon bread pudding over to a frazzled mother and father of four under four. "Here you go," Molly offered, pelting them with a generous look of sympathy she felt compelled to offer regardless because, damn, that was a lot of kids. "And some road snacks for the kiddos." Molly shoved the final popsicle sticks topped with maple-leaf-molded amber taffy she'd been saving into four tiny fists. "Enjoy! Hope it makes for a quieter ride home."

With an exhausted nod of thanks, the family herded their hoard behind the rest of the attendees who were all shuttling out to the parking area. Another few minutes and she could officially shut down her booth and lose her damn mind like a normal person.

Molly glanced at her phone. Three forty-five. Sundown was at four fifteen.

Thirty minutes.

Belatedly, she remembered what Benny had asked her. "Nah, the festival's almost over. Just sell what we've got."

"Yes, chef."

Chef. That word was the culmination of so much hard work

and sacrifice for so long, and yet even as she stood at *the* food festival, after giving her card out and schmoozing with countless food industry VIPs, the glory of that moniker was the furthest thing from her mind. The truth was, whatever part of her that had been all smiles and shaking hands was a paid actor. On the inside, Molly was going through the motions with mud in her veins. Whatever fanfare and promises of follow-ups she'd experienced had felt like literal drops in the sea compared to what Brass was facing.

Just the mere whisper of his name through her mind had her looking to the corner of her booth where, true to sentinel form, Brass stood like a snarling gargoyle watching over the crowd as they ambled past. He'd chosen to flank that side, where she spent most of her time processing payments on her tablet and restocking the paper cups from the crate beneath, whereas Bronze had taken the opposite end. While the other angels had rotated around, some staying at the booth and others patrolling the festival proper, Brass hadn't moved from her side.

"Any sign of her?" Molly asked, offering him a sip of her coffee.

He didn't accept it, however, and instead just stared out into the milling crowd. "No."

That was when Molly noticed how much Brass had changed over the past several hours. Poking above his high-necked leather trench coat, a thin sheen of sweat dappled the underside of his jaw. The stubble that had been shaved off the day or so before had returned, casting a haggard look upon his stony features. Tension carved out runnels beneath his cheekbones, and his eyes couldn't maintain their amber color for more than a minute or two. Even as she spoke, his irises fluctuated from honeyed gold to that of a blazing sun.

"Brass," Molly whispered. "Your eyes."

He stilled, seemingly doing some sort of internal check, before squeezing them shut. Then he quickly gave the crowd his back, though he remained mindful of where Benny stood as the man scraped out the last of the baked beans into serving ramekins for the stragglers.

Shit. Not good.

Molly grabbed Brass by the arm and turned to Bronze and Benny. "We're going for a walk. Back in ten to help break down."

And then she yanked him as far away from people as possible. The most unsettling thing of all was that he let her.

She dragged him toward a bench on the far side from where the tents had been set up and promptly shoved his ass onto some hardwood. "Sit. Head between your thighs. Now."

"I'm not a child, woman."

"Good. Because otherwise, what we did last night would be ten kinds of wrong, and I'm too cute to go to jail. I wouldn't survive. Now, keep your head down for a thirty count and just breathe for a hot minute."

"If she finds you here—" Desperation she hadn't known him capable of clawed through his deep voice.

"Then Iron can slice her head off with that nice, shiny ax he was sharpening earlier in between mouthfuls of cider donuts." Then she leaned closer and massaged away the knots of tension at the back of his neck. "Do you really think they'd let her get anywhere near us right now? Or, for that matter, why would she bother with the element of surprise when there's a standing appointment on the books already?"

"Stop making so much damn sense, will you?" he ground out, leaning into her touch.

"Only when you tell me the truth about what we're really up against."

He peeled his eyes away from the ground to look at her, and she'd never been more grateful to see them lose their golden brightness. Then, faster than an inhale, he sat up and gripped the back of her neck. Their foreheads met in a soft caress that held more words than either of them had time left to say. Once his heated skin met hers, a flush of warmth fled his reddened cheeks, returning his skin to its usual vibrancy and tone. The sigh against her lips accompanied each knot melting away its strain, until the only heat that remained was the kindling worked up to smoking by the frenzied worries of her heart.

"Are you sure you can do this?" Molly asked for the fifth time since they'd been there.

Even through her narrow range of vision, she couldn't miss his annoying grin. "Ask me again, and I'll think you don't want me to win."

"I'd kindly ask you to check your male arrogance at the door, but seeing as we're outside, I'll table that for now so you can tell me what's going on."

"Noted." The scent of rich spices and fermented fruit clung to the leather of his coat. She recognized the fragrances from the gun oil he'd prepared his weapons with before they left for the festival. With all the spaces that male could hide something lethal, he never let her know just how many weapons he had on him, whether bladed, bulleted, or blunted.

It was a heady thing to know her soul bond could surprise her in this manner.

Brass grabbed her hand, the one bearing his mark beneath her high-cuff convertible mittens, and relaxed against the bench. When he didn't address her comments right away, she geared up for a second pass.

"Do you really think she—"

"Doesn't stand a fucking chance in hell," he growled, and that ferocious venom he'd let loose in the alleyway returned in full force.

"But you shot her with your angel fire, and you saw what she did. She popped those puppies out of her eyes like she was shelling peanuts. Her *eyes*, Brass. As in, actual organs."

He met her gaze and, despite his tense state, still managed to wink. "Those *puppies*, as you call them, weren't my full fire."

"They weren't . . . what?"

"I forgot that I hadn't replaced the bullets in my guns yet. What was stored in the chambers was still laced with my limited celestial fire from before you and I bonded."

It had been a long time since Molly had felt the delicate stirrings of hope. Oh, her stomach had seen no shortage of butterflies and rocks depending on the occasion, but hope?

Hope had always been for the lucky ones, not her, so when Brass looked at her with a twinkle in his eye instead of the pained wince she'd been used to seeing lately, she wasn't sure what to make of it.

Or the palm-sized velvet box he held out to her.

Molly's breath hitched. "If that's—"

"It's not. At least, not yet," he said with a boyish smirk.

And boy, did *that* stir up some feelings she'd been trying to ignore because velvet boxes usually meant rings. Rings usually meant copious usage of a certain four-letter word that neither of them had mentioned or even discussed yet. Soul bonds, sure. The deed had been done on that front, and with her help, Brass had gotten his powers back. But jewelry contingent upon emotional attachment to a cursed fallen angel who was about to face down an immortal witch goddess and possibly lose his soul?

She'd had Thanksgiving grocery lists with fewer things to sort through.

Brass broke through her spiraling thoughts. "It's something I want you to have. Open it. Please."

Slowly, as if the thing were about to bite her, Molly unhinged the rich blue velvet box. Nestled within a powder-blue bed of satin lay a brass sundial highlighted with raised Roman numerals and accented with verdigris and gold. Across the top of the dial, curving around the vertical stick that pointed northward, were three Latin words: *Sine Sole Sileo.*

There wasn't a diamond on earth that would have shone more brightly for her than the palm-sized sundial.

"Without sun, I am silent," Brass translated the inscription. "There isn't a creature on this planet that is immune from the sun and its charms. Cyro's demons must hide from it. Ragana's elements and moon cycles rely on it. It's the thing that unites humanity and pulls us all under a common umbrella, regardless of motives."

Then he lifted the sundial from the box and placed it in her hand. "This should remind you that you are so much more than what others have carved out for you. You're not just an orphan, Molly, or a restaurant owner. You're not merely a best friend or a soul bond. You're a woman with boundless humanity and love, and you are *not* alone." He paused for a moment, as if choosing his next words carefully. Her heart stopped beating until he spoke again. "Know that, as long as there is a sun in the sky, I will find my way back to you. Always. Whatever happens tonight, I will find you, no matter how long it takes."

He kissed her swiftly and surely, capturing her shock and any unspoken words she hadn't yet managed to conjure. The kiss was a burning promise against her lips. She clawed at his collar, desperate for more, yet somehow she knew her desperation wouldn't be enough to keep him there. Soon, the bite of the cold swooped in and replaced the warmth he had enveloped her with.

Heated tears traveled down the closed fan of her lashes and landed on her wind-burned cheeks.

When she opened her eyes again, he was gone.

CHAPTER 29

As far as last stands went, Brass figured a football field was as good a place as any to make his happen, especially at one with near-perfect conditions for what he was about to throw down. Like clockwork, Aurora High School students had been officially let out for winter break at two fifty that afternoon, with teachers and staff fleeing the premises at a precise two fifty-five.

Good. No one would be around to see the fireworks, and fireworks there definitely would be. With his full angel fire thrumming just below his skin, he'd worked up enough concentrated power to melt the rafters and star in a one-man fire-and-brimstone performance.

A few more minutes and it would all be over. His curse. Ragana. Everything he'd sacrificed for nearly two thousand years. All his torments would settle into the past like ashes beneath his boots.

Brass walked out onto the fifty-yard line with the weight of all he was leaving behind dragging at his heels. It'd been selfish to steal that kiss from Molly and then vanish. The memory of it ghosted across his lips with so much regret. Hit-and-runs had never been his style, but he'd had no choice. If he'd stayed, if he'd lingered one more second against her perfect mouth, he wasn't certain he'd ever have been able to leave her side again. Even during the briefest of moments when he had to lift his lips from hers and reposition himself to take more of her, the madness had already begun to creep in. As long as he was touching her, scenting her, filling his lungs with her in some vital way, he was whole.

Without her, however . . .

With great effort, Brass put Molly from his mind, let his eyes fall closed, and lifted his chin to the sky. Without the benefit of his sight, he knew the exact hues of what he'd find cresting over the stadium's high western walls. Burnt oranges illuminating amorphous gray nimbostratus clouds heavy with the promise of snow. The thinnest line of scarlet spanning the horizon's edge before a pregnant sun sank into shadow.

They were all things Molly, praise the mages, would see again and again if his plan worked.

All he had to do was buy himself time and breathe through the pain. Even as he stood there, armed to the teeth with firepower and fury, it was all he could do to keep focused. Sweat dripped down the back of his neck in a terrifying seduction. His temples pounded with promises not his own.

Fire warred with a rage that snapped at its confines. One more vicious bite and it would all be over.

Never.

Hang on just a little longer . . .

"What a sight you make, sentinel. I do say, red is most definitely your color." Ragana rose to her feet from the bleachers to his left, commanding all the regality of a queen who'd lost her throne to a younger, prettier monarch only to win it back after a messy beheading. Crimson robes had been traded for a hunter-green velvet gown. A golden-stitched bodice hugged her torso like an intricately woven plate of armor, while the low neckline offered up her breasts like the ripe sins they were.

Then she vanished from sight, leaving the silver metal seats as empty as he'd found them, only to reappear in front of him before he'd had a chance to blink.

"Did you miss me? Or rather, more to the point, did you enjoy my gift to you?" She stepped forward and trailed a long claw down the open collar of his coat. "I do wish I could have been there when you fucked her for the final time, but watching animals rut is not something that stirs my blood." She leaned in closer, caressing the curve of his ear with her tongue. He shuddered at the oily inkiness that slithered across his soul at the contact but fought to remain still as long as possible.

Soon. Let her get close.

"No," she crooned, "I much prefer being the one doing the rutting, especially when they're *my* animals."

"Eat shit and die," Brass barked.

"I'd rather eat you. Oh, your rage will be delicious on my tongue, especially after you've destroyed that cooking wench. As a matter of practice, the mad do always tend to go after what they love the most when they first turn, rather like a rabid wolf that wants to play with its pack, only to discover that its manner of sport has turned from belly rubs to bloodshed."

At the mention of Molly, Brass finally let the tether free. He grabbed Ragana's throat and, with a roar that shook the ground beneath them, engulfed them both in his full celestial angel fire. Once the dam had been opened, there was no stopping the power that poured forth. Rage and fire drowned them both in a monsoon of destruction.

Ragana screamed and flailed in his arms. The pale skin that she'd exposed so much of crackled and puckered beneath his fingers, causing corrugated deltas of fire to snake up her body. Mahogany hair caught in the flames and incinerated into the night.

It was working! Brass propelled his fire higher, hotter. He threw all of himself into it, even as it meant sacrificing his defenses against the rage within that had finally been unleashed.

Balance will be restored once she's dead. Just keep going . . .

Yes. More. One more push . . .

A blinding flare of power slammed into his chest and catapulted him across the field. His back smashed into the frozen earth with such force, the compacted soil split beneath him. His body sliced a trench several dozen yards long. Once his momentum had finally ceased, he hurried to his feet again, called upon his power, and . . .

Found nothing.

Through stilted mental movements, he frantically tried again to reach within himself for the power only he could command, that he *needed* to end this nightmare.

What reached him, instead, was a familiar feminine cackling that had haunted every single sunrise for two thousand years.

Ragana stood before him as healthy and hale as she'd been when she'd first arrived. Skin an unblemished porcelain. Hair a mass of silken waves.

Coal-black eyes promising that his death and the deaths of those he loved would not be swift.

"How?" he forced out through strained lungs and a body that wouldn't listen.

Ragana stood over him and flicked a speck of dirt off her bodice and onto his cheek. Then she leveled him with a tempestuous sneer. "I am the goddess of death, sentinel! I am fire and pain and fury and birth. Your power was mine the moment I cursed you. Again, you question my benevolence? Allow me to demonstrate it one final time, so there is no mistaking what your new existence holds for you."

With a swipe of her hand, the rage that had filled every muscle in his body so quickly it had begun to blind him receded to that familiar cage within his core. Brass cried out on a shuddering exhale of relief and flopped onto his back. Chest heaving, mind whirling, and limbs frozen to the ground, he had no choice but to lie there and listen.

"I'll never understand why you threw your lot in with mortals. They are ungrateful, worthless swine who are as fickle as the wind." She stormed over to him, knelt by his face, and, with a single claw depressed under his chin, turned his head from side to side. "Always looking to what new thing can serve their purpose, what they can exploit and corrupt for their own gain." She took her hand away and stood but not before she drew her heel back and kicked him in the ribs. He grunted behind the gag of her magic. "They never appreciate what had sustained them from the beginning, what had allowed them to thrive into the beings they are."

Ragana drew away from him. "Two thousand years ago, I was one of the most revered goddesses. Every new spring, mortals would leave me abundant sacrifices and carve my name into the stones of their people. Men would sing of me, while women would weave tapestries of my glory. Every fatted lamb, bowl of new milk, and rag of virgin blood smeared on my altars was such exquisite praise that I delighted in the mortals' prosperity. I ensured their herds remained healthy, their crops free of winter's frost and pestilence, and gifted fat, crying babies to their women. I gave them everything, and then one day, all the sacrifices stopped."

The whisper her words had fallen into was as short-lived as the sun as it finally fell below the horizon.

"I had been too generous for too long, it seemed. They'd gotten so used to the abundance that they'd forgotten the goddess who granted it all in the first place. With one blink, I could rob the milk from their cows and infest their fields with any number of vermin." Her upper lip curled while her eyes danced with freakish delight. "With a snap of my fingers, every single woman in that tribe would have wombs bleeding in rivers down the great mountains. They would feel my rage and remember exactly whom they had forsaken." Then her eyes refocused with solemn clarity. "But the cycle would have all started over again eventually. A new tribe, new sacrifices, effusive gratitude, and then . . . nothing. Until Cyro came along with a most intriguing proposal."

Brass's heated blood boiled in his veins as she spoke the demon ruler's name with such syrupy seduction.

"He found me and made me a quite delicious offer. Why rule among ungrateful mortals when I can rule among doting demons?" She smiled as the pieces clicked into place in Brass's mind and his eyes widened in horror. "Yes, sentinel, you have guessed correctly. In exchange for me providing his charmers with mortal souls to extinguish, he would provide me with a place of power at his side, an opportunity to rule the unruly." Then her features twisted into the fury he was expecting. "His apex—*my* apex—Sorig, had been the key to everything. He was Cyro's harbinger of death, his second and equal to no other charmer, as he was the first demon his master had ever created. The original apex. And he was brutally exquisite. He was to be my assurance, my guarantee that Cyro would not turn his back on me the way so many mortals had done." Claws lengthened at the tips of her fingers. "And I loved Sorig! Loved him enough to fuck him in any flesh form he took, male or female. Enough to scorch a thousand fields fallow for the promises of power he assured me he'd help me rise to at Cyro's side. And you took him from me!"

Her voice dropped lower, taking on the vibrating growl of a beast. "So now, as promised, I will take from you. Most completely." Her taloned fingertips stretched toward a spot on the field he'd not noticed before, but once the solar-powered lights kicked on around them, Brass saw the vision of his nightmares.

There, frozen by magic, was Molly.

THE TOES of Molly's boots bent back the blades of grass as she was dragged through the air by some unseen force. The constriction around her middle took hold of her breath, allowing it to release or catch at the whims of another. Never, in her thirty-one years of life, had she felt so utterly helpless and terrified . . .

Until she saw Brass, filthy and feral, writhing against the same hidden bonds that held her. His wild eyes met hers as she was pulled closer, near enough to see the tendons threatening to leap from his neck and his shoulders nearly popping with strain against what confined him.

"Do you know what my favorite pastime is?" Ragana trilled, breaking Molly's focus from the wrath etched on Brass's face. "I believe the term you mortals use nowadays is *people watching*. It's truly amazing what you learn when they think no one is looking." Her onyx eyes slid toward Brass. "How the most heroic among us often behave no better than the vilest scavengers, always slithering over those beneath them to rise to the top and protect themselves. So, imagine what shifting into the simple form of a hound afforded me. Oh, I did, indeed, learn so much about our fearless sentinel, as well as his human lady love."

Molly blanched at the use of the term but did her best to conceal it. Her neck vibrated with the need to turn and watch Brass's reaction. She couldn't. She wouldn't. He'd confided in her how he despised the looks of pity on his brothers' faces when he mentioned his curse, and she'd be damned if she had to experience the same expression painted on his face but aimed at her.

"Shut your *fucking* mouth," Brass hissed as he surged against his invisible bonds.

The lascivious crimson smile that curled Ragana's lips would forever remind Molly of blood welling up over bone. "Tell me, Molly, has he shared with you what he's discovered about your true nature? Why he's spent so much time in your company as of late, lapping at your heels and running around your little restaurant like a dog begging for scraps?"

"I don't care about anything that comes out of your mouth," Molly fired back.

"You will," Ragana assured her. "Especially when my mouth reveals more about your beloved than perhaps his own." Then she whirled away from Brass, her skirts flaring out around her ankles, and skewered Molly with those dark eyes. "Do you have headaches? Unusual bouts of heat coursing through your veins, even among the coldest temperatures? Or, perhaps, a general unease beneath your skin, like there are thousands of burrowing midges crawling throughout your very bones."

Molly continued to thrash and struggle, but something about Ragana's saccharine words stilled her efforts. She cranked her head in the witch's direction, fully prepared to douse her with a dose of murderous stink-eye, but instead, tendrils of truth pulled her to hear the rest.

"That's right, my dear. *You* have magic."

The bonds around Molly vanished, and she crumpled to the ground. A dizzying rush of oxygen to her long-deprived limbs gave her all the coordination of a newborn giraffe as she got her legs under her. "No, I don't. I'm human."

"Are you?"

Distant words surfaced to the front of her mind. Words that had been spoken against her bare neck in melting, drugging pleasure back when her largest concern was lusting after the employee who'd said them.

Oh, little witch . . . I love how responsive you are. Where shall I touch you next, hmm? What will make your magic sing?

Molly glanced sidelong at Brass but addressed Ragana. "We're soul bound. It's why my body has felt different lately."

"Is *that* what he told you? Oh, my dear. Men are truly the consummate liars, aren't they? And yet women are always painted as the conniving she-devils. I'll never understand why men always turn to deceit when the truth is so much more powerful to play with." Then the witch took Molly's hands in hers and stared down at her with the devotion of a mother imparting hard-won wisdom to a naïve adolescent. Brass's golden eyes tracked Molly's hands, which had grown heavy with the weight of her doubt, especially as she didn't remove them from Ragana's grip.

"You are an empath with a wonderful burgeoning magic of your own. I dare say it's gotten stronger with your little love connection, but it's the reason your angel sought you out in the first place and why he can't help but stay at your side. Your power draws his emotions into you, lessening the burden he'd been doomed to carry alone. It's why my curse has been regrettably less prevalent in his mind when he's kept you near. It has nothing to do with your little bonding, unless, of course, you count the return of his full celestial power. That he *did* need you for."

For some reason, the legend of Icarus shot to the forefront of Molly's mind as Ragana released her hands and they fell motionless at her sides. Beeswax wings had always been part of the standard tale, but Molly had always enjoyed the version that spoke of the individual feathers more. How they had been constructed of metal first, before being cobbled together in a leather framework using beeswax. It was a small distinction but a significant one.

Foundations, after all, were truly nothing without the bonds that tied them. As an orphan, she knew that better than most.

Standing before Brass, however, still innately leaning into his magnetic strength that relentlessly called to her, she couldn't help but see the cracks beginning to form.

Or perhaps how long they'd been there when she was too blind to see them.

"Is that true?" she whispered. "Do I have magic? *Real* magic? That you knew about?"

Ragana's singsong voice chimed throughout the arena, filling Molly's heart with dagger-like shards. "Do be honest, sentinel. Show her that honor you're so proud of."

When he didn't answer, Molly stepped closer to him with sluggish steps. "Brass?"

And then she saw the one thing she'd fought so hard her entire life to protect herself against. It was etched on the rigid outlines of a face she'd memorized and had formed in the fires of a gaze her soul called its own.

Pity. Regret. Shame. And the truth.

"Yes," he ground out. "But—"

"No buts. We're done. You are mine." Ragana curled her fingers into a fist, and a wave of magic blanketed Brass. Molly screamed as she felt the instant his tether on his rage snapped. All other magic binding him fell away, and a red haze fell over eyes that had once consumed her in their undying emotion and unspoken promises.

Then he stood, and Molly's heart broke for the second time.

Brass was no longer her angel but a cursed beast.

CHAPTER 30

A manic cackling echoed through the night, growing louder as Brass's metallic wings spread from his back. Everything Molly had come to recognize about him had vanished with the swiftness of clouds as even they scuttled to get out of range.

"No!" Molly ran to him, tears streaming down her cheeks, but an invisible wave of magic rippled in front of her and blocked her path. Through the waves, that disorderly thatch of hair she'd smoothed back countless times fell over vermilion eyes that were not Brass's and never made a move to land on her.

Molly screamed at Ragana. "What did you do to him?"

"Only that which he reaped upon himself," the witch hollered back. "Your kind never did think of consequences or what might happen when it was time for actions to be answered for. Now, thanks to *my* sentinel, I can resume what I started two thousand years ago."

Ice formed in Molly's veins. "What are you saying?"

"I'm saying," she sneered, "that Cyro's need has not changed, and neither has our bargain. Souls for status. That was the arrangement we struck, and for ones such as us, time is of little consequence." Then she swept her hand toward Brass, and he immediately took to the sky, pumping his powerful wings against the night. "The more souls my sentinel extinguishes, the sooner Cyro will be able to make his advance on the Empyrean and the sooner we will both reign."

Panic crawled up Molly's throat as she stood, helpless to stop what was happening. She had no way to reach Brass, if he was even still aware of her, and likewise, she had no weapons. Desperation clawed at her like a wild beast. She was no match for Ragana. Whatever power the witch insinuated Molly had was clearly unhelpful when it came to combat. Once again, Molly was alone, overwhelmed, and—

"Now, I don't generally like to use the B-word, but when one finds the perfect embodiment, one must pay tribute, you hear me?" A flash of reddish-brown metal swept across Molly's vision toward Ragana's direction. Bronze, fully transformed and armed with a halberd that looked like it had severed a head or two before breakfast, kicked the witch's legs out from under her and hovered his weapon above her to strike. "Light's out, bitch."

Ragana shook off her surprise and hissed into the night, then brought her palms together in front of her face, redirecting the blade's trajectory. With a fire of her own, the witch countered the attack, slamming beams of flames into Bronze's chest.

And that was when the other fighting sounds registered. Behind Molly, the rest of the angels had arrived and split the flank, half taking on Ragana while the others tried to subdue a raging Brass. Wings, blades, and guns peppered the night sky with streaks of angel fire. Bodies clashed with roars that shook the stadium. In midair, Iron and Titan flew predatory circles around Brass. Against the darkening sky, weapons dangled from fists that had yet to unclench as they delivered blow after blow among brothers.

With the magic shield around Molly lowered and forgotten,

it allowed her to do the one thing she'd spent a lifetime perfecting.

She ran, bolting toward the nearest set of bleachers.

This can't be happening. They shouldn't be fighting each other. They should be fighting her!

Just as Molly reached the metal benches, another voice flared to life in her mind. This one, however, was sweet and sultry and, hell if she knew how, but *warm*. Warm like the sun's kiss on her shoulders. Warm and safe and soothing.

Molly. Only you can prevent this. Embrace who you are, and Ragana will be no more.

Molly jolted mid-step and grabbed at the chain-link fence for support.

"Who said that?" she cried, whipping her head in all directions.

Someone who has watched over you and yours since the ice first formed along the shores of the north.

"That's not fucking helpful," she screamed and gasped as Brass kicked free of Iron's hold midair and used his brother's stolen iron mace to wallop Titan on the side of his head. The angel went down in a devastating spiral and crashed into the ground, leaving a crater in his wake.

Help yourself, Molly, as you always have. Ragana was only half right about your magic.

"Magic? What magic?" she cried to the thin air.

You are not just an empath but an empathic siphon. Only you can free your cursed angel and destroy Ragana. Use his rage. Use your bond. Take his fury unto yourself, and propel it with the spark of the Eternal Flame that now joins you both. His full celestial fire has returned to him. Feel that power and embrace what your bond can do, what only you can do, Molly.

"Oh, you've got to be kidding me." But the voice had abandoned her on a brisk current, though what it left behind was neither chilly nor unsettling.

The flutter began in her stomach. Just a little tickle, but enough for her to realize it grew in intensity each time she laid eyes on one of the battling angels. When she finally found Brass among the melee, his furiously twisted features and snarling expression fanned her body's awareness into something tangible.

Yes, Molly. Use your gift. Instinct will guide you. Trust the bond.

Out of options, Molly closed her eyes. God, what was she doing? What in the actual hell was she doing? She should be looking for a weapon or something, not standing by, becoming one with her feelings while the only family she'd ever known destroyed themselves.

And then every pore, muscle, and vein in her body filled to bursting with a rage not unlike the most volatile volcanoes. Brass's curse slammed into her with the force required to split atoms, to create entire solar systems. It was light and energy and emotion all coiled into a ball of pure pain that made her weep for every living thing that had ever and would ever know sorrow.

Was this what Brass felt? How could one *not* go mad at the mercy of that devastation? It was too much, too crippling, too—

Now, Molly! Now is your chance!

The voice punched through the din of the emotional destruction Molly was harboring. Her tear-filled eyes flew open as her chest heaved and pain wheezed out of burned lungs. Then the fire came. Blue flames circled her limbs in a protective fury, fueled by an indestructible tether between her soul and Brass's. She almost screamed at the sight of her arms amid the flames, but Brass's reassuring words from earlier punched through her fear.

My fire will never harm you, Molly. It recognizes you now. You have to know that.

Ragana was on the field, one palm swirling a whirlwind around her wrist while the other commanded a tunnel of drenching water. Together, they created a typhoon of torment against the angels, who sputtered and gasped for the air Ragana had robbed them of.

But while the witch was focused on those in front of her, she'd left her back wide open.

"Bingo."

Molly didn't have time to figure out the whys and hows. Instead, she just let go, relinquishing every cursed cry from her body into a beam of celestial fire straight into the witch. Ragana roared at the impact. The green velvet of her gown ripped away, leaving her skin exposed to the flames of the cursed magic Molly hurled at her. Pearlescent skin flayed into ribbons of torn flesh and blood under the onslaught of Molly's siphoned emotions.

"*No! NO!*" The witch's screams were swallowed up as more of her body was incinerated by the force of her own warped curse and Molly's soul-bound power. Blood gave way to bleached bone. Charcoal eyes exploded under the pressure of the onslaught. With one final flare, Ragana's remains were reduced to ashes upon the earth.

The din soon settled and quickly gave way to an assortment of grunts and groans croaking from various battered angels.

Bronze was the lightest on his feet, by far. Made sense, as most of his injuries seemed to stem from the gaping shoulder and the neck wound he sported. "Molly! Are you hurt?" He helped her to her feet with his one good arm.

"How the hell can you ask me that when you look like you just got into it with a vampire and forgot to use your safe word? And why the hell are you running? I can literally see blood pumping out of holes in you."

He waved her concerns away as if she'd just made him aware of a marinara sauce stain on his favorite graphic tee. "A night or two underground and I'll be good," he said with a carefree smile, though she did *not* miss how labored his breathing was. "You scared the shit out of us, though. What happened to you? One minute, you were in front of us walking to your car after the festival. The next, you were swallowed up by some soupy mist."

"Ragana," Molly confirmed, while she took off her mittens and held them to his neck. "Some sort of magic."

After she skewered him with a *don't be a bro, take the damn mittens* look, he wisely pressed them to his wound. "Took us a minute to find you guys. Brass was much easier to track."

The mention of his name caused her heart to tighten, and she forced herself to look out onto the field. At the far end from where she stood, between the away team's goalposts, Brass was being helped to his feet by Iron and Titan. The causes of their injuries seemed much less magical and elemental in nature and far more blunt force trauma related. Brass's right shoulder hung lower than his left. The clavicle supporting it had been broken and flattened, while his gait was slowed significantly by a knee that wouldn't bend correctly.

"Molly," he cried and leaned on his brothers for support as the three of them hurried closer to her.

For the first time, though, Molly didn't move. She was beyond happy to see him alive and breathing, but her heart . . .

The three of them had just passed the thirty-yard line when a flare of white light at Molly's back blanketed the field, halting everyone in their tracks. Once Molly was able to blink away the floaters obstructing her vision, her consciousness settled on yet another beautifully regal woman towering over her.

Bolts of golden shimmering fabric draped like honey over the woman's shapely curves. Her brown shoulders were bare, save for the woven silver shawl wrapped around them in a comforting embrace. Curls of spun straw were piled high on top of her head and were anointed with the most opulent crown of glittering golden tassels Molly had ever seen, not that she'd seen many. Perhaps one or two in those Baltic mythology texts she studied as a teenager when she wanted to learn more about her birth heritage.

As the shock of seeing the woman began to bake off, Molly finally analyzed some of the pieces that shone before her. The gold, the crown, the solar imagery woven into the woman's shawl . . .

And then, with a smile of knowing encouragement, the woman leveled her sunburst eyes directly at Molly.

Holy. Shit. She can't be . . .

"I am Saulé, goddess of the sun, protector of the earth's fertility and its orphans and shepherds, and guardian of the unlucky and unloved."

Of all the possible things to do in such a scenario, Molly executed the first one that came to mind. Her knees hit the grass before her body could protest.

"None of that, young one. I don't require such servitude. It is *I* who exists to serve my people."

Molly yanked Bronze down next to her and spoke in frightened tones to the goddess's gold shoes. "I'm happy to stay down here, just in case you change your mind."

"Rise," Saulé stated in a commanding voice. "Rise and hear me, for I have much to say."

One by one, every broken and battered person hobbled to their feet, some with the help of others. In her case, it was with the help of her disbelief.

When she was fully ambulatory, the stunning smile that radiated from the goddess, along with the noticeable lack of weapons being drawn around Molly, was enough to calm her nerves long enough to at least convince herself she wasn't about to die within the next five minutes.

"You were the voice in my head," Molly confirmed.

"That I was. I have been your guardian for some time. The moment your parents perished and you were left alone in this world, I have kept my eye on you."

Molly swallowed back a cold, distant worry. "How did you know that my—"

The goddess's hand floated up to play with the gold pendant at her neck. "You are descended from ancient Baltic tribal elders, ones who, two thousand years ago, refused to make further sacrifices to the goddess Ragana and instead brought those sacrifices to a cliffside altar in the north, where they gifted me the best of their livestock, food, and vegetation."

Understanding bloomed in Molly's mind. "The tribes Ragana mentioned, the ones she said abandoned her and took for granted the abundance she offered, they gave their wares to you instead."

Saulé nodded, the tassels dancing about her temples. "Yes, except Ragana's reasoning, like so much of her ideology, was flawed. There had been a blight plaguing neighboring lands and villages to the east. People were disappearing, and entire tribes were being whittled down to unsustainable numbers. Your ancestors, concerned as they were about it reaching their own tribe, prayed to Ragana for aid, as they always did in times of strife, but that time, nothing changed. So, they then turned to another deity and offered me their sacrifices in exchange for my help."

"The charmers," Brass croaked out. "I remember. They were stealing souls and destroying them. Robbing children from their beds, slaughtering entire families."

Molly stiffened at the sound of his voice, which had moved closer, but she kept her focus on the goddess in front of her.

"Yes, sentinel. But unlike in their request to Ragana, the prayers they offered to me held a different ask." Saulé lifted her chin high. "The elders pleaded to me for their tribe's safety, that is true, but they also begged me to watch over the souls that had gone missing from the neighboring tribes." A sadness dimmed the vibrance in her eyes. "While it is not within my power to protect those souls which have moved on from the mortal plane, no matter how cruelly they left it, it is my sacred duty to guide the orphans and unlucky on their paths while they exist here. You, Molly, are a descendant of one whom I was asked to protect, one of the ancient tribal elders who first sought me out to watch over his people."

A fogginess misted over Molly's understanding, even as her heart lightened from a relieved burden that had been a vice around her soul since the day she was born. "What?"

Saulé held up a hand, urging Molly to save her questions. Golden rings adorning the goddess's long fingers winked beneath the stadium's solar lighting. "There is one more thing. You have more in common with the elder you are descended from, Valdis, than you realize. Because of Valdis's desire to help his people, I gifted him and his bloodline with the power of empathic siphoning. Not merely the ability to feel what others feel but to take it within yourself and use that source of energy for good. Valdis chose to use his skills to temper the fears of his tribe and direct their energy into the growth of crops, felling wood for lumber, and calling the sea to him with favorable waves so his people could fish and travel. Over the centuries, however, the power had grown mild and mostly dormant in Valdis's descendants, as tribes thinned and larger cities formed. That is, until you bonded with your angel."

Molly hardly had time to dwell on the fact that she had magic—real *magic!*—before she was forced to reexamine her fresh hurt. "As unbelievable as all this is, what does the soul bond have to do with it?"

In the corner of her eye, Brass stiffened. He hadn't missed that she didn't refer to him by name.

Saulé cast a forlorn glance in the area behind Molly where she knew Brass to be. "Your magic sought out your soul bond because the emotions you would share in coming together would be enough of an empathic event to awaken your full magic. Much, I gather, in the same way your angel came into his full celestial power."

"I'm right here," Brass ground out. "You can talk to me."

"I'd rather not, sentinel." The look Saulé cast him was enough to wither a thousand-year-old redwood. "It was only through your combined powers that Ragana was destroyed. Goddesses, I assure you, are not easy to kill." The threat lingered in the air, turning their breaths icier. "It is only through my protection of Molly, and my power passed down to her, that she was able to break your curse. Soul bond or no, that does not entitle you to betray her trust."

Pinpricks stabbed at Molly's eyes at the sharp reminder of what he'd done and the mess between them that was not so easily swept away.

Through her blurry lashes, Molly could just make out the golden straps of Saulé's sandals crisscrossing the goddess's feet. Then under the insistent force of a slender finger beneath her chin, Molly met the goddess's face. The contact was what Molly imagined it would feel like to touch a star . . . without the whole burning to a crisp bit. Latent humming energy, the kind that gave succor to every plant and planet, flowed from the contact point, drying her tears instantly.

"Hear me, Molly Resnick. You were not born under a bad star, as you have always feared. Quite the opposite, in fact," Saulé said with a smirk.

You have to love a goddess with cheek.

"You are a creature of the sun like Valdis, and your power comes from those you feed. If you ever doubt yourself again, look to the sun and know you will always find your path. I suspect, in many ways, a part of you has always been drawn to the sun, hmm?"

Molly thought back to all her solar trinkets. Key chains, paintings, things she'd never made a connection with until now.

All this time . . . Had she subconsciously known this about herself all along?

A soft snort rumbled at her elbow. "Well, don't look directly *at* the sun. That's a recipe for retinal incineration. Totally not worth it." Bronze laughed at his joke, but all Molly heard was several male groans and a muttered, "Fucking idiot," that she hoped had escaped Saulé's notice.

It hadn't.

The goddess turned her attention to Bronze. "One word, sentinel, before I depart." A sly smile curved her lips. "Not all curses are created equal. Some require more skill than luck to defeat them. One day soon, you shall meet a woman to challenge you in this regard."

At that, his eyes lit up. "A woman, eh?"

"Yes. I wish you luck. Lycans are so very fond of their games."

If Molly had a pin, she would have run back over to the bleachers and dropped it just to confirm everyone would have heard it as it clacked onto the metal bench in an eerily silent stadium.

All levity left Bronze's face. "What?"

A final blaze of light illuminated the field. Molly and the others all threw up their arms to shield their eyes. By the time she risked a glance, Saulé was gone.

Don't go.

Molly wasn't sure whether her silent plea was born of a daughter who'd just found her true family or from a woman who wasn't prepared to face what was currently lumbering up to her from behind.

"Molly," Brass cried. "I can explain everything."

I can explain everything. . .

Were there ever four words in the English language that were more symbolic of guilt? Entire talk show episodes had been programmed and cast around the *I can explain everything* setup. The admission of guilt and subsequent groveling were instant ratings fodder.

Well, she wasn't in the mood to be someone's entertainment. Or their regret.

"I have questions," she said, cutting off his next line of bullshit. "And if you cared for me at all, you're going to answer them."

Brass elbowed his brothers off him and forced his weight on his mangled leg. Worried panic shone behind his strained eyes, and didn't that just gut her heart even more? When he nodded tightly, seemingly already knowing he didn't have a horse in the race, she bit back a sad laugh.

Still no words for me.

But oh, she had plenty for him.

"Did you know I have magic?" Molly trained her gaze on him, never once glancing at the others. If she saw pity there, she'd fucking lose it. It was by some miracle she was even holding it together at all.

"I did."

"And is that what drew you to me? Is that why you ripped down my *Help Wanted* sign and never let me out of your sight? Because it calmed your curse?"

Brass's jaw ticked on words she wished he'd say. Oh, how she wished he'd say no, that her wit or food or, hell, she'd even take cute ass, were the true draws, at least in the beginning. How some part of her that made her *her* was worthy of the closeness they'd grown to share.

Just say it. Say it so I don't have to wonder.

"Molly, please . . ." The desperation in his voice was almost enough to drown out the desperation in her heart.

"Just say it!" she cried, tears already leaking out of the corners of her eyes.

Brass's auburn head lowered. "At first, yes, but it wasn't—"

"When did you know? Hmm? When did you suspect I have magic?"

"All the *fucking* time!" he roared so loudly that she had to take a step back. "When I saw you in the alley and was slammed with the look of shame on your face that another man had caused. I almost lost my fucking mind then and nearly melted the dumpster with a thought. Instead, it was *your* thoughts that nearly did it. When *my* angel fire erupted in the dumpster on its own, that was when I first wondered whether you had something to do with it. The next time was in your apartment, when I blew the fucking door off its hinges in my rage. One kiss from you then had taken it all away. You'd done more to lessen my fury in two seconds than I'd managed to do in two thousand years. And let's not forget the blown pipe and what preceded it." His eyes darkened, quickening the pace of her bruised heart as they both recalled the sexual tension that had nearly consumed them, along with her entire restaurant.

"Every single time my rage and emotions were about to get the better of me, you were there, absorbing it all into your slim frame and redirecting it. The writing was on the wall, Molly. Yes, I knew you had magic," he seethed and lowered his eyes in anguish. "I knew it from the moment you used it to steal my soul, when I realized I would have given it to you regardless."

Molly's heart shattered. Hearing the grocery list of their encounters, and the vitriolic delivery Brass had recited them with, was a blow-by-blow of faults laid at her feet from the one man who had never faulted her for anything.

It was enough to hasten one final question to the surface. "Were you planning on telling me?"

Wild dread spread across Brass's face. "Molly, please let me—"

"If you say my name one more fucking time, it'll be the last time you ever say it. Now, answer me." She wasn't yelling anymore. There was no point. Her lungs had already gone on strike, her tears dried up.

Only her heart, shriveled, worthless thing that it was, still hung around so it could witness the final swing of the executioner's ax. Damn thing always did have a flair for the dramatic.

"Were. You planning. On. Telling me."

Then the deeply resonant voice that had whispered her to sleep and coaxed her wildest dreams to the surface also pounded the nails into her coffin.

"No," he relented.

Molly kept her eyes to the ground, refusing to look at him as she tunneled into her pocket and heaved the sundial he'd given her at his feet. It landed with a thud in the chewed-up earth. "You're right about one thing. I *am* so much more than what others have carved out for me, including you. Don't ever come looking for me again."

She made it out of the stadium with no apologies or pleas chasing her. No explanations or grand gestures.

As usual, Brass's silence spoke volumes.

CHAPTER 31

Three weeks later

Brass decided that, when it came to the seasons, winter was a mean girl.

Her frosty face could be so serene and whimsical, pumping out the fresh powder and dusting mountains with snowcaps of unmatched beauty. But all it took was a dirty look and a dip in pressure, and she hammered out storm after storm of freezing rain, nor'easters, and spite.

Fucking lucky. If only all tantrums were so easily tolerated.

The park bench he warmed had been his permanent late-afternoon perch since Molly had not only dressed him down but castrated and condemned him. The worn wood had long since lost the warmth of her when he'd kissed her there last, though his senses still sought it out regardless.

All because he couldn't fucking say what Molly had needed to hear. A thousand times since that night, he'd stayed awake replaying the battle in his mind. Not the battle against Ragana but the one against his heart. He'd always chosen his words carefully and had long since learned that it was better not to say anything than to say the wrong thing. Would it have helped her to know that, yes, he knew she had magic but it terrified him? Did she not see the havoc magic had wreaked on his life already? Magic wielded at the hands of a woman?

A woman who was not your soul bond. A woman who perpetuated far more crimes against you than the one whose only crime was giving you your life back.

Brass crunched his boot down on a clump of ice, then growled when the block shattered all too quickly.

Damn, he needed to break something. To throw himself into the sea, to have the frigid ocean batter his flesh until he could no longer feel the hollowness that had been left behind these past three weeks. He needed to—

"You know, the sun will set whether you're there to watch it or not." Rhode's approaching voice did more to scratch at Brass's wounds than soothe them.

"Are you the babysitter du jour, then?" Brass inquired over his shoulder. "Who drove you?" As sour as he was, he knew better than to highlight the fact that since Rhode had been returned to them, he had not yet been able to call forth his wings.

Rhode settled his weight onto the bench. "I drove myself."

Brass lifted an eyebrow.

"Oh, don't act so surprised. I've been driving for over a month. You'd know that if you bothered to spend time with anything other than your bad mood."

"I am *not* in the—"

"Mood? Yes. I just established that. Mages, man. Did the woman rob you of your memory in addition to your good sense?"

"What do you want, Rhode? I'm tired."

The angel's heated umber gaze raked over Brass's profile in

silent challenge, but Brass kept his eyes trained on the horizon. On the extremely short list of things he wanted to do that day, getting into it with Rhode wasn't one of them. Besides, the sun would settle soon, taking the day and his connection to Molly along with it.

"I realize it is ironic for one lost angel to provide guidance to another lost angel, and yet here we are."

Brass's spine tensed at the allusion. It wasn't lost on him how significant such a statement was. Ever since Rhode's captivity, the angel's secrets have been his own. Often, he'd blame his silence on tampered memories, but Brass hadn't endured two thousand years of torment not to recognize it in another's eyes.

"I don't need sympathy," Brass remarked, keeping his suspicions to himself.

"Good, 'cause you'll not get it. Least of all from me."

"For fuck's sake, speak plainly."

Rhode cast him a droll look and crossed his ankle over his knee with a casual grace Brass had always envied. "You're lost, brother. You need a map."

"A map," he parroted, letting his disbelief linger on the P.

"Yes, a map. How are you expected to see the way forward without guidance? You've been sent astray for two thousand years, Brass. As I've been made to understand, you've been here but not really. Alive but barely. Of course it's impossible to see the next move when, until now, every road available to you has been paved with booby traps. Terrible phrase, that," he muttered under his breath. Then he leaned forward and rested his forearms on his knees, adopting the same frustrated sitting stance as Brass. "But even the most intrepid mortal explorers found ways to push through."

Push through? Was he serious?

"I cannot simply *push through*," Brass snapped, then swept a hand out in front of him. "There is no navigating this for me. Molly won't speak to me. She won't even look at me, and I refuse to dishonor her further by forcing her to hear explanations on why she should forgive another man in a long line of men who have betrayed her."

He heaved out lungfuls of an emptiness he couldn't escape, knowing that a darker fear always rushed in on the heels of his laden breath. One he'd never given a voice to . . . until now.

"But she's my *soul bond!* The one creature in this existence who carries the light of the Eternal Flame within her soul, which has, against all odds, found my own light's spark. And she has *magic!*" He dropped his head into his palms. "Do you see? Do you see why, after all I have endured, the idea of being that close, that vulnerable, with a woman who possesses magic has me clawing for a way out?"

There it was. The pin in the grenade that he couldn't stop fiddling with. With Molly at arm's length and her magic kept at a distance, it didn't matter how her true motivations would manifest over time, because he ensured she'd made a decision that was for the best.

Even if the grenade did go off, he'd be free of the blast zone.

Eternally miserable but free.

"What if she uses it against me? Maybe not today but one day," he wondered aloud.

Rhode met his anguished plea with a sympathetic silence, before responding with, "And what if the sea rises?"

"Don't do that," Brass barked. "Don't ask those asinine questions. You know what I mean."

"Fine. I won't if you won't."

Brass whirled on him. "Are we children now? This isn't a game to me. This is my life!"

"Yes, it is," Rhode conceded. "So go and fucking live it." His words took on a harsher tone, one Brass had not heard him use since they'd fought in combat together before the Fall. "Some of us would give what's left of their dark souls to have the mere chance for what you have, what you're throwing away."

"And what do I have?" he asked more calmly.

The waning light of the setting sun cast a sparkling brilliance across Rhode's tense features. Still, there were shadows. Brass suspected there always would be.

"You have someone who's only ever required the truth from you. Somewhere in this impossibly tiny town, your soul's other half exists—and she's alone." He cast a weary glance toward the vast expanse of empty field around them. The faraway look in his eyes spoke of more than snow-covered grass. "We all fought. For every soul in the Empyrean, we fought. Has your mate ever given you a reason to prove she is also not worth fighting for?"

Brass leaned back against the bench and watched as the final rays of light sank below the horizon. Once the shadows had fully descended, he pulled his hand from his pocket and ran his thumb around the raised edge of the sundial he'd given Molly.

The sundial she'd tossed back at him.

What *had* Molly proven to him? Certainly, her tenacity when it came to owning and operating a business on her own. Her everlasting marathon toward greatness, whether it was perfecting a souffle or working around a perceived flaw. She'd gone as far as to secure a lucrative deal with a local baker just to supply her patrons with the very best baked goods, regardless of her faith in her skills. She'd proven her infuriating kindness toward strays, whether they be benevolent chefs with a doting uncle complex or a maniacal witch-turned-wiry hound.

And then there was her ability to ignore her better judgment, despite what life had taught her, and hold out a hand to him, of all people, when he needed it most. Repeatedly.

"Fuck." Brass groaned as he pulled at the frayed ends of his hair. "I don't know how to do this. I don't know how to get past all this. What I feel for her, what she means to me, it's far more significant than any curse. I feel changed *in here*," he said, poking at the cavern where his heart cried out. "It feels far more elemental than any magic. No, it feels *essential*, indestructible, but I don't know for sure. How can I know?"

A firm hand settled on his shoulder. "That's just it. You can't, because it's not up to you. Fate has a hand in it, yes, as it does for all of us, but the answers you seek can only come from Molly, and only if you actually talk to her."

"I have. I've tried."

Rhode pegged him with a glare. "Use your words, Brass. Several, in a row, all at once. Repeat as necessary until she loves you back."

"I know how to— Wait, what did you just say?"

Had Rhode just said *loves*? The emotion was so foreign to him, yet instantly settled into the darker parts of his soul, working to mend the damaged bits and testing the new concept. Could Molly ever love him back? To accomplish that, it would mean he'd have to love her first.

Do I?

The thought humbled him, not for the enormity of all it entailed, but for the absurdity that he hadn't realized it sooner.

Holy shit. He *loved* Molly.

"I love her," Brass breathed, stunned by how simple it all was.

Rhode looked to the sky in exasperation. "Thank the mages, he's finally figured it out."

"The mages have nothing to do with this," Brass assured him as he leaped to his feet, heart thrumming with anticipation of what he must do. "I'm through banking on what-ifs and maybes."

Only Molly's certainty mattered. He just prayed that once he finally told her everything, it would be enough to include him in it.

CHAPTER 32

There were certain drawbacks to being an empathic siphon, Molly quickly learned. Chief among them being that, when everyone around you was basking in their post-holiday happiness that snowballed into the ramp-up for their Valentine's Day merriment, she felt it *all*. It was as if the giddiness of every single one of Grandma's sugar cookies had been crammed into a capsule, shot with a champagne cocktail of cheer, and then chased with boink-inducing bonbons. And try as she might, she'd not been able to summon Saulé again to ask for advice. That was, if one could even summon a goddess anymore. It wasn't like Valdis had left her instructions on the finer points of her ancestral heritage.

Seriously, did nobody ever think to write these things down?

So, instead, she did the only thing she could under the duress of nursing a betrayed and broken heart while getting up close and personal with everyone else's: she cooked.

After closing the restaurant an hour before and officially sending Benny packing on a much-needed trip to the Dominican Republic with his wife for two weeks, she threw herself into her deeply favorite pastime: baking spinach knishes.

She liked to think the copious amount of potatoes mixed in with the spinach was implied, but she still preferred to lean on the spinach's more fiber-friendly reputation when thinking about the delectable treats. An eerily empty kitchen that held far too many memories for her liking was enough of a judgmental beast. No need to add carb-shaming to the list because up until that point in her life, pounding out a tray or three of pillowy golden brown pockets stuffed with salty mashed potato and garlicky spinach had reliably been the only thing that *hadn't* let her down.

For obvious reasons, churros had been removed from that list.

Molly cinched her apron tighter around her waist and arranged her workspace to her liking. Except, where the sight of a dough ball the size of a corpulent baby usually sent her heart a-flutter, the only thing it produced this time was a pang of loneliness that did excellent work of poking at her ever-present wound.

Rolling out her knishes, she remembered all too late, was a two-person job.

"Shit," she muttered, thoroughly annoyed for allowing herself to stumble, ass-first, back into the cavern of depression she'd only begun to crawl out of.

Well, *thought* about crawling out of. One day. Maybe.

Molly threw some plastic wrap over her dough baby and rested a hip against the counter in exhaustion. Even empty, the kitchen still held hauntings of Brass. She couldn't walk through the door to the dining room without remembering how he'd always held it open for her *just* before she got there, with his bus tub filled high with dishes and perched securely on his strong shoulder. Or the heat at her back while he watched her as she punched in ticket orders and remembered the kisses he'd stolen in her office moments before.

No, he'd never watched her, she corrected. He'd *studied* her.

She knew that now, with no little bit of shame. He'd been studying her for any signs of magic and locking his findings away for his benefit. What that benefit was, exactly, she didn't know.

Because he'd never freaking told her.

And worst of all, that small, hurt part of her desperately wanted to give him the benefit of the doubt. Somewhere over the past few weeks, her well-honed self-preservation had abandoned her and was inclined, instead, to throw its lot in with the male who'd made any hope of finding happiness a fool's errand.

Even though he'd finally begun to feel like the home she'd always been searching for.

Being a soul bond, it seemed, was worth its weight in bullshit.

Three consecutive knocks at the door drew her from her brooding. "Why does no one want to read anymore? We're closed!" she hollered to the person crowding out the tiny window of the restaurant's front door. Backlit by the fierce late-afternoon light, the figure was all sloping shoulders and shadows and very much not welcome.

"We're closed," Molly said to the glass panel. "We'll open again tomorrow at—"

Molly froze when the curl of a familiar forelock stood out in relief against the glass. A fine misting of fluffy snow had built up a decent skim coat on the top of his head. White puffs of breath fogged the glass in strong, quick spurts as his breathing quickly began to match her own.

Brass.

Her heart tumbled backward on itself at the sight of him. Eyes a familiar shade of misery. Mouth a grim line that looked like it had forgotten how to smile. Brows sunken into a pleading slant that begged for something her battered heart could no longer offer.

But he was outside her door. After three weeks of radio

silence, which had sent her hemorrhaging heart into full-on *do not resuscitate* status, he was there.

Were they doing this, then? Did she even *want* to do this?

A part of her wanted to donkey-kick him into the street, then throw the ineffectual chain lock home for emphasis.

A part of her wanted to rip the door off just to drink him in.

In the end, curiosity won out as she undid the deadbolt, pretended to undo the chain lock she always forgot to engage, and threw the door open.

"Hi," he said quietly.

"What do you want?" she snapped at him.

A sorry desperation sparked through his amber eyes. "You." He'd proclaimed it like a general would shout it to his soldiers at the forefront of battle. It was a rallying cry bolstered with the force of hopeful victory among most certain defeat.

It nearly gutted her.

"You and everything else I was foolish enough not to fight for," he added.

There was something about seeing a wounded animal that, no matter how malicious or vengeful it may be, always softened her heart. Or in her case, what little was left of it.

She didn't invite him in but simply turned from the door and walked back into the kitchen. A moment later, the door *snicked* closed, and that recognizable heat at her back returned. Damn if her body didn't react on contact, warming beneath the gaze her skin had memorized and traitorously missed. She didn't say anything, however. Couldn't.

Because when she turned around to face him, Brass simply held out a picture to her, and any autonomic lung function she'd previously laid claim to up and vanished.

Sooo not helpful.

"What's this?" she asked as she took what he offered with trembling fingers. "A postcard?"

She *really* wished people would stop handing her shit like that.

Quaint picturesque brick buildings with mismatched russet and black roofs huddled together in the old-timeyest of old-timey city squares against the sunset backdrop of a lava sky. A bulbous cathedral stood sentinel above the tiny cityscape. In the background, the cable-stayed Vanšu Bridge she used to sketch pictures of in high school stretched along the Daugava River, shuttling travelers into Latvia's capital city of Riga.

Talk about random and breathtaking.

"Why are you showing me this? This isn't a stand-in for basic open-mouthed communication. I've had three weeks of silence from you and now you're sending me a literal postcard? You went to Europe. Congratulations."

He had the base-level decency to look chagrined at the picture her connected dots revealed. "Probably could have worked on the delivery a bit."

"You think?" Then she tossed the card onto the counter. "Why are you here, Brass? To hurt me some more? I'll give you the heads-up now that I'm standing in a room of very sharp knives and I'm ambidextrous. Expertly two-handing a set of Benny's meat cleavers is most definitely a skill I possess, in case you're wondering."

His eyes shifted to the knife blocks for a beat before returning to her. "Because you need to know I love you and I fucked up."

Molly cringed. "You fucked up because you love me?"

"What? No! I fucked up because— Mages, dammit, that's not what I meant."

"Then what did you mean?" she challenged with a hand on her hip.

Brass pinched the bridge of his nose. "I mean, I was afraid of losing the one person I can't live without because of what might happen if you learned of your magic and one day decided to use it against me."

A different chasm opened up inside her, separate from the one that had swallowed her happiness. "You really thought I would hurt you? *That's* why you kept your knowledge of my magic from me?"

Shame, hot and fresh, darkened Brass's features. "Yes," he said quietly but still forced himself to look at her. "Ragana's curse, it . . . it did something far worse than I think even *she* ever intended. Males who wield magic, they're always ruthless, but they're also always the same. Predictable in their offensive attacks, outward displays of power, you name it. But Ragana? Her ruthlessness was in her patience. Her magic was a slow, drawn-out torture that I hadn't been prepared for. It ruined me and sent me to a dark place I didn't think I could ever come back from." A shattered breath rattled out of him, stripping away his defenses as well as some of her own.

"When I first sensed that you had magic, I went back to that dark place. The worries, the concerns, the paranoia. I kept wondering, what if you would eventually be the same? What if, after you'd learned of your abilities, you'd figure out a way to manipulate the men around you? Mages know you have more than enough reason to do so, especially after how so many of them treated you. How *I* treated you." He took a deep breath and stepped closer. "I was wrong. So very fucking wrong, Molly. Your magic wasn't this evil poison I thought it was solely because you happened to be a woman. Ragana was the poison, not all women, and certainly not you." He risked a step forward and dipped his forehead low to caress hers. "Never you."

But before she sank into his heat, a worried prickle pulled her back. "You lied to me. Humiliated me in front of your family . . . a family that had begun to feel like mine, too." Heat flared beneath her cheeks, forcing some of the mortification she'd worked so hard to forget to come bubbling to the surface.

Brass rushed to grab her hand and wouldn't let it go when she tried to pull away. "I lied to *myself*. And believe me, my brothers were more than happy to call me out on my bullshit. Chrome melted down my favorite gun, saying he'd make me a new one after he finished training you on how to use it."

A small snort left her nose, interrupting the groveling session, but Molly sucked it back in and steeled the rest of her features. Just the mention of Chrome and the others was enough to cast a pall over a life she'd worked too hard to illuminate. "I miss him. I miss Drea, too, but I can't bring myself to look at either of them now. It hurts too much."

"They're waiting for me to fix my fuck-up before they can bang down this door and snatch you up again and are more than happy to vote my ass out if I can't get the job done."

Molly stared at him with a renewed interest, trying to ignore the spark that was beginning to brighten within her chest. Feeling a change of subject was better than examining how she was further hurting, she gestured toward the picture on the counter. "What's with the card?"

Brass's chest lifted. "During the past few weeks, I've been thinking about family a lot. How I have one that's willing to melt me down into literal scrap, and you've just found out your ancestral family was blessed by a Baltic deity. So, armed with knowledge about your family I didn't have before, I did a little digging." He leaned over the counter and pointed at a moderate-sized building not far from the cathedral. "That's a hotel in Riga. Small place, but as it turns out, the owners are from a town not far from where you were born. They, uh, knew your parents. Your birth parents, I mean. Remember them."

The dam holding back Molly's impossibly large wave of emotions was a hairbreadth away from creating a civilization-ending event. "You found where I'm from?" she said in disbelief.

He nodded with the certainty of a man who had decided long ago that there was no going back. "The hotel is not far from a museum dedicated to, get this, Baltic mythology. I've been in touch with the museum director, and he's been putting me in contact with the right people to set up some hikes and tours of the area."

"Tours?"

"Well, not, like, on a bus or anything. I was just given some guidance on the best places to see and how to get there. The travel's all on me." A sly sparkle played in the amber depths of his eyes. "There's no better way to see the countryside than flying above the treetops around it, especially while I'm holding you close to me."

Molly's jaw lowered. "When you say, 'the travel's all on *you*,' you mean . . ."

"I want to be your guide, Molly. I want you to be in my arms and beneath my wings as we discover the forests, seas, and countryside of your ancestral homeland. I want to give you back the family you lost and the family that loves you. I want to learn and explore your magic right along with you." He stepped closer and gathered her hands against his chest. "I want to clean up every single dish that comes out of your kitchen and bounce every single fool customer who doesn't deserve your talent. There are lifetimes I've missed out on. Entire species have grown into existence and succumbed to extinction in the time I've been in the mortal realm. And I'd endure all those long eons again if you'd only be waiting for me at the end of them."

"I'd never ask you to do that," she said, still reeling from the shock of his words.

"Family doesn't ask, and neither do mates," he said, lifting her face to his. "It's my job to anticipate your needs, to care for you as the other half of my soul. I love you. Nothing will ever change that, whether I have your forgiveness or not."

She blinked away the tears gathering on her lashes. "I love you, too."

And she did. Like, with her whole damn chest and all the

gooey parts inside of it. It was the most liberating feeling she'd known and the happiest confession she'd ever shared.

"Oh, thank the mages," he breathed against her mouth before claiming it with a leashed ferocity born of separation and uncertainty. Their tongues melded in a dance that had become familiar and whole, where no part of her was a stranger to no part of him. There was a wild tameness to the act, as though their joining needed to establish roots again before it could grow wings.

It was more than enough when their souls could take it from there.

When they finally parted, she beamed up at him. "You know, it's a good thing you showed up." She nodded down at her dough ball. "I was just about to make spinach knishes, and it's a two-person job. This puppy needs to be spread tissue-paper-thin across this whole counter, and two hands aren't enough. Or maybe I should put a *Help Wanted* sign in the window."

Brass's smile tickled her cheek as he nibbled a line of kisses along her jaw. "Well, I know a guy. Kind of broody. Definitely the silent type. Prefers cleaning to cooking. But he also knows a great chef in Latvia who can give you a few pointers. The chef's name is Georg. I can introduce you when we check out the tasting menu he's going to prepare for us when we visit."

The squeak that reverberated through all the kitchen's stainless steel was enough to trigger a mild earthquake. "A tasting menu? Really?"

Brass wiggled a finger in his ear, trying to let some of the sound back in. "Yeah. Just give me a date and it's all yours."

Molly sighed against his mouth, placed one final lingering kiss there, and wrapped her arms around his neck. "I'm yours. Always. I love you."

Then he held her to his heart, and she smiled against every answering beat. "Now *that's* the kind of magic I can get behind."

EPILOGUE

Several Months Later - The Spring Equinox

ood-roasted chicken and charcoal-braised lamb
perfumed Aurora's downtown with the sweet
steam of the annual Spring Swing Festival, the
greener and more grill-friendly version of its winter counter-
part. For Molly, the festival signified many things.

One, Chunky's Churros was now offering its spring flavors,
including her absolute favorite, lemon curd. And two, it was the
confirmation that she'd never work another festival again. Kind
of hard to twist her arm on the subject when she was still
hobbling around on sleepy sex limbs after a certain angel
convinced her that lazy Sunday mornings were better spent in
other ways.

Brass in her bed and the automatic start set on the coffee pot
were quickly becoming an addicting combination.

Yeah, she wasn't mad about it. Especially when, once they
finally made it out the door, he'd promised to acquire her the

crown jewel of the festival. The pièce de résistance. The Holy Grail of gastronomic acquisitions. The—

"Dumplings! Two o'clock! And the line isn't long yet. Oh my gosh oh my gosh!" Molly tugged on Brass's arm as if it was an air horn in an eighteen-wheeler and started dragging two hundred and ten pounds of muscle through the unsuspecting crowd. "Excuse us! Coming through!"

By the time Molly's heels had skidded to a stop at the end of a food truck line six customers deep, she finally allowed herself to inhale. And oh Lawdy, was she happy she did.

"Breathe with me, Brass. We've reached Mecca. C'mon, in through the nose, hold it for a two count, then exhale." Her eyes fluttered closed as she allowed the scents of the Dumplin' Buggy, the once-a-year spring festival proprietor of the most delicious dumplings to ever have been hand-pinched, flow over her. "I can already taste the choices," she said to Brass, still with her eyes closed. "Sweet chili oil, soy-marinated chicken, maybe some sort of hoisin-sweet potato-ginger combination."

"If I didn't know any better, I'd say someone scouted the joint before we came over here," Brass remarked.

She smacked his deliciously hard abs. "Quiet, I'm trying to work out their theme. And no one says *scouted the joint* anymore, not since *N.Y.P.D.* went off the air." Molly inhaled again, smacking her lips. "There's just one more flavor I'm not nailing down yet. Szechuan peppercorns, maybe?"

"Try jalapeño and cream cheese with a spicy chili aioli."

Molly's eyelids swung open. "Yes! Wait. How did you—"

The sly grin that had gotten Brass's mouth in trouble more times than the words that left it tempered Molly's fury when she saw the four Styrofoam cartons balanced across his ridiculously strong and apparently heat-resistant forearms. Nestled within each tray were perfectly pinched pillows of rice flour dumplings. Their seared little bottoms sat on top of lush beds of green seaweed and sticky rice and were drizzled with glistening sauces and hefty chunks of vibrant scallions.

In other words, four little palate orgasms.

Brass held out a set of paper-wrapped chopsticks and, knowing better than to try and find a free park bench, marched Molly and their haul back to the sanctuary of her closed-to-the-world (for a day) restaurant.

Once they'd tucked into their treats, after no fewer than a dozen porn star moans elicited on Molly's part, she looked around at the small space she'd carved out for herself and how different it would look in a few weeks. "I bet Amelia likes dumplings. She strikes me as a dumpling lover."

"Who doesn't like dumplings?"

"No one I'd ever invite to my birthday party, I can tell you that much. If it was up to me, I'd have a dumpling-shaped birthday cake."

Brass chuckled into his napkin. "Filled with dumplings?"

Molly's eyes widened with wicked delight. "I *knew* there was a reason I kept you around. That's it. When my birthday rolls around in a few months, you're on cake duty."

"That I can manage, if Amelia's up for decorating it."

"She definitely would be. Speaking of which, do you think I made the right move there?" she asked around a mouth full of ginger garlic chicken.

"Partnering with Amelia? Hell yeah, I do. This place's kitchen space is huge for the amount of tables you turn over. It's like drawing a stick figure with a 3D printer. It gets the job done, but boy, is it overkill. I think connecting with her at the Winter Whimsy Festival set you on a path for success with the restaurant. It'll take you in a new direction than what you previously envisioned, for sure, but an exciting and better one."

Amelia Bosas—owner of the online New England confectionery sensation Sweets, Eats, and All the Treats—had followed up with Molly a month or so ago after their brief introductions at the festival and broached the idea of a partnership. Namely, Molly had the kitchen space, storage, and foot traffic, while Amelia had the online presence, perfect small add-ons to larger ticket items, and regional kitschy charm that paired well with Suerte and Honeysuckles's touristy clientele and vibe.

And money. Amelia had money . . . and candy. She was the literal answer to Molly's financial prayers, not to mention the sweetest (ha!) human being on the planet.

The arrangement had officially been inked the past week, and Amelia was going to move in within another week or two, which coincided perfectly with Benny and Marisol's spring vacation.

"I don't think I'll mind having bags and trays of confections to sell around the place. I can certainly think of worse fates."

"You're stuck with me. So, tread lightly there. No backsies, remember?" Brass stole a rare moment when Molly wasn't bringing a dumpling to her lips and snagged her hand to place a kiss on the back of it.

"You are so damn cocky."

"You like it," he said with a wink, and she squeezed her thighs together at the illicit memories his smoldering gaze conjured.

Bastard.

Brass was just about to slip a dumpling into his mouth when his phone pinged. He looked at it briefly before rolling his eyes and shoving the thing back into his pocket.

"Trouble?" she inquired before dunking her dumpling into soy sauce.

"If you mean what happens when Bronze is left alone in a library, then yeah."

"Oh?"

Brass put his chopsticks down. "He can't get what Saulé said out of his head."

"About the lycan thing?"

"Yes. He's already exhausted every text we have, and now he's moving on to mortal myths."

Molly chewed the idea around in her mind. "*Are* lycans real?"

"Not to our knowledge, but then again, there's so much out there we don't know about. Who are we to say definitively just because we've never seen one? Wow, I can't believe I just said that," he muttered, shaking his head, then looking around as if he were expecting a lycan to magically jump out from behind Molly's potted plants.

Molly sat back in her seat and waved a chopstick in his general direction. "Look at you, being all sagely. Just so you know, with wisdom comes—"

He arched a brow. "Great responsibility?"

"No. *Words*. You can't be wise if you don't share what you know, and you can't do that without talking. Oh, and speaking of sharing sage advice, just tell Bronze that if he's looking for lycan research fodder, he should focus on anything *not* produced by Sony Pictures Entertainment."

Then Brass's eyes darkened to that toe-curling caramel that only ever came with a chaser of her favorite kind of trouble. "I'll be sure to let him know, right after I keep you in bed for the next several hours telling you about all the things I'm going to do to you."

A dumpling dangled precariously in front of her open mouth while a suggestive drop of glistening soy sauce jumped ship and plunged onto her tongue. "Oh?" she repeated, barely registering the salty morsel.

"Oh," he confirmed as he stood from his seat and took up the chair next to her. "Starting with how I'm going to book you that first-class ticket to Latvia next month." He brought his warm lips to her neck, sending shivers down her spine. "Then I'm going to hold you close to me as we recover from jet lag in the most luxurious bed the Old City has to offer." Another nip along her jaw and she lowered the dumpling back down to the tray.

"I'm going to fly with you through forests I've not seen in two thousand years. I'm going to stand beside you as you converse with people who are part of your past and console you if it gets to be too much."

A swell of emotion tempered the fire he'd stoked and wrapped her in a warmth like no other.

Molly finally turned to him and let every ounce of love and happiness she felt for her angel shine through in her smile.

Brass rubbed soothing circles into her hands with his thumbs. "I'm going to love the hell out of you and tell you every damn day until you're sick of hearing my voice."

"Impossible. Not on the love thing, but on the voice thing. Your voice is damn sexy."

Then he leaned forward and brushed a kiss on her lips. "My plan's a working theory. I'm only in the early stages of testing. Lots more R and D to go."

"Well, best get to it, then."

"Always so bossy," he chided, reminding her of a time, months ago, when he'd first warned her of the same problem before getting her gloriously naked. "And thank the mages for it, because I wouldn't have you any other way."

BRONZE JUST CAN'T GET Saulé's taunt about some supposed lycan woman out of his mind. Imagine his surprise when he stumbles upon an exquisite and unconscious princess during his nightly patrol . . . a princess who just so happens to be a lycan, and is in desperate need of a competitor to win her hand lest she be mated off to a lycan warlord of her brutal father's choosing. Find out what happens when Bronze must decide whether to fight for her, or stay true to a sacred oath he'd long ago sworn to another. Start reading *Angel's Conquest!*

. . .

CAN WE KEEP IN TOUCH? Are you curious to see what happens when Molly and Brass take their first trip to Latvia as soul bonds? It comes with no small amount of pampering on Molly's part, and a super secret surprise on Brass's part. But when Molly's old Boss Lady habits flare up, she turns the beauty crew on Brass. Find out what happens when the tables are turned and Brass is subjected to the same beauty tortures as Molly, and whether, despite his (newly preened) and ruffled feathers, he can still deliver the surprise of her life. Claim your BONUS EPILOGUE when you sign up to my newsletter to learn more about the surprise in store. Enjoy!

THANK you so much for reading *Angel's Temper!* If you loved seeing Molly and Brass's relationship grow, let your friends know. Help other readers fall in love with this couple, and all those hunky angels, by leaving a review.

SCAN THE QR code to start reading *Angel's Conquest* and the BONUS EPILOGUE today!

ACKNOWLEDGMENTS

No matter how much I think I know everything, the universe always seems to take great delight in proving me wrong. Thank you, universe. I owe you a few choice words, to be clear, but probably a drink as well. Without you, however, I would never have read Elizabeth Gilbert's *Big Magic* and I would never have found the tiny but mighty tribe of writers who you've thrown into my orbit. I will be forever grateful.

As always, the hugest of acknowledgments goes to Ben, who always insists I'm doing exactly what the universe intended me to do. Thank you times a million.

ABOUT THE AUTHOR

Aimee Robinson is a lover of romance novels in all forms. Her absolute favorites, though, are the ones that offer a little bit of something *extra*: time travel, guardian angels, good old-fashioned meddlesome grandmothers with a supernatural secret to hide, you name it.

She believes romance novels should transport you from the humdrum to the swoonworthy, preferably while being curled up on the couch with chocolate and tea (or a martini . . . or both!). Aimee's overactive imagination lends itself to fun tales with emotional adventures, sexy snark, and happily ever afters.

When not writing or reading, Aimee enjoys spending time with her husband and keeping up with her two young sons.